The Crandall Haunting

By A.H. Gilbert

Toad Song Publishing

FREE PREVIEW!

Want more? Preview the first two chapters of the next Emerson Crandall novel, *For Sissy*, at the end of this book.

For Sissy

Violence has come to Creeley County, Colorado.

Here to defend himself for crimes committed by his father, Emerson Crandall is suddenly implicated in a string of grisly murders. As a killer prowls the night with an insatiable compulsion, Emerson becomes the prime suspect.

What Emerson doesn't know is that his daughter is the only surviving witness to a crime, and she is in the killer's crosshairs.

Now, with more to lose than his freedom, Emerson must outsmart the police and catch a killer. But with the killer already stalking his next victim, is Emerson too late?

Acknowledgement

Many thanks go to my beta readers, Mary Chepetz, Shannon Glazer
and Adrienne Glazer Salvagni, for their valuable help.
Also, my thanks and love go to Jenny, for always being generous
with her knowledge and time.

The Crandall Haunting is dedicated to
Gibby, for his love, patience and support,
and to Peg, for her enthusiasm and encouragement.

Do you want to know more about *The Crandall Haunting* or
A.H. Gilbert?
Visit **ahgilbert.com**.

Chapter 1
Colorado, 1897

The diamonds didn't start the trouble. The possibility of diamonds did.

The possibility of diamonds brought Silas to this dark, hot house, his searching hands in a desk drawer, the muzzle of a pistol pressing against his temple.

"What are you looking for?" said a husky, male voice behind him. Silas realized it was Asa, the rancher who owned this house. And he knew that things were about to go bad.

Silas could tell that Asa hadn't noticed Lonnie, standing on the dark stairs. Lonnie had time to take aim. There was a quick flash, a loud crack and Asa fell forward into Silas, splattering him with blood.

"The woman!" Silas said, shoving aside Asa's limp body. Lonnie headed to the bedroom, gun still ready, while Silas stepped through the puddling blood and followed.

Mayla, in bed, had pulled a pistol from under the pillow. But the dim moonlight shone on her, while Lonnie and Silas were shielded by the home's inner darkness. She didn't have time to aim, and Lonnie was ready. His bullet penetrated her head, blasting it open and spattering the pillows with blood and brains.

"Damn, Silas!" Lonnie whispered, horrified. They crept toward her, unable to take their eyes off the sight. Silas fumbled for the room's lantern, found it, lit it, held it out toward her. The light cast feebly white, and long shadows stretched across the bed. The woman's face was gone, her head a pulpy mass.

"Oh, Jesus, Silas."

They looked, spellbound by the horror. Silas' thoughts flitted back to earlier in the day, when they had stealthily watched that woman. She had bustled around the chicken coop, gathering eggs and cheerfully scolding the annoyed hens. Lonnie's rifle had blasted that life away, leaving a hot, headless mess. Silas felt his stomach heave, his heart pound. Then his attention was distracted by a bit of pink cloth, mostly hidden by the bloody pillow.

"What's that?"

"What?"

"There."

Silas jabbed a finger at it.

Lonnie tucked the rifle against his body, still pointing it at the woman, as if she might come back to life. He reached out with his other hand, keeping as far back as he could, pulling at the piece of silk. It was a small bag, closed with a drawstring. When he almost had it free, the woman's body slipped, falling toward his arm. Blood gushed out, over his hand, soaking the little bag.

He yelled and yanked his arm away, dropping the bag on the floor. It landed with a thud and a shimmering pink stone slipped out, glittering in the white lantern light.

"Oh Lord, Silas," Lonnie whispered.

"Pick it up. Let's go."

Lonnie grabbed the bag, shoving the stones back inside and tightening the drawstring.

"Wait. Look." Silas nodded at the woman's neck. A large, pink diamond dangled there, mounted on a heart-shaped pendant, wet with blood. Lonnie held his breath, then reached out and gingerly lifted the pendant. The woman's body started a slow descent, slipping out of the bed. It hit the bedside table, toppling onto its shoulders, the rest of the body following, sinking to the floor, blood pooling beneath it. Silas fought back the urge to be sick.

"We got to go," Lonnie said. "What if someone heard?"

"No one could have heard." Silas remembered the miles of distance to the nearest home.

"Someone could have heard."

They hurried through the front room. Silas paused to check Asa's body, and found another large pendant under his nightshirt. It was a diamond, set in silver wire, hanging from a leather tie.

So, it was all true, the stories of the diamonds. Now he knew.

He tried yanking the pendant, but the leather was too strong and Asa's body jerked forward, his head snapping back weirdly. Silas used his knife to slice the leather.

"Go," he said.

They slipped out of the house and mounted their horses. They started fast, trying to put plenty of distance between themselves and the carnage. The moonlight was bright, and they had no trouble seeing the road. But as they topped a hill and started down the other side, they saw dark storm clouds rapidly crossing the moon, rolling toward them over the valley. This surprised them, and they pulled their horses to a halt. They didn't want to be stuck on the prairie when a big storm hit.

"Did you have any idea there was a storm coming?" Lonnie said.

"No."

Their horses, blowing hard, put their heads up, looking toward the storm, ears alert. They snorted and jigged on the road, unable to hold their feet still. Lightning flashed and, at the same time, a crack of thunder rumbled across the mesa. Lonnie's horse reared straight up and turned quickly, catching Lonnie off guard. He fell, hitting Silas' horse as he went. Silas's horse bucked twice, dumping Silas, hard, on the road, stunning him for a moment. By the time Silas could sit up, the clatter of the horses' hooves was far in the distance. The storm continued to pour in around them, and big, heavy rain drops struck them like ice. As bright as it had been just minutes before, it was now dark. Silas couldn't see Lonnie.

"Silas? You OK? You there?"

"Here."

Silas crawled forward, his head throbbing, and now shivering in the sudden cold. He reached out, trying to find Lonnie. His hand closed over what he thought was Lonnie's arm.

"Here," he said again, squeezing.

"Where?"

Silas was startled. Lonnie's voice sounded ten feet from him. He squinted through the heavy rain, trying to see what he was holding. Through the darkness, he thought he saw someone, or something, rising up next to him. A scream started deep in Silas' chest. He tried to release the icy thing he was holding, but his hand was clamped on. He could not get it free. He sat back and kicked out, screaming.

"Silas?" Lonnie whispered, his voice tight with fear. "What's happening?"

Silas was staring in horror at his hand, still locked on what seemed to be an arm. Straining his eyes in the darkness, he saw his hand was turning white and hardening like ice. The crackling ice traveled up his arm as he screamed, trying to push away with his feet. Then the cold traveled up over his shoulder to his neck, where it spread down his body. It crept up his face, freezing him, hardening him, his scream abruptly silenced.

"Silas!" Lonnie stumbled toward him, tripping on Silas' body, now hard and cold. "Silas!"

Lonnie thought he saw movement, and looking up, he saw a dark and shadowy figure rise up before him. He gasped and tried to stand, tried to run, but something caught him in mid-stride and burned him with intense cold. His scream turned into a ghastly gurgle, and he fell on the road, clattering like a block of wood. The hardened bodies of the two men continued to change, now drying, becoming a fine gray powder, blowing this way and that in the gusting wind, until no trace remained.

The bloody pink bag had fallen from Lonnie's shirt and hit the ground, spilling its contents across the wet dirt. The diamonds sparkled in the last flickers of lightning as the storm rolled over the horizon.

When the sheriff and his men investigated the murders, no one was entirely sure of the motive. It seemed robbery was probably the intent, but both corpses were found with their diamond necklaces in place, and the pink bag of diamonds was tucked under Mayla's pillow. How could the robbers possibly have missed them?

Chapter 2
Present Day; Syracuse, New York

Emerson's cell phone chirped as he finished his fiftieth push-up. Good excuse. He was going to add ten more today, but instead, he pushed himself up with a grunt and found the phone.

"Hello?"

"Hi, Emerson, is that you? Well, of course it's you. What a silly question. Who else would answer your phone, using your voice?"

"Hi Gary." His partner.

"Well, I've got some bad news." Gary was uncharacteristically direct.

Emerson took four strides to the refrigerator that rattled in the tiny indentation he called the kitchen.

"Let's hear it." He tucked the phone against his ear with his shoulder and opened the refrigerator, reaching for the carton of orange drink.

"We're canceled."

He paused, carton halfway to his lips.

"What does that mean?"

"We're done, man. The Aggies canceled our funding. They said they have to reallocate their funds to the Asian Longhorned Beetle, which, to quote, 'is rapidly becoming an epidemic in virtually all varieties of maple in Massachusetts.' As well as attacking the ash and poplar, I might note."

"I know what the Asian Longhorned Beetle is."

"Apparently the Asian Longhorned Beetle is considered to be of greater importance than the hemlock looper."

Emerson put the carton down and stepped to the window. A plump, dark woman was walking a fluffy white dog across the street. It pulled on the leash, lunging against its harness to get its nose to the base of a light pole. The woman didn't notice its frantic tugging, and she dragged the frustrated creature along easily at the end of an orange leash as she talked into a cell phone. Emerson watched her dully, a distant gaze in his dark blue eyes, his thoughts darting around Gary's news. It was bad.

"Can we appeal the decision? I mean, they pretty much guaranteed us another two years."

"I suppose we can write to someone. The board, the committee, the president, the Royal Canadian Mounted Police. But you know how stubborn Aunt Aggie is when she makes a decision."

"Aunt Aggie" was one of Gary's many nicknames for the U.S. Department of Agriculture, which funded their research.

"So what do we do, just turn off the lights and lock the lab?" Emerson ran one long hand across his forehead and into his dark hair, which hadn't seen barber's clippers in a few months.

He noticed a rusty hatchback pulling into a "no parking" zone across the street. The driver, a middle-aged woman, turned to the child in the seat next to her, taking hold of the young girl and hugging her.

"Well, we could stage a protest, let the loopers loose," Gary was saying. "That would show them. Do they have any hemlocks on the grounds of the Department of Agriculture in D.C.? Maybe we could fling some loopers at the President's motorcade. Can you imagine the coverage? The news coverage, I mean, not the coverage of the motorcade with loopers. Hey! We could get sympathy donations from the anti's and professional protesters. No, wait, they're always broke."

Emerson turned away from the window as Gary prattled on. They would actually probably have to kill the loopers, an odd thought, after he had worked with the little, striped caterpillars for so long.

"Maybe we could ask the Saudis," Gary was saying.

"Alright, Gary," Emerson cut in. "I've got to think. I'll talk to you later."

"Sorry."

"Me too."

"Bye."

Emerson sat on the bed. He hadn't yet folded it back into a couch.

Great. No more money for their research also meant no more income for him, meager as it was, just enough to keep this cheap studio in a questionable neighborhood, barely enough to keep gas in his ailing, 12-year-old car. Enough to buy imitation orange juice, but not real orange juice. He couldn't say they were close to finding a way to eradicate the looper, but they were definitely making progress. This sudden change made his last two years of work seem, well, useless.

Useless. He had heard that word so often. The image of his smirking father wedged its way into any fleeting optimism he tried to muster. While Emerson was in college, his father never missed a chance to harangue him about his choice of majors, although, admittedly, he did help pay for it. To his father, biology was only useful if it led to medical school. Its leading his only child to a solitary, low-income life in a lab full of insects was, to his father, a complete waste of time and money. To his father, it made no sense to work so hard at anything that didn't involve a big financial payoff or notoriety, or best of all, both. Any conversation they had attempted in recent years revolved around his father trying to belittle and bully Emerson into forgoing this work and, instead, coming to work with him. The concept repelled Emerson as much as it enthralled his father, who longed to have his son working by his side. Now Emerson was about to become destitute, with funding hard to find, but he still couldn't tolerate the idea of going to work with his father. The thought made him feel almost physically ill. He would have to be nothing less than desperate to do it. Emerson couldn't imagine ever getting to that point. Even a job waiting tables or serving burgers would be better than that. He could just hear his father's disgust if he heard that his master's-degreed son was working in a fast food restaurant.

Hell, it would probably pay better than his research grant.

He sighed and stood, stepping toward the shower, which was set, with a sink and toilet, in an alcove off the kitchen. A plastic, accordion-style door separated it from the rest of the room. Just then he thought he heard a quiet tapping on his door, two little knocks. He froze, naked, and listened.

Tap-tap.

"Just a minute."

He rummaged in his dirty clothes hamper for a pair of shorts. Stepping to the door, he put his eye to the peephole. He could see the top of a small head.

"Who is it?"

"It's me," said a little voice, almost too quiet to hear.

Emerson pulled back the chain and turned the deadbolt. He opened the door to see a girl about three feet high with straight, dark brown hair and deep blue eyes. She looked up at him with an expression of mingled curiosity and fear. A lanky six-foot-two, he towered over this little person. He scratched the hair at his chest absently as he looked back at her.

"What can I do for you?" he said, not quite knowing how to address a little kid.

She took a deep breath, stared at his knees and spoke as though she were reciting something she had memorized. "My name is Courtney. I'm seven. I'm in second grade. You're my father."

That stated, she glanced up at him shyly and then looked back at his knees. As her words sunk in, a woman appeared in the doorway. She bore an overall rumpled appearance, with a tired, middle-aged face. Her body was soft and pudgy, bulgy under a baggy, long-sleeved T-shirt and sweatpants.

"Are you Emerson?" she said.

"Yes," he said.

"The bug guy?"

"Yeah, you could say that. What's going on?"

She thrust a pink, child-size knapsack in his hands. "This girl is yours. Her mother was in an accident and can't take care of her. She's in a coma. Hit and run," she added, anger flitting across her face.

"What?" He heard her words, but they didn't make sense.

"I brought her all the way here for you, because she's a good kid and she has a good mother. But that's all I'm doing. I've got too much." Her face was sad, and utterly exhausted. Then she looked at him with a hardened expression and said, "Ask the child. She has all the information for you."

Her eyes rested for a moment on the girl. Then she said, "Good bye."

She hurried down the hallway and out the front door with surprising speed.

Emerson looked at the little girl, who was staring back at him. He heard a car engine start and he hurried to the window to see the hatchback pulling away from the curb. He tried to open the window, but it was painted shut, as he already knew.

"Hey!" he yelled, slapping the glass as the car disappeared down Fourth Street. "Hey! Stop!"

"Can I come in?" Courtney asked quietly, glancing uneasily down the dank and dingy hallway. Muffled shouting came from one of the other apartments, and the hallway stank of old fried food and cigarettes.

"No!" he said, feeling panicky, stepping back to the girl.

"My mother said if I ever met you, I should show you this."

She held up a glossy, color photo. He took it, frowning. It showed a group of people on the dock of a lake. They were holding cans of cheap beer and smiling. He was one of them, and he had his arm around a woman.

He remembered that day. It was a graduation party, a small group of the science students, celebrating the end of their college careers. They had earned their degrees and were preparing to start jobs. Barry Ross had invited them to his Dad's cabin on Loon Lake, up in the Adirondacks.

He gazed at the woman in his arm. He remembered her, too. Annie Hughes, a sweet, smart botanist who had been in some of his classes over the previous couple years, and who surprised everyone that weekend by revealing a delightful, bikini-clad body. Since she was normally hidden in baggy shirts and loose jeans, Emerson would never have guessed that she could be so appealing. Apparently she liked him pretty well, too, because they ended up making love several times over the course of that weekend, in the lake, in the woods, in the tent. It was sweet, and fun, but it didn't last beyond those intense, forty-eight hours. She was slated to start research on the Aleutian Islands the next week. He was coming to Syracuse to work on a study aimed at preventing the emerald ash beetle from spreading into New York. They sent a couple e-mails and had tracked each other on social media for a while. But they both seemed to know that it was just one of those goofy, horny episodes that was never meant to be anything else.

Except, apparently, it had become something else, and that something else was standing in his doorway, now looking like she was about to cry.

He watched her with consternation. Emerson's total experience with children was limited to conducting school field trips at the nature preserve. Watching her eyes fill up with tears, he knew he needed to stave off her crisis so he could focus on his own. He drew on what he could.

"Want to see a really cool bug?"

The girl looked at him in surprise, then nodded.

"Come on."

She stepped through the door and he closed it behind her. He showed her a lighted glass terrarium atop a pressboard stand. "Can you see the bug?"

She looked intently through the glass. He watched her dark blue eyes examine mossy sticks, leaves and rocks as she turned her head this way and that to see under objects.

"Where is it?"

"I'll give you a hint. It looks like a stick."

She continued to look, but, after a moment, said, "I can't see it!"

"Look up."

A long, greenish brown bug was perched upside down on the screen covering the terrarium. It was four inches long, no thicker than a cocktail straw and had long legs with knobby joints.

"I see it!" she said. "That's a bug?"

"It's called a walking stick."

"Why does it look like a stick?"

"For camouflage. It looks just like a stick so birds won't see it. That way it won't get eaten."

She looked back at the bug in wonder.

"What's its name?"

"I haven't thought of one yet. Maybe you can think of one. I'll be right back. I have to make a phone call while you're thinking of a name."

He set down the knapsack and looked up the phone number to the police and punched it on his phone. He looked back at the little girl who was watching the bug and thinking hard, her almost-black hair falling across her pale cheek. On impulse, he stopped the call and went to his closet. Reaching up, he pulled out a worn photo album. In its first few pages, he found what he was looking for, his kindergarten photo. He looked at the photo and back at Courtney's thin face with those deep blue eyes surrounded by long, dark lashes.

His face was different now, of course, with his straight nose, long arching brows and angled jaw, but still, there was no doubt about it. They could have been brother and sister. Or father and daughter. He felt weak. He sat down heavily on the bed.

A daughter!

If he called the police, what would happen? They would try to find that woman, maybe, and the girl's mother, and the girl would be sent to temporary foster care. That was probably the best solution, he thought. Then his mind abruptly bounced across memories of news stories of foster parents starving their children, keeping them in closets, abusing them. Surely, they weren't all like that?

The girl noticed his intense gaze.

"You could call him Sticky," she said.

"Sticky?"

"Uh-huh."

"That's a good name. OK, from now on, she's Sticky."

"She?" Courtney grinned, showing tiny, slightly uneven white teeth. Braces as a teenager, he thought, same as me. He realized he needed more information before he could figure out what to do.

"Courtney, where do live? What's the name of the town where your mom is?"

Courtney looked down. Her lip trembled. He got up from the couch and went to the kitchen. He pulled out a chair at his Formica table that he had found at the Good Will store.

"Here you go. Have a seat."

She sat. He reached for the orange drink, deciding she wouldn't suffer from a few of his germs, from his habit of drinking out of the container, and poured her a cup.

"I had to come here, with Lois." she said, her voice sad. Then apparently remembering something, she went back for her small knapsack, unzipped a pouch and pulled out a large, tan envelope. Handing it to him, she sat down again.

"That's from her."

He looked at the envelope with apprehension. On the front, "Open in case of emergency," was written in large, red block letters. It had already been opened, and now he pulled out the contents. The first document was apparently this girl's birth certificate, with a social security card clipped to it. He read the birth certificate and felt a surge of adrenalin when he saw his own name on the line for "father."

He stared at it so long that Courtney said, "There's a letter for you, too."

It was in a plain white envelope with "Emerson" on it in small, round cursive. He unfolded the single sheet of lined paper, dated a year earlier, and started to read.

Dear Emerson,

I hoped you would never have to read this note, but if you are, it's because something has happened to me, something that is preventing me from taking care of Courtney, so here goes:

Courtney is our daughter. I know you'll see it, just looking at her. And I gave her your last name. Don't ask me why I didn't tell you. I just didn't think it was fair to force you into this, once I made my decision to have her. You were just starting out, too, and you didn't ask for this.

But now, if you are reading this, it's because I don't have anyone else I can trust to take her. I know it isn't fair, and I'm sorry for that. But I couldn't bear to see her go to foster care. One of the reasons I am so messed up is because I spent my childhood with some really bad foster families. PLEASE DON'T DO IT TO HER.

I know that you and I didn't stay close, but I also know you are a good, gentle man. I have followed your research, and you are doing important work.

Courtney is the sweetest girl, with a big heart and incredible curiosity, and she is so smart. Please, please keep her safe.

Thank you, Emerson. Thank you.

Sincerely,

Annie Hughes.

Emerson's stomach tied itself in tighter knots with every line he read. He put the letter down and shuffled quickly through the few remaining documents. He paused over another note that listed his name and current address as Courtney's custodian in the event that Annie was unable to care of her. He had moved here a couple years ago. She really had been keeping tabs on him. The packet even included a photo of him, taken from a news article when he received the looper grant. The bug guy.

It was so weird to think this had all been going on without his knowing – the baby, Annie's careful planning, her keeping his address current in these documents. But why the heck had she kept this a secret from him?

He stuffed everything back in the envelope and went to the little girl. Kneeling on the floor, he put his hands on her shoulders.

"Courtney? Where's your Mom?"

Her eyes got wide and round. Bright orange drink stained the skin above her upper lip.

"Where does she live?" he said, more urgently, panic creeping into his voice. "Who is Lois? Courtney!"

He gave her a little shake.

Tears burbled out of her eyes and ran down her face as she stared at him. He pulled his hands away from her.

"I'm sorry. I didn't mean to scare you."

15

She jumped up from the chair and ran to the door, trying futilely to open it, not able to reach the deadbolt. Emerson was horrified.

"I'm sorry," he said. "It's OK."

He went over to her and kneeled down again.

"No!" She yelled, giving him a furious, useless shove. "Go away! I want my Mom!"

She dissolved into sobs, clutching her knapsack. He tried to hold her, but she cried louder and fought him off. He jumped up and walked to the window, picked up his phone, put it back down. He turned to his laptop and punched in Annie's name, starting a search, but not really knowing if it would produce any magic, useful information or a solution. He focused intently on this endeavor for a few minutes, but didn't get far before Courtney's quiet crying snapped him back to the room and the physical facts in front of him, mainly, a real girl, huddled miserably on the floor like some soggy pile of pink and purple rags. He sat down next to her, his back against the wall.

It was too much. His research. This kid. What in hell was he supposed to do now?

Chapter 3
Present day, Colorado

It was getting harder. Harder and colder. Clara couldn't describe the feeling, even in her thoughts. She just felt a sadness settling over her, like a layer of dust. A dusty, cold, frail old lady, she thought. Might as well add lonely, while she was at it.

Cars rushing by in the cool afternoon light stirred up a crisp chill that burned her cheeks. She opened the heavy wooden door to Toby's tidy office building and slipped inside. A draft blowing in under the door chilled the stairwell.

The cold spell they predicted was officially here.

Clara sighed and started up the long staircase to Toby's office, clutching the banister with both hands. It didn't hurt to walk, at least that's what she said, when asked. And it really didn't, not much anyway. Just normal pain for her age, she figured, stiffness, arthritis. What was really hard was balancing. She remembered reading once that humans performed an amazing combination of timing and balance, just to keep their big bodies from tipping over as they walked on two small feet. With her ability to balance leaving her, she saw the truth in that. She had fallen once. Now, walking was just a little scary. She knew a broken hip at her age was a death sentence. She would never come out of the hospital, or the home. What was it? A skilled nursing facility? Whatever. She knew that once she went in one, she wouldn't be coming back out. The thought gripped her with sadness, and she paused on the stairs, her knobby knuckles clutching the rail ahead of her, regaining her composure. Eighty-one years old and afraid to die.

"Get moving, fool," she said to herself.

She finished the last few steps and opened the heavy wooden door with its brass knob and small brass plate that read, "Tobias Landy, Esq. Attorney at Law."

"Hello," she called.

"Hello," came his voice from the library. "Hello."

Toby stepped through the large doorway, framed in dark oak, glasses perched over his thick brows. He carried a big book in both hands, supporting it with his firm, round belly.

"Hello, hello," he said warmly. "Good to see you, Clara."

"And you, Toby."

He set the book on his neat, leather-topped desk and took her hand, holding it gently instead of shaking it.

"To what do I owe the pleasure of this visit? Ah, here to finally sign your will, I'm guessing? Not just here to grace this old man with your delightful company?"

"Well, maybe I can do a little of both," she said, smiling into his round, blue eyes. "But I can't call you an old man, unfortunately, since I've got at least twenty years on you."

"No matter. You act and look fifteen years younger."

She was pleased at the comment, even though she knew it was a lie. Oh well, some had told worse lies in their time. Not Toby. He only told white lies, out of kindness. He watched her closely, still smiling, but a look of concern crossed his face. She must look winded, or pale, she thought. He led her to the chair by his desk.

"Here you are. Please sit down. You know, I keep meaning to move to a first-floor office. Those stairs are getting tougher on me every day."

"Oh, you couldn't leave this handsome office. You don't see buildings like this anymore, with all the hardwood trim and the antique glass." She nodded toward the large, sunny windows, their leaded glass etched with a swirling design, made by hand decades ago.

"Oh, I suppose." He was flicking through the files in a wooden cabinet drawer. "All right then, Clara, here it is."

"Do you remember how Maddie used to play under this desk?" asked Clara, smiling.

He handed her the document, titled "Last Will and Testament, Millicent Clara Stanton."

"Yes, I do. And the secret drawer? I used to hide little trinkets in there for her to find."

"I remember! She used to be so amazed to find something special in there. I still have the cigar box she kept those little goodies in, up in her room. Let's see. There's a marble, a little horse figurine, a baseball card, a kazoo."

She looked down at the document in her hand and sighed.

"Are you sure I should sign this so soon?" she said. "I mean, what is the hurry?"

His mouth opened in surprise and she could see he was trying to come up with a tactful way to respond. She laughed, and then so did he, relieved.

"You got me with that one," he said. "You shouldn't tease me, Clara. You know I'm kind of slow."

"Sure. You're about as dull as a diamond."

She started reading. Beyond all the legal necessities, the will was simple. It left everything to her niece, Maddie, who had spent so many summers and holidays with Clara that she was more like a daughter. The will also had a provision to care for her pets, Joe Todd, the Jack Russell terrier, and the old stock horse, Bugle. Joe Todd would probably outlive her, since he was only five years old, but it was a toss-up between her and Bugle. The bony old paint's joints were about as stiff as hers. If it weren't for the regular TLC of Clara's horse-crazy, 13-year-old neighbor from up the road, he might not have made it this long.

Her will also specified that the land should not leave the family, and should not be divided. When the last blood relative died, it would be granted to a local land and wildlife conservancy, guaranteeing that the land would be kept in its present, natural state forever. Or, at least, for a very long time.

Her property was more valuable than anyone knew, excluding Clara and her long-gone ancestors. But she would tell Maddie soon, as soon as Maddie got back from South America. She looked forward to that.

"Well, I never saw anyone smile while they read their will," said Toby.

"Oh, I was just thinking of the surprise I'll be giving to Maddie when she comes back home," Clara said. "I have some documents – other than this will – that I think she will be very interested in. And a few little trinkets that I want to give her now, before I'm in the grave."

"You've mentioned those documents before," said Toby. "You know, Clara, I'm not comfortable with your keeping valuable documents in your home. I'm afraid they might be vulnerable to theft or to being lost. What sort of documents are they? Stocks?"

"Don't worry about that. They are very safe. I have a spot that is entirely hidden. Believe me, nobody could find it."

"They say the thief always knows where to look."

"I appreciate your concern, Toby, I really do. But you don't have to worry."

She didn't want to tell him that she couldn't trust anybody, even him, with those documents. She had protected them for so long, and so had her father before her, and his father and finally her great-grandfather, who claimed the property back in 1875.

"Well, this looks fine," she said, reaching for the pen held in a heavy, red glass orb on his desk.

"It's pretty straightforward," he said. "Hold on. I need to call Antonio to come witness." He picked up the phone and spoke a couple of words into it. In a moment, they heard steps on the stairs and then Toby's downstairs neighbor, Antonio Torres, knocked and stepped in. Antonio owned an insurance company, and he served as a witness when Toby needed a second one.

"Good morning," Antonio said. "My fingers are warmed up and ready to sign."

"Ah, just in time," said Clara, and she signed her name. "Thank you, Mr. Torres."

As she passed the document to Toby, she said, "I always sign my full name on important documents. Millicent Clara. On everyday papers, checks and what-not, I just use Clara. But when it's really important, I know I have to include that awful 'Millicent.' Never could stand it. That's why I switched to my middle name when I was little. I just refused to answer to Millicent any longer – or especially Millie –– and, eventually, my parents gave in and switched to Clara, too."

"There's nothing wrong with the name Millicent," said Toby. "I have to say this: Do you declare this to be your last will and testament, being of sound mind?"

"I do."

Toby signed the document and passed it to Antonio, who signed and said, "Is that it?"

"Yep. Thanks, Tony," said Toby.

Antonio stepped to the door.

"Back to the underwriters," he said cheerfully, waving his way out.

"OK, ma'am," Toby said, stamping the document with his notary seal and adding his initials. "That's a wrap."

"Okie-dokie." She started to rise, pushing hard at the arms of the chair for balance. She got to her feet, holding the back of the chair until she was steady. Toby held her elbow lightly. She took a couple of small steps, then stopped, remembering something and looking at him with shock.

"Oh no, Toby. I owe you money, don't I?"

"Oh, please don't worry about it. There's no rush. No rush at all."

"Nonsense! How could I be so forgetful!"

She wasn't being totally truthful. Money had just been so very tight recently, with the property tax bills being due, and the new furnace she had needed and, well, to be honest with herself, her Social Security just wasn't enough to cover all the bills lately. Milton's veteran's checks were shrinking, thanks to some ridiculous new legislation in Washington, and her small savings were long gone.

She opened her handbag and pulled out her checkbook. Turning away from him slightly, she checked the balance. Six dollars and forty-eight cents. She opened her wallet and found a twenty dollar bill and the grocery coupons she had planned to use to stock up. She checked her change purse and found a fair number of coins, at least a few dollars.

"Here you are, then." She handed him the bill. "That's a start anyway."

"Oh, no, Clara. Don't be silly. I'm not in a hurry. And you don't have to pay me cash, for heaven's sake."

They both knew the twenty dollars was just a small fraction of what she owed. He handed it back.

"No, no. I insist. I'll have the rest for you in no time. I just have to move some money between accounts, and I'll get it right to you."

She started her small, careful steps toward the door. "And I really am sorry to make you have to wait so long for it. You have done such good work for me."

Toby sighed, holding the bill upright in his hand as another troubling thought entered his mind.

"Clara, why don't you sell that old place to Crandall?" He spoke with urgency. "You would have more than enough to live on comfortably. Move into a nice adult community, your own little apartment, closer to other people. You're too far away from town out there on the ranch. Let it go, Clara. It's an insanely generous offer."

"Absolutely not."

"If it's Maddie you're worried about, you'll have plenty to leave her – and it will be in cash. She won't have to worry about what to do with the land! Don't you think she'd rather see you comfortable, warm and safe and ..." he hesitated.

"That old piece of land is more valuable than what Crandall's offering," Clara said. "And I've got a lot more to offer Maddie by giving her that property."

"Clara, what can I possibly say that can convince you that it would be much healthier for you to sell it and move?"

"You can't convince me, Toby. I know what's right, and keeping that land is right. It's more valuable than you know, or even that crafty old Crandall knows."

He sighed and smiled. "You are being very mysterious. And stubborn."

He opened the door for her, then held her arm all the long, slow way down the stairs. At the bottom, he took her hand again.

"Thank you, Clara. Remember what I told you, about those other documents. You get them to me or to a safe deposit box."

"I'll consider it. And thank you. You did a terrific job on my will."

"You are very welcome. Let's hope we don't need it for many, many years."

She smiled.

He opened the door and put his arm lightly on her back, quickly slipping the twenty dollar bill into her coat pocket. A bitter wind blew in, causing them both to gasp.

"Woo. Cold," she said.

"Yeah. I'm glad this kind of weather only hits us every few years. I don't know how anyone could stand it for more than a few days. You get home soon and put the heat up."

She turned, waited until she was balanced, then started down the sidewalk, remembering the overdue notice from the electric and gas company. When had she received that? Ten days ago? Two weeks? Surely they wouldn't shut it off in this weather. One of her old friends ran Stony Valley Electric and Gas. She looked back at Toby.

"The heat. Yes, I'll do that," she said.

"Can I call you a cab?"

"Oh, no, thanks. I'm going to stop by the store before heading home."

"All right then. Take care." He sighed and watched her small, bent frame treading away. "And think about what I said."

She waved her hand at him without turning around, dismissing his comment. He sighed again. Eighty-one years old, frail as a sparrow, living alone, obviously short of funds. It just didn't bode well. He couldn't shake the feeling that she would be in trouble if she didn't get out of that cold, lonely ranch house.

Chapter 4

"I told you, Kellerman, this is not a significant problem. The old lady is just holding out for a better price. Who would think a little old lady could be such a sharpie?" Crandall attempted a confident, good-natured chuckle, which even he thought sounded artificial. Maybe Kellerman didn't notice, the imbecile.

"Well, you better figure out what she wants, and it better be fast and it better be reasonable," Kellerman said. "I'm not waiting. You think you're the only investment I could make? I've got a desk full of offers. I've got office buildings in Hong Kong. I've got veal farms in Canada. I've got oil drilling in Peru. Hell, I've even got an offer to invest in a cocaine plantation in Guatemala. I don't need to wait all spring to see if some stubborn old bat is going to sell you a run-down ranch so you can build your little play land for the rich and famous. Got me?"

"Oh, yes, I read you loud and clear." Who couldn't? When it came to reading people, Kellerman was the large-print variety. "You don't have to worry. I've worked with the regulators for the main buildings, so that the second she sells, approvals will be almost instantaneous. And I have got all the other permits in place, the ones for the surrounding properties. We are ready to break ground for the gas and electric lines, so we can get that started. And the equestrian facilities, if we want. Everything is in place, just waiting on her."

"And she is not budging."

"Like I said, she's just waiting for that last dollar, to see what the best and final is." Crandall ran one hand up the angle of his jaw and into his short, neat hair, which was still mostly dark, with a touch of gray at the top and temples. He grabbed some hair in his fist, giving it a nervous yank and said, "It's just a minor obstacle."

Just then, Crandall glanced through his hotel window and caught sight of Clara Stanton, shuffling like a little wind-up toy down the sidewalk. There was his minor obstacle now. It looked as if, should she stopped walking, she'd tip over sideways. She could barely even stand up, yet she stood stubbornly between him and the biggest hotel, casino and luxury housing development east of the Continental Divide.

"Well, you better get on with it. You've got another twenty-four hours to tell me we're golden, or you can kiss my hairy ass goodbye."

I wish I could, Crandall thought. If it weren't for all that money that went along with kissing that hairy ass. He glared toward Clara. She had stopped to chat with a fat woman who was carrying a tiny, black dog. It was a brief conversation. Too cold to linger.

"Twenty-four hours. Got me?" Kellerman said. "Got me?"

"Yes, I do."

Clara was heading for the dollar store down the block, Crandall guessed. It was the only thing that could possibly interest her on this crappy block. He watched her intently.

"I surely do. I'm going to talk to her today. She'll get my best and final offer, and she'll take it. You don't have a thing to worry about. You will be very glad you stuck with me, when that resort is full and those luxury homes are being snapped up by our darlings of the ten-digit variety."

"It better happen." Kellerman hung up abruptly.

Crandall focused his attention back on Clara Stanton, who was laboriously pulling on the handrail to get herself up the wheelchair ramp at the store.

Why wouldn't that old coot budge? He could not understand why an old lady would want to live by herself on a dilapidated ranch on the edge of nowhere, with no neighbors for miles.

Unfortunately, her home was also the center of the most beautiful piece of real estate he'd ever laid eyes on. From the moment he saw it, he knew it was the spot he had been looking for. It was far enough away from the beaten track to be attractive to those who want some seclusion, with almost perfect weather – if one discounted the current, highly unusual arctic cold front that was blowing through. It was in a trendy location, but not too trendy, and still close enough to major airports. But then, most of the people who would be staying at the resort or buying homes in the hills would probably be flying in and landing on the mesa in private jets. Oh, it was perfect. And it was his. He found it. His destiny. He had found the perfect place and the perfect idea to show them exactly what E. Rexham Crandall could do. And to think that this tiny, hunched up, old lady who didn't weigh more than ninety pounds was keeping him from his destiny.

Clara had finally finished her long, slow and painful-looking climb up the ramp and entered the store.

Crandall brought his fist down on the windowsill. It was intolerable. For some irrational reason, she wouldn't sell. Why would she want to live by herself in a five-bedroom ranch, eighteen miles from town, with nothing but a squatty mutt and a bony nag for company? He could understand the appeal of the acreage, even to someone who didn't want to develop it. A big spread, being the lord - or lady, in this case - of all you could see, that was an American dream. But she could barely see two feet in front of her anymore, and she was all alone. The pasture fences were a tangled menace, most of the barn had fallen in on itself years ago from neglect, leaving only the small stable area intact. Her only living relative was thousands of miles away, chasing rodents around the jungle, or some such nonsense. And the house was in desperate need of repair.

Crandall's gaze went from the store to his own, faint reflection in the glass. His dark blue eyes were lined with age and anxiety, and he felt his stomach burn and his intestines knotting. He had to get to the bathroom. Despite keeping himself in great condition and watching his diet, colitis still bothered him in times of high stress, after all these years. He sighed and turned away from the window. Rummaging through his briefcase, he found the property development proposal, and carried it into the bathroom with him. He dropped his pants and briefs and sat, just in time.

He opened the proposal and thumbed through it to the location map. Three thousand acres of some of the most beautiful rocky hills and prairies ever seen. And a deep, winding creek and a waterfall to a lake that did not dry up, even in the summer, sitting right in the middle of it all. Of course, that lake, creek and the Ponderosa forest that surrounded it also sat right in the middle of her property. He already owned 1400 acres but the rest, that precious remaining 1600, that was hers, Clara Stanton's.

Unfortunately, he did not really believe what he had told Kellerman, that she was just holding out. There was something else going on. She was not motivated by his money. She wanted to keep that property for some reason he couldn't understand. It wasn't spite. Other people did that, not Clara. And it wasn't because she was using it. She didn't even drive around the land or walk on it. And it definitely wasn't because she wanted more money from him. That was the hard part. That meant that she didn't speak his language, and he had no way of even beginning to speak hers. He simply did not understand her. What he knew, though, was that she stood in his way.

Sometimes, and especially in this case, in E. Rexham Crandall's way was a very bad place to be standing.

Raised in a crumbling, Upstate New York town in the Rust Belt, Crandall's childhood home was contrived of several converted rooms in a drive-up motel, owned by his parents. The family — his parents, sister and brother — made their living from the passing guests who drove up to the motel, a seasonal business that started falling behind when his parents resisted the changing modes of competition, the advertising and rating systems that came with the Internet. Spending many nights at the front desk of the empty lobby,

Crandall was in a hurry to leave behind this musty, rundown motel of his past, and his parents along with it. When he was 18, he moved to Buffalo and put in long hours on overnight shifts in increasingly more respected facilities, learning and moving up, eventually becoming a manager of one of the nation's largest hotel chains. But that wasn't enough for him and there came a point when he was done with other people's rules. He had left his good job and used his savings to start developing land. He found he had a knack for matching the land to just the right sort of development that suited it — hotels, housing, office parks, malls.

Now he was ready to do something big, really big, something beautiful, that would far exceed anyone's expectations of him, especially his parents, though they had died several years back. This new project would blast him up to world-class status. It would be a luxury resort with condos, skiing, a casino, horse sports. The only problem was that this dream was extremely expensive. He needed other people's money – and Clara's land – to do it.

Another thing he had a knack for was getting his way. He was willing to try the nice way first, negotiations, big buy-outs. But there were other ways, and he was fully capable of trying every one until he reached his goal.

His thoughts flitted briefly to his wife. They often did when he was driving so hard toward something he wanted this much. The memories were twinged with pain. He couldn't have loved a person more, but long ago stopped asking himself why she had left. She could no longer tell him, anyway. What would she look like now, if she were still with him, his beautiful, tiny, girlish bride? How would she carry herself at age fifty-three? She would still be lovely, he was sure, and maybe she would be less solemn. Maybe he would have helped her find joy; maybe his passion would have spread to her, and she would be full of the vigor he was sure she could have developed, given time.

He refocused. Now, with Kellerman's ultimatum, there really wasn't any more time to mess around.

With a sigh, he tossed the proposal across the floor and flushed. Crandall really hoped the old lady would agree to the nice way. Otherwise, he'd have to change his tactics.

Chapter 5

Unaware of the twenty dollars in her pocket, Clara knew she had enough change for a can of tuna, a tin of dog food and bus fare home. She made her purchases, then waited under the plastic-sided shelter for the bus. It was bitter cold. The shelter blocked the worst of the wind, but not all. Clara thought of the gas bill again briefly, but forced the worry out of her mind. They wouldn't cut her off in this weather, and she was expecting Milton's check anytime, probably today. She thought it would be a good idea to stop over to the gas and electric offices to tell them that she should be able to pay in full by Monday. But then she saw the bus coming. It would be at least forty-five minutes before the next one, and it was getting late.

So she boarded the bus, gave the driver her fare, told her where to stop and went as quickly as possible to a seat. The driver kindly waited until she was seated before pulling out. She was a plump young woman with slightly greasy black hair, tied in two ponytails on the sides of her head. She smiled at Clara in the rear-view mirror before pulling out, and Clara smiled back.

With all the stops, it took almost an hour before the bus arrived near Clara's house. It was so warm and cozy on the bus, and Clara was so tired from her long walk, that she dozed off.

"Here you are, ma'am," the driver said in a friendly voice.

It took Clara a few moments to stand, catch her balance and start down the aisle. She felt the impatient looks of the few remaining passengers, but she couldn't go any faster. The bus driver stood and helped her down the bus steps.

"Now you get home quick where it's warm, honey. We are supposed to get some major weather tonight."

"Thank you. I will."

The kindness of the driver reminded her of Maddie. She would be so glad when Maddie got home. She really could use the help of someone she trusted. She checked the mailbox at the end of her drive. Finally! The veteran's check had arrived.

The dirt drive to her house measured two-tenths of a mile. Clara walked steadily along. The wind blew through her long wool coat, chilling her ankles and the bare place between her gloves and sleeves. Joe Todd started barking as soon as the bus pulled away, and his cheerful yips were a beacon, guiding her to the front door. His powerful little white and tan body leaped joyfully behind the front window, almost flipping over with each jump.

"Hello, Joey," she said through the glass. "Hello little man."

A blast of arctic wind lifted her coat, and she quickly opened the unlocked door and went inside. She tore open the envelope as Joe Todd jumped on Clara's legs, yipped, scooted around the entrance rug, then jumped on her legs again.

The check was more than enough to pay the gas bill. She was glad, but realized now she would have to turn around and get back to town, walk down that long driveway, wait for the bus. It would be back by there in only about twenty minutes. The thought was unbearable. It was so cold, and her back ached along the spine. Her feet felt swollen and sore. But it was Friday, with Monday a holiday, and she had to pay the bill.

Then she realized she didn't need the bus. Now that she had a little money, she could get a cab. She would call the gas company and tell them she was coming, and not to close up until she got there, and then she would call a cab. She reached for the phone, found the gas notice in her small, wicker bill basket and dialed the customer service number. Holding the phone to her ear, she reached toward the door and let Joe Todd out. He sped away, barking into the brush. The phone at the other end did not ring. She must have left off a number. She pressed the "off" button, then the "on" button and listened. No dial tone. She turned it off and back on.

"Oh, please no!" The phone bill. She had not paid it. She rummaged through the basket and found the bill. It was overdue by six weeks. She looked at the due date on the gas bill. It was dated more than two months back. Now she knew she had to get back out there to get that bus. She quickly wrote a personal check for the amount due. The bank would be closed now, but she would give Fred the check and get to the bank on Saturday, deposit the money, and by Tuesday, the check would be good.

"Joe Todd! Joe Todd!" Her voice was carried away by the wind. She heard the dog's frantic barking and then saw a car coming down the driveway. She didn't know who it was, but she decided right then that it didn't matter. Whoever it was, he was not getting away without taking her into town. It could be a serial killer for all she cared; he would take her to the gas company so she could pay her bill.

The dark sedan eased up to the door. The tinted glass made it impossible to see more than a silhouette of the occupant. When the driver's door opened, and a tall, lean man emerged, she was not pleased to see that it was Rexham Crandall. She sighed. She was already so tired, and he was here to try to wear her down. She braced herself.

Joe Todd leapt at Crandall, not biting, but definitely not friendly either. He looked like a white and tan missile, launching repeatedly at the man, who tried to look amused, hiding annoyance.

"Joe Todd, that's enough," Clara said. Joe Todd took two more Super Dog leaps, then contented himself to marching purposefully behind Crandall, eying his calves menacingly.

"Hello, Mrs. Stanton," Crandall offered a full smile, his teeth unnaturally white and even, except for the two pointy canines. He took off his dark hat as he approached her, his long, black coat swishing in the wind, and proffered a thick, gold box.

"I don't know that we actually need a peace offering," he said. "But I thought you might enjoy some chocolates."

She recognized the box; they were top-quality candies, and she had a serious sweet tooth. Her stomach rumbled audibly.

33

"I hope I haven't interrupted your dinner,"

"No, I just got here myself, actually."

He stood there holding out the chocolates and smiling expectantly, his dark blue eyes watching her.

She took them, imagining how delicious they would be, and said, "Well, thank you. Please come in out of this cold."

She turned, grasping the box in both hands, and allowed him to open the door for her.

Once inside, she decided not to offer him a chair.

"I hate to sound inhospitable, but I really must get back into town. I'm assuming this is not a social visit?"

He shut his eyes, smiling still, and nodded slightly before opening them.

"Well, of course you are correct, and I appreciate your being direct. I shall be as well."

He held out an envelope and watched her closely.

"What is it?"

"Take a look."

She gave him a skeptical glance then opened the envelope. When she saw what it was, her brows raised in surprise. It was a check, made out to her, for $1.7 million.

"And it's just a down payment, as you know, a fraction of the final amount," said Crandall, huskily.

Clara needed that money and he knew it. It alone was enough to provide her with all that she needed, pay her debts and keep Joe Todd in the best dog biscuits, until he was as fat as a piglet. And it was only a third of the amount he had offered – just a down payment, as he said. Her gaze drifted from the check out the window to an enormous ponderosa pine, some one-hundred yards away.

That tree had been there since before her great-grandfather moved to this land. Of course, if she took this down payment, she would give up this home, this land, that tree. She sighed. She knew she could not give it up, and she could not let down her last blood relative, Maddie. Maddie was the only person left on earth who had a chance of finding, in this land, its fullest, truest potential.

She put the check back in the envelope, closed the flap crisply, and handed it back to Crandall.

"No, thank you."

His eyes narrowed. He looked into her face, studying it, assessing all indications of emotion. She looked away from him, uncomfortable.

"Now, as I said, I really have to get back to town."

He smiled narrowly and took the envelope. He set it on the hall table and gave it a small tap with his index finger.

"Well, I'll just leave it here for you to consider," he said.

"No, you won't." She picked it up and handed it to him. "I don't want there to be any 'misunderstanding' about whether or not I accepted this check. I do not accept it, and if you will excuse me, I'm going to miss my bus."

"Bus? Now, wait a minute. Why do you need to go back to town so urgently on an evening like this one, by bus no less?" Crandall actually seemed to have dropped the gamesmanship for the moment. "Good heavens, woman, it's ten degrees out, with a wind chill of minus fifteen."

"That's exactly why I have to get back to town." Clara caught herself. She didn't want to reveal too much to this man. "I just need to drop this envelope off at the gas and electric."

He looked at the little pink envelope. It looked like a "thank you" note.

"Is that all? Well, that's hardly worth going all the way back to town for, especially when I'm heading downtown now. Please, let me deliver it for you."

Clara looked out the window again. That would be perfect. Then she could just eat her tuna, the chocolates, and turn up the heat. It seemed colder in here than it should. But she hated to be indebted to him in any way, even on something as small as this.

He was watching her closely again, seeming to read her thoughts with that narrow-eyed gaze.

"Oh, honestly, Clara. It's just a small thing I can do for you. Here. I'll take back this check. No pressure. I'm just trying to save you the long, cold trip into town. Surely you don't dislike me that much, to not even give me a chance to do you this small favor?"

He sounded quite sincere, after all. "Oh, alright then, Mr. Crandall. I do appreciate it. I would rather stay here tonight, and not have to go back out."

"I don't blame you one bit." He slid the envelope containing the check into the breast pocket of his coat and held the pink one in his hand. "Well, I'll make sure this gets to its destination in just a few minutes. Now you collect your little dog." He glanced at Joe Todd. The dog sat like the Sphinx in front of the door, and curled up his lip in a snarl. "And crank up the heat, settle in with a good book and that box of chocolates, and don't worry about a thing."

Clara sighed. "You know, Mr. Crandall, that sounds like an excellent idea. Thank you, and good afternoon."

"Good afternoon." He stepped quickly through the door, the wind catching his coat, flying it wildly behind him as he strode to his car.

Chapter 6

Clara watched as Crandall pulled away, then quickly tore the plastic wrap off the box of chocolates and opened the lid. Inside were sixteen plump truffles, white, dark and milk chocolate. She popped one into her mouth and chewed it quickly, swallowing it down and reaching for a second. She ate three before she realized she had barely tasted them, so she put the lid back on the box and carried it and the cans of dog food and tuna into the kitchen.

"Here you go, Joe," she said as she peeled back the lid and plopped the dog food on a plate, setting it on the floor in front of the little dog. He dug his teeth eagerly into the can-shaped mound.

Clara wanted to join him in a meal, but her conscience was nagging her about Bugle. She hadn't checked on him that day. Since the candies had taken the edge off her hunger, she thought she'd better get everything done before indulging in her simple meal. That way, she could really enjoy it. But it meant going back outside. She sighed and put on her barn coat and boots. She also picked up her cane. She never used it in town, but here on the ranch, she relied on it to help her over the uneven ground.

"I'm just going to check on Bugle, Joe Todd." The dog acknowledged the statement only with a polite quivering of his short tail, still intent on his food.

The wind was bitter at her back, shoving her painfully along toward the stable. The small structure, made of broad, hand-cut boards many decades ago, stood solidly in its peeling white paint, although much of the original barn had fallen down around it.

Bugle nickered at her approach, his black head poking out the open top of a Dutch door. She switched on the dusty bulb hanging over his stall. The lanky paint, with his white body and a few big, black spots, had once been roundly muscled in the rump and shoulders. He had put in a full career as a working ranch horse, not to mention his side jobs at local horse shows with various young girls aboard, both relatives and neighbors. Even Maddie had barrel-raced him in high school, and brought home a ribbon or two. Now his hips protruded, his teeth were long and yellow, and he had puffy lumps around his leg joints. He was an old friend, and Megan, the girl in braces and blue jeans who lived a few miles up the road, pedaled there every day to give him hay, fill his water bucket and muck his stall in exchange for the pleasure of grooming and riding him.

Clara loved to watch them trot off together across the prairie, Megan sitting up proudly on the old gelding. Bugle would jog stiffly, joints clicking, but with his head up and ears pricked, just as if he was searching for a last little heifer to chase.

"Hello, old man," Clara said, running her hand down his straight, bony face. His lips pulled playfully at her glove and she took it off to stroke his soft muzzle, so warm, even in this cold. Megan had been there that day, Clara saw, and had put down fresh bedding, filled the water bucket and supplied him with plenty of hay. Clara hadn't been able to buy grain for some time, but a cattle farmer neighbor ten miles south had extra hay this year and supplied her with enough large round bales to get Bugle through the winter, charging almost nothing. Actually, his story about the extra hay and the low price was hard to believe, but Clara opted to believe it, for the sake of her horse's health.

"Well, I guess we should shut that top door, so the wind isn't blowing in on you. What do you think?" She turned back to look at his dark, interested eyes with their long, black lashes. The horse nuzzled her face and hair gently.

"You're a good old fellow," she told him, stroking his neck for a minute. Then she shut the top of the two-piece door, hooking the latch. "There. Now you'll be toasty."

She made her way to the stable door.

"Good night, Bugle," she called, switching off the light and walking carefully, using the cane to find the path. The wind was in her face now, and biting cold.

Back inside, she was glad to hear the furnace blowing. The house was warming up. Joe Todd greeted her happily as she took off the coat and boots. She was about to head toward the kitchen again when the headline of the free, weekly newspaper caught her eye. It was a story about the son of an old friend who discovered a dinosaur skeleton when digging out a foundation for a new house. She carried the paper into the living room and settled in her cozy chair, turned on the lamp and began to read. Fighting that cold had been so hard, though, and after all the walking she was exhausted. Before finishing the article, she dropped into sleep with Joe Todd curled in a tight white-and-tan ball on her lap.

"Damn her!"

Crandall barely noticed the road, he was so consumed with frustration.

"What is the matter with that crazy old bat? She wants that money!"

It had been obvious, how much she wanted it. Why did she give it back?

There had to be a reason that was very important to her. What could it be? Was she simply saving the land for her niece or granddaughter, or whomever that girl was? That didn't seem to be a big enough cause to turn down $1.7 million cash. Maybe it was part of it, but it wasn't the whole reason. He was going to have to find it out, this reason. He considered going back to Clara's, insisting that she talk to him and tell him what was actually preventing this sale.

There was no room to pull over safely on the narrow, cliff-side road, but when he cleared the canyon, he pulled off to the shoulder. Though it was dark, he knew that before him stretched the fertile chaparral-covered countryside, rolling its acres toward the rocky, purple and black hillsides, covered with spotty scrub oak, aspen and ponderosa pine. His land. The land he had to have. The last piece before he put together the puzzle that would be the Crandall Resort.

He started to turn around when his eye fell on the pink envelope Clara had given him, the one he had promised to take to town. Without a moment's hesitation, he pried it open and pulled out the contents, a flowered note card containing a personal check, addressed to Stony Valley Gas Company. She had jotted a few lines in graceful, cursive writing, written in a style painstakingly learned by people her age, long ago, in grammar school.

Dear Fred,
Here is payment in full for my outstanding heating bill.
Thank you for being so patient with me on the matter of my account. I know I owe it to you that my "home fires" have been kept burning, even though I have been very delinquent.
Sincerely, with much respect and gratitude,
Clara Stanton

Crandall tucked the card and check back into the envelope. A dark little thought began to form somewhere in the back of his head. He didn't let the thought really take shape, though. Instead, he set the envelope down on the passenger seat and pulled the car back onto the road toward town.

It was very cold out there, getting colder, with a long weekend ahead.

After about half a mile, he approached an intersection. If he turned here, he could take the back route to town, a treacherous but lovely pass over the hills. It would take him past the waterfall that would be the focal point of the vista from the windows of the resort lodges he would build along the ridge. It was shorter as the crow flies, but even the most hardcore locals usually stuck to the main road to get where they needed to go. The pass was narrow, with sharp curves, and unpredictable in terms of what might be blocking it at any time – mud, rocks, even cattle. It would be especially difficult at night, with this driving wind blowing dust and debris all over the place, but it did show a spectacular view of the very land he coveted. He glanced at the dashboard clock. It was 4:15 p.m. He immediately turned off the main road, making his way slowly toward the pass.

During the drive, he allowed that dark little thought to emerge. If he didn't get that payment to the gas and electric company in time, would the company turn off Clara's power? What would happen to a frail old lady with no way to get to safety in this coming blizzard? Surely, she would die, and it would be such an easy death. Didn't people who freeze to death just go to sleep? He really didn't know, but he rather liked the idea.

By the time he turned back onto the main road, it was 5:15. If they were going to shut it off, wouldn't it be done by now, after 5 on a Friday? He had never looked into the rules about such things, but now he had to know. He turned the car back toward Clara's ranch.

Tiny bits of freezing rain were pinging against his windshield, starting to form a glaze, making it tough to see the dark country road. But when he stopped at the end of her long drive, he was pretty certain he saw a glow of lights in the distance. So, the electric company hadn't shut her off. Crandall stared glumly down the driveway. The idea had been too convenient, he knew. What were the odds of the power company shutting off a little old lady before a holiday weekend and during the blizzard of the century? But now that he had the idea, Crandall couldn't let it go. As he mulled the situation, her unreasonable resistance to the sale, his growing desperation that he would lose his funding, he stared off at the house as it glowed warmly through the sleet, and he slowly put together the pieces of a new idea.

What was keeping him from shutting off her power himself? It would really be a gentle way to remove this problem.

He drove into the driveway and pulled his car out of sight. He buttoned his collar up around his neck and stepped out into the wind. It was howling and he was fairly certain even that menace of a mutt wouldn't hear him approach the house. It was easy to spot the location where the electric wires attached. He used the penlight he always carried, contemplating them nervously. He didn't want to electrocute himself. The insulation on the thick, ancient cables looked cracked and tarry. He didn't dare touch them. He glanced around for another option and saw the old entryway to the basement. It wasn't locked. He pulled open the rickety wooden hatch. A few stone steps led to a door, which he was able to open with some pushing. Something fell on the other side, and Crandall held his breath, waiting to hear a bark or footsteps. All he heard was the wind. He dropped into the basement, a dank and cluttered spot, probably untouched for decades, except for occasional additions to the pile of broken chairs, cracked mirrors, lawn games and the other odds and ends a family collects.

The only new thing in the basement was the furnace, whirring away. When he finally got there, it was a simple as flipping a switch. He snapped it downward, and the motor's hum slowed into silence. Crandall slipped away, back out, into the storm.

His first stop when he got to town was his office. He pulled out the check and practiced copying Clara's signature several times. Forgery was one of the many dubious talents he had picked up over the years. Once he was satisfied, he wrote a graceful, "Clara Stanton" at the bottom of his land sale contract. It was perfect, just the right amount of old-school handwriting, a little tremor from age, matching her loops and "t" crosses exactly.

"Damn I'm good," Crandall said to himself.

But now he had to hurry. He couldn't risk missing Toby Landy.

It could work, but if it didn't, he was in big trouble. He had a lot riding on the possibility of an old lady's freezing to death. What if she didn't die?

Crandall hated loose ends. Maybe he should have done something more direct. But he needed to keep this death as natural-appearing as possible, or everything could get held up. He would lose the opportunity.

He shook the thought away. The path was decided. Whatever had to happen, he would make sure it did.

Chapter 7

Clara awakened when Joe Todd stood on her lap to reposition himself. She saw by the wall clock that she had slept for about half an hour. Her stomach complained that she was past due giving it a good meal.

Back in the kitchen, she opened the can of tuna and plopped it on a plate. The house felt cold. She went into the dining room to check the thermostat. It was sixty degrees. That didn't seem right. She pushed the tiny lever to the right, to eighty degrees, and went back toward the kitchen.

"You know what would go well with this?" she said to the dog, who licked his now empty plate hopefully. "One of those carrots in the garden."

Her small garden had yielded a nice assortment of vegetables last year, and the ground still housed carrots. They kept fine there over the winter. She took a heavy kitchen spoon, put on her barn coat and plodded through the icy wind toward the patch of garden. She eased herself down on her hands and knees to scratch at the ground, a difficult endeavor. Her stiff hand could not generate enough pressure to get the spoon through the cold ground. It must be too late. The ground was hard as cement. She pulled at the top of a carrot, but the old greens broke off in her hand. She scratched the spoon around the top of the root, managing to expose some of the orange vegetable. Her breath was so white it felt as though she were working in the fog as it puffed out around her face. She was shaking in the cold as she exposed more of the carrot. Finally, prying with the spoon, she was able to coax the yellow earth to slowly release the short, fat carrot.

"Ahh!" she said. She took her time getting up, first sitting back, then standing carefully, using the cane. Once up, she waited until she was sure she was balanced, then turned and went back to the kitchen door. Joe Todd barked happily, as if she'd been gone for a week.

The house offered relief from the wind, but it was still cold. She checked the heat grate in the kitchen and felt nothing. She listened and heard no indication that the furnace was preparing to generate warm air. She went back and checked the thermostat. The temperature was down to 50.

A frightening thought entered her mind. What if they had shut it off?

No, she just couldn't get herself to believe that the gas company had shut off the heat on her. Fred would not have let that happen. It must be a delay, a little interruption because they hadn't gotten the check. But they would soon enough, and everything would be all right. Still, it was very cold outside. It was even cold enough for someone to possibly die of exposure, without heat. In fact, she realized, that could happen to her.

Maybe she should try to get to her neighbor's. Clara looked out the window. The wind was raging, now bringing sleet. She could hear ice hitting the windows. In the barn light, she could see the bits of sleet flying by sideways. It still wasn't coming down heavily yet, but there was no way she would make it to her neighbor's. She would just have to hunker down and ride it out.

Hungry though she was, Clara knew she had to work quickly. Still in her barn coat, she hurried back outside, moving faster than she preferred, collecting all the scrub oak and ponderosa branches she could carry. She brought them back to the house, her spine aching. She dropped the little pile – hardly anything, really – by the fireplace and reached for the box of wooden matches on the mantle. She had stopped receiving the daily newspaper several weeks back, it being an added expense she couldn't accept at this time. She went back to the table and collected some fliers that had been mailed to her, and the free weekly paper, and the other junk mail and bills she had not yet opened. She wadded the paper into loose balls and piled the twigs on top of them in the hearth. Lighting a match, she set the flame first to the back of the paper, then the front, blowing on it gently to encourage the flame to burn hot. The little twigs caught, and she added a few larger pieces. But she realized she really hadn't collected enough of the larger pieces to sustain a decent fire. Shivering, she stood, using the back of her easy chair for balance, and started to the coat closet. She pulled down a canvas tote bag that hung from a nail there and headed outside again. Joe Todd exploded out of the kitchen and burst through the open door, his wild barking swallowed by the wind as he disappeared from view.

"Joe Todd, no!"

She couldn't go after him. It was all she could do to plod along toward the ponderosa, hoping its ancient structure had yielded some sizable branches. It seemed to take her forever to reach its base. She was so cold, her fingers, nose and chin were numb, and she could not feel her toes. To her relief, the tree had dropped several manageable branches. She stuffed the bag full of the smaller pieces, then laid it on the ground and piled some of the bigger pieces on it. Before starting back to the house, she felt along the base of the tree for the small twist of rope that marked the opening to her safe. It was there, well hidden under the roots of the tree. Satisfied, she began to drag the bag of branches, walking backward, toward the house.

Her pace was intolerably slow, and she had to stop several times to stand up straight, trying to prevent her back from cramping, and to catch her breath. She finally made it back to the house, and pulled the pile of wood in behind her, ignoring the pine needles and dirt that trailed in after her load.

The little fire she had started had long since burned out, so she had to start over. She was a proficient fire builder, though, and soon she had a small blaze again. This time, she could add a few larger pieces to sustain it. When she saw it was going to stay lit, she stood again, and then sat in the easy chair, resting. She was exhausted and very hungry.

Right about now, the folks at the gas company would have received notice that her bill was paid, and would start flipping switches, or hitting computer keys, probably, that would start the gas flowing to her house once more. Surely, it couldn't take much longer. Mr. Crandall had left more than an hour before. She just had to wait it out.

She stood slowly and checked the thermostat. It was 43 degrees. She pushed the little lever up to 85, so when the heat came on, the house would really warm up.

She continued on to the kitchen, where she rinsed the carrot and collected the plate of tuna. She returned to the fire. The little pile of wood she worked so hard to collect didn't really amount to much, she noticed. She would have to go for more, if the heat didn't come on in a few minutes. But for now, it offered a pleasant warmth.

The unexpected cold had distracted her from the main mission of the evening. She had decided earlier that day to write a note to Maddie, telling her about the diamonds.

She placed another small branch on the fire, trying to be conservative, and ate a forkful of tuna. The little fire started to warm the room, and she was satisfied for the moment. She sat down, with blank paper, to write.

Dear Maddie,
I want to tell you a story that is wonderful and exciting and maybe hard to believe. I'm writing it instead of telling you so you can absorb it privately, at your own pace. Before I start, let me assure you that I have not lost my marbles. Look at the other documents and other things I'll include with this note, and you'll see that, while my body isn't doing so well, in mind and spirit, I'm just as sound as ever.

To really do this right, let me go back to when my great-grandfather, Asa Ramsdale Cunningham, first inherited this land back when Colorado was still a territory.

Chapter 8
Colorado Territory, 1875

Asa chewed quickly, swallowing down a large chunk of lamb. It seemed like the best meat he had ever eaten, so tender, with a black char on the outside, pink on the inside. After months of fire-cooked wild game or leathery jerky, this piece of lamb was amazing. He wanted to savor it, but he just couldn't stop himself from gulping it down.

The tavern door banged open and two men came in. Asa glanced their way. One was tall with strong, lean shoulders and dirty, hay-colored hair. The other was shorter, square-faced, with dark eyes and black hair. The tavern was small, and the men seemed to fill it up as they chose to sit at one of the two tables, the one closest to a dusty, upright piano.

"You never did break that mare, and if you say you did, you're the worst kind of liar," the dark one said.

"I did too. You can ask Terry if I didn't."

"Terry's a worse liar than you."

"Evening Jake, Cal," said the tavern keeper.

"Howdy, Darwell," the dark one said.

"What you got that smells so good?"

"Lamb."

"Any good, mister?" The tall one turned to Asa, appraising him and his plate with interest.

Asa swallowed a bite of meat and took a longer look at the young men. The tall one was toothy with hazel eyes and a deer hide vest, wearing the challenging smile of a joker. The other one had a thick neck and chest, and a nose that had probably not started out that shape, but had been reworked sometime in his young life, maybe by a fist, maybe by the neck of a bucking horse. Under a veil of caution, his dark eyes were kind.

"Good doesn't even come close," Asa said, smiling back.

"Well, that's good enough for me," said the one in the vest. "Serve it up, Dar."

"Me too! And don't be charging us no four cents for the bread. Bread is supposed to come with it."

"It's four cents," the barkeep, Darwell, said, pouring whiskey for the two men.

"You ain't from around here, right?" the taller man said. He walked up to Asa and held out his hand. "I'm Cal Johnstone. That's Jake St. Bonaview. He carries a fancy name, but nothing else about him is worth a nickel."

Asa shook the man's hand.

"Asa Cunningham."

"Well, well," Cal looked at him with interest. "Pleasure. We help keep ranch up at McAllister's place. You heard of it?"

"No."

"Well, I'll warrant it's the biggest spread in these parts. Got three standing Hereford bulls, a whole passel of longhorn cows and some of the best cattle horses you'll find for a thousand miles. Mr. McAllister was one of the first men in this territory. Wait 'til you see those new calves he's got on the ground."

"Oh?" Asa said, not knowing how else to respond.

"You finish that lamb, Mr. Cunningham, but after that we want to hear where you're coming from," Cal said. "It's been weeks since we saw a stranger come through, and this town is boring if it's anything."

Asa pondered this request as he continued eating. He ran the end of his bread around the lamb drippings on his plate and chewed the thick, damp crust. It was so good, he might have licked the plate if the others weren't watching him.

"All right, then, Mr. Asa Cunningham, pray tell your story before that meal hits bottom and you'll be wanting sleep," Cal said, coming up behind him with his whiskey and leaning his back against the bar.

"Why don't you buy him another drink, since you're so keen on loosening his tongue?" Jake said, joining them on Cal's other side.

"That's a deal. Come on Darwell, get it flowing!"

The barkeeper poured drinks and Cal nodded at Asa expectantly. Asa sipped and cleared his throat.

"Well, I came from Toledo on horseback. I left in the spring. There's not too much to tell for most of the trip. I met up with some other men. Traveling days, sleeping out at night. But when we got near here, we had some bad trouble with the Indians."

"What's that, Arapaho?"

"Don't know, but they were at the last big pass east of here. 'Twas five of us, by then. That morning, another fellow and I headed out after some elk we had seen over on the east mountain. We didn't get any though. We were about two hours out and two hours back to the others. When we got back, well, it was just terrible."

"They killed 'em?" Cal said.

"Yes, but it was worse than just killing.'

"Torture?" Jake said.

Asa sighed. He didn't like to remember the sight. "By the time we got to them they were bled dry and half-cooked, tied over the fire."

"May they rest in peace," Darwell said.

"We cut them down, but then we had to get out of there." Asa sipped his whiskey. "I have regretted that ever since, that we couldn't bury them properly."

"So, did you get even with those sons-a-bitches?" Jake said.

"No. We heard them coming back our way. We were just the two of us left. We didn't stand a chance. We ran."

"Did they give chase?"

"Yeah," Asa said. "And they were keen on catching us."

"How'd you get away?"

"Well, I reckon I don't know. That afternoon, it seemed like they were getting close. Up ahead we had a choice of a rocky pass or a low, wet plain. We decided our luck in the hills had not been good, so we went low. As soon as they saw where we went, the Indians just stopped. They watched us for a while, discussing it among themselves. Afore long, they took off."

"What did you make of it?"

"I'm not sure. We reckoned maybe we were heading toward quicksand or some other calamity. But we were so glad to be rid of them we decided we'd just take our chances. We never saw them again. We were a good ten days' ride from here, where we last saw them."

"They probably decided they chased you far enough," Cal said.

"Maybe you went into their enemy's territory," suggested Darwell.

"No," Jake said. "It's just like up on the Mesa. Most of the Indians won't go near it. They think it's evil, full of bad spirits."

"It is," Cal said.

Asa looked at them curiously. "What mesa is that?"

"Black Rock Mesa, south of the village," Cal said, sipping his whiskey and squinting shrewdly at Asa. "Prettiest land in the whole area. Got a creek to a waterfall, into a lake, lots of flat land, plenty of forest and hills. But there ain't a man who can use it. Not even the men who claimed it. Funny thing," Cal said, looking hard at Asa. "The last one who tried was named Cunningham, too."

"Yes, that sounds like my land," Asa said quietly. "That sounds like the land my cousin described."

"I thought so," Cal said, "as soon as you said your name was Cunningham. Your cousin was Caleb Cunningham."

"He willed it to me."

The men were quiet as they absorbed this information.

Cal finished talking and sipped his whiskey. Jake and Darwell, who had heard Cal's story before, watched Asa, waiting for his response. He cleared his throat and looked away from Cal.

"Well," he said. "I don't know what it could be you saw out there. With all due respect, I reckon you might tell a tall tale now and then, just for fun."

"He does," Jake said.

Cal shrugged, not looking at him. He didn't look like this was a joke.

"However," Asa said, "I just received 1,600 acres of land. If Cousin Caleb wasn't exaggerating, it's fertile and rich and ready for just about anything I want to do with it."

"It is that," Jake said. "A creek crosses through it, and it drops about forty feet at the base of the cliffs and goes on to make a lake at the center of the property. And that lake don't go dry, no matter what the weather is doing. Any man would be proud to be the owner of that plot, no question."

"Except for the fact that it's possessed by evil spirits, right?" Asa said, smiling wryly at Jake. He glanced sideways at Cal, who was stoically ignoring them. He was so serious, Asa felt bad for teasing him.

"I'm not trying to poke fun at you," He said to Cal.

"Yeah, Cal, stop being so cool," Jake said. "How do you expect the man to act when you pop out with such a wild tale the first time he meets you?"

"You know, I didn't think of it like that," Cal said, turning around so his back was resting against the bar again. "I usually like to tell much wilder tales than that when I first meet a fellow. Like the time I came upon a mama grizzly and her babies up over the Sandy Ridge."

Jake, Darwell and Asa relaxed, relieved. Asa sipped his whiskey.

"Well, sir, she was eight foot tall if she was a inch, and I was feeling I was about six inches tall when she stood up in front of me."

The men exchanged stories for an hour or more, then Asa said goodnight. He was groggy with good food and drink, and exhausted from his trip, and nothing would feel as good as a real bed in the rooming house up the street.

As he undressed for bed, he felt unsettled. Until tonight, he had felt nothing but impatience to get to this place, and excitement to see his new land. But now, as he thought over what Cal had told him, he couldn't fight off the tiny tendril of fear that wound round the edges of his thoughts and followed him to sleep.

Chapter 10

It was the first time Asa had slept past sunrise in months. The soft feather bed and thick, cotton quilt were a welcome change after his dirty bedroll and the ground, and he barely moved in the night. Curtains prevented the sun from waking him, and, since his horse was safely bedded down with feed at the livery, he had no reason to wake up at any particular time.

When he finally arose, he was as stiff as if he'd been hibernating over the winter. He also had a pulsing pain behind his right eye, a sure sign he had slept too long. He sometimes got these headaches after periods of prolonged stress. Once the stress let up and he felt some relief, and got some rest, then the headache would occur as if some sort of final punishment. His mother had been the same way. He remembered many Sundays when she couldn't get out of bed, even to go to church. It usually occurred after some period of unusual exertion, such as the slaughtering.

He tried to sit up, but motion, together with a sliver of sunlight from the window, caused the throbbing to flair. He pressed his palm tightly over his eye and lay back down. He wished desperately for the two things he knew could help: a cold pack and a cup of coffee. He couldn't bear the thought of getting up to seek help from the proprietor, so he tried to doze through the pain.

As he lay there, he felt a strange, cool breeze swirl around him. It was as though something, or someone, had entered the room, disturbing the air just slightly. Asa's heart sped up and he opened his pain-free eye and looked cautiously around. The room was empty. The window was not open, so the breeze couldn't have come from outside. Still, he had the eerie feeling that someone was in the room with him. Then he felt something like a hand on his forehead, right over the spot where the pain was throbbing. He opened both eyes wide and pulled away, causing the pain to flare again. He didn't see anyone in the room.

He decided he must have imagined it. These headaches sometimes brought on odd feelings, usually visual changes, like wavy lines in his vision, or sparkling lights. Maybe this was just another symptom. He lay still and shut his eyes. Soon he felt the cool breeze again, and the invisible hand again touched his forehead. This time he didn't move, convincing himself that the headache was still causing this strange sensation.

Now he felt heat on the spot where the hand seemed to touch, and then he noticed a strange smell in the room, sweet and earthy. He opened his eyes again, but there was still nothing unusual there. The smell grew stronger, as did the heat over his eye. This continued for some minutes, and then the heat faded. As it did, Asa was astonished to feel the pain diminishing with it. With each pulse, the pain decreased until it was gone. Then he felt the cool breeze again. He sat up and waited, expecting the pulsing pain to begin again, but there was nothing. He stood. Still no pain.

He was surprised. Never had one of these headaches ended so abruptly, and certainly not under such unusual circumstances. Asa stepped idly to the window and looked down at the street, dusty in the cool sunlight. Several people were going about their errands. A wagon clattered by, pulled by a single, heavy horse with a thick mane and no tail. The wagon was loaded with caged chickens and driven by a man with a straw hat pulled low over his eyes.

Asa's gaze was drawn to a small woman standing on the wooden walk across the street. She was dark skinned, with long, black hair, clad in a deer hide dress and leggings and soft, buckskin shoes. An Indian, obviously, but he couldn't guess her tribe. Others passed her without noticing, but Asa's attention was captured by her. He felt a prickle on his neck as he realized her dark eyes were looking directly at him. He felt as though she had been standing under his window, staring up at him, for some time, as though she were waiting for him to appear. She kept her intense gaze on him for a moment as Asa's heart pounded, unaccountably.

There was something so strange about her. Why was she looking at him like that? How had she known he would look out the window? Then, her intense gaze suddenly relaxed. The smallest of smiles crossed her face, fleeting, happy. Then she turned and walked slowly away down the board sidewalk, her slender hips swaying beneath the leather dress. Asa watched her, moving to the other window so he could see her slowly saunter out of sight.

"What in the world was that?" he said aloud.

Since his headache was gone, Asa dressed. After so many weeks on the trail, his only remaining clothes were filthy and shabby. He had some money, so he decided to purchase a new pair of pants and a shirt — after a bath, haircut and shave.

Later, dressed in his new clothes and with a warm breakfast in his belly, he went to the livery, saddled Buster and headed out to investigate his land. The sun was already past the midway point, but he figured he still had about seven hours before sundown. It was a clear, sunny day, with wispy clouds across the deep blue sky. There was no sign of bad weather and, despite the cowboys' tales from the night before, Asa felt cheerful. He was not one to spend more than a moment's thought on ghosts and evil spirits, considering them to be inhabitants of the imagination.

He asked Buster to pick up an easy jog along a wagon trail by a cliff. Buster, in top condition, had also received a good night's sleep and two good meals, not to mention a hoof trim, and he was frisky, throwing a few bucking hops into the jog. Asa recognized it as good spirits and laughed instead of scolding the horse, who then settled into a smooth and comfortable gait.

They had traveled more than an hour before Asa spotted the turn off that Cal had described – a narrow path separating from the road. From there they set out across a mesa, rich with grasses and shrubs, surrounded by hills, shrouded by tall pines and shimmering aspen trees. It was some of the loveliest countryside Asa had seen. He surprised deer, elk, and plenty of gophers and hares. He was delighted with his good fortune when he finally came across the boundary marker of his land.

"This is it, Buster old boy, our new home. Let's go take a look."

With that, they set foot on the property for the first time, 1,600 acres of hills, streams, woods and flatland. Asa felt joyful.

As soon as they crossed the boundary, however, he noticed the weather seemed to be changing. A cool breeze picked up from the north, and the sky darkened.

"Well, this could be some bad luck, then," he muttered as he pushed Buster toward a hill. He wanted to get a full view of the land from up there. The hill was wooded, and they wound their way along what looked to be a deer path. The wind was starting to howl and it grew overcast and dark. It was now so cold he could see his and Buster's breath.

"What in the world?" he said. "Buster, you ever seen anything like this before?"

Just then the horse's head popped up and his ears pricked toward the path ahead. He stopped and snorted so loudly it made Asa jump.

"You fool, don't scare me like that," he said, peering ahead to try to see what had startled the horse. Buster leaped sideways and tried to spin around, attempting to go back down the trail and rocking Asa in his saddle.

"Oh no, you don't," said Asa, pulling the horse back around and urging him forward.

Buster reluctantly continued up the trail, his ears still pricked and his nostrils flaring. Asa was alert too, both to see what was scaring Buster and to be prepared in case the horse tried to jump sideways again. The wind was howling through the trees. The thin aspen branches flayed about and the ponderosas hissed. A thick branch slammed to the ground, barely missing Buster's face. The horse reared.

"Let's get out of these trees!"

He pushed the horse into a gallop and they crashed through the woods, Buster leaping logs and brushing Asa roughly against trees. Asa kept his head down by the horse's neck so as not to be whipped by branches. At last they burst onto a clearing at the top of the hill. He slowed Buster to a walk as he tried to get his bearings. It was so dark, there was no way he could get a view at this time, and he looked for shelter. Just then lightning flashed, thunder cracked, and the wind blew up a tumble of leaves and twigs that stung Asa's face. Heavy rain now pounded them.

Buster panicked, running across the dark hilltop. Asa couldn't stop him. The horse that had been brave through the many dangers they had already faced now hurtled on, blind with fear. Asa felt the terror and held on helplessly, forgetting all he knew about stopping a runaway horse. In the next lightning flash, Asa saw with horror that they were running toward a cliff.

"Whoa! Whoa!" he yanked on Buster's reins, but it was as though some powerful force was rushing them straight toward the edge. Asa had no choice. He threw himself from Buster's back, hitting the ground with first his left hand, then his shoulder, tumbling against rocks. Pain snapped through his left side and cracked into his head. He rolled upright and watched as Buster continued toward the cliff's edge. The horse was about to go over, head first, when out of nowhere a figure appeared. The figure, a slight silhouette, stood right in the horse's path, on the cliff's edge, arms spread wide, robes flapping crazily in the raging storm. To Asa's amazement, Buster stopped, just inches away from driving himself and the figure over the edge. The figure gathered Buster's reins and patted the horse. Buster calmed down immediately, as though he had not been frightened to the point of killing himself and his rider only seconds before. Just then, Asa became dizzy and everything went black.

Chapter 11

Asa was aware that he was being pulled roughly along the ground. He was dragged over rocks and uneven earth, and each bump made his head and arm throb in pain. He opened his eyes and tried to focus. Rain dripped into his eyes. Ahead he could make out Buster, walking placidly next to a small person, a woman, he thought. Two poles were tied alongside Buster's saddle, and they connected to a crude frame to which a thick hide was lashed, and on which he was lying. He bumped along, his head padded on a woolly sheepskin. As he tried to figure it all out, Asa's vision suddenly closed from either side, and he passed out.

Asa remained either asleep or in a murky, semi-conscious state for several days. In his rare moments of consciousness, he could spot Buster grazing nearby, and realized that the woman was caring for him. He was aware of his arm being braced, his head being cleaned and bandaged. He sometimes awoke enough to vomit, his empty stomach twisting painfully. Occasionally he thought he saw a huge, reddish bird nearby, a terrifying vision that led to nightmares. The woman offered him sips of bitter water that must have contained medicine, for whenever he swallowed some, he sank into a comfortable, groggy state that led to more sleep.

One day he finally emerged, clear-headed, because the smell of roasting meat made his stomach rumble urgently. He saw the woman tending to six plump partridges on a spit over the fire. As he watched, the huge, red bird flew in and dropped a rabbit near the woman, then hopped up in a tree, folding its wings and settling them with a little shimmy, causing bits of feather and dust to cloud around it briefly. Asa now realized that the bird was real, and that it was some kind of eagle.

"Thank you," the woman said to the bird. She grasped the rabbit, swiftly gutted it and brought the innards to the eagle, which hopped down to a lower branch and ate the morsels from her fingers. It was not gentle, but it also did not bite her fingers. Asa had never seen an eagle behave that way.

"How did you train it to do that?" he said. The eagle, the woman and Buster all looked around at him in surprise. The woman's face was at first as still and stern as the eagle's, but then she smiled, and this changed her face completely to one of girlish delight. That smile made her beautiful, he noticed.

She came back to the fire and sat, the rabbit in one hand, a knife in the other.

"I h'aint trained it," she said. "I just asked it."

She worked on the rabbit as she spoke, finished dressing it and adding it to the spit of meat.

"You asked it?" Asa sat up slowly, feeling weak, but otherwise well. The pain in his head and arm was minimal. "And what did it reply?"

"That should be obvious."

"Did you stop my horse from running off the cliff?"

"Yes."

"And pulled me here? Bandaged my arm?"

"Mm-hmm. It was broken."

"Well, thank you." He noticed the sun was setting. "How long was I out?"

"Six days."

"My God. Longer than I thought."

She said nothing, just turned the spit.

"What's your name?" he asked.

"You couldn't pronounce it, I'm sure." She said something he didn't understand, and she smiled again. "It means 'Healer Woman.' You can call me Mayla. It's easier." She pulled four of the partridges from the spit and offered two to him, keeping two for herself.

"Thank you," he said enthusiastically. The meat was too hot to eat, but he attempted it, burning his tongue and then having to wait. When they were finally at an edible temperature, he ate both birds quickly and looked at the others, still on the spit. She noticed and gave him the last two, letting the rabbit continue cooking. This dark young woman with the pretty smile suddenly looked familiar.

"Were you in town before?" he said. "I think I saw you."

"I saw you, too."

"What're you doing way out here?"

"I'm in town but little. I spend most of my time here. In fact, my people have lived here since the beginning. This is our place." With the sun setting behind her, Mayla's face was shadowed.

He might have a head injury, but he definitely understood her point. He thought about it, considered letting it go without comment, but realized he couldn't.

"Well, actually, it's my place," he said. "My cousin bought it and left it to me. I have a deed in my name, officially filed with the United States government and the Colorado Territory. He had to work pretty hard and pay a lot of money to pick up all those connected parcels in order to own this acreage. Alas, he died, so I'm here to carry on and make this place a ranch. And my home."

"What your cousin did makes no difference. What you want to do makes no difference. Neither I nor any of my people sold this land to the United States government. You can show me all the papers you want. They have no meaning to me." She spoke toward the fire, but when she finished she looked at him, her face dark in the twilight.

Asa knew this was a problem, but he also knew it was a battle she couldn't win. This saddened him, for her, but it wouldn't stop him from taking possession of this property and building his ranch.

As if reading his mind, she said, "Yes, the white man's law is on your side, but I have this land on my side, and all of its creations. Here, there are things more powerful than your law."

"I'm not trying to be disrespectful by saying this, but what you have is not powerful enough."

She suddenly laughed, and its musical trilling surprised him. He wished she wasn't laughing at him, because the sound, and her smiling face, were so charming.

"Let me tell you some of this land's history," she said.

"Sure. I'm interested. But it won't change matters."

"When the white people first came here, they killed my grandparents while they slept in their bed, but they didn't realize my mother was left alive. She was just a little girl, but she had a powerful friend. She asked him to kill the white men who had murdered her parents and stole the land."

Mayla checked the rabbit and repositioned the coals under it.

"Did this friend do it?"

"A grizzly bear killed them."

"Oh."

"So yes, the friend did do it."

"I don't understand." Asa poked at the fire, accidentally stirring up ash that floated up and clung to the rabbit. "Are you trying to say that the friend got a bear to kill the people?"

"No, the bear was her friend."

"People can't control wild animals," Asa objected mildly. "But that is quite a story."

Mayla smiled. "No, not control, but we can ask for their help. She asked the bear for help. It knew the white men were a threat, too." She shrugged. "So, it helped."

"That was very nice of it. But I doubt a girl can make a grizzly bear do anything. Even if she asks nicely." He peeled the breast meat off the last partridge.

"Can a woman get an eagle to bring her game?" she said. "A rabbit, maybe?"

Asa stopped chewing and glanced over in the direction of the bird. It was gazing at the horizon, relaxed, its feathers puffed out softly.

"Why did the men kill your grandparents?"

"They were after pink diamonds. It seems they are very rare."

He was surprised.

"Oh?"

"Yes, they grow in the ground here. We use them for medicine. For healing. For decoration."

"Diamonds? Here?"

"I reckon sometimes the whites use them to make tools, because they are so hard. But they like them mostly for jewelry, like this."

She pulled out a necklace that had been tucked under her tunic. It was made of about a dozen clear, pink stones the size of peas, intricately beaded together with turquoise and silver.

Asa looked closely.

"Those really do look like diamonds," he said. "But I haven't seen any that color. And, to be honest, I wouldn't know a diamond from glass."

"Definitely diamonds," she said. "They're powerful. And dangerous."

"I'm sure it's true," said Asa. "So, carry on with your story."

"My mother, she was the one who asked the bear to kill the whites. She grew up and married an Arapaho man, and afore long, they had me. They were murdered, too, by white people who wanted this land. They had heard about the diamonds."

"That's terrible," Asa said. "I'm sorry about your parents."

She nodded. "I was alone then, and when the white Christians heard of me, they stole me and forced me into their school for a spell. It's how I learned English. But I got help, from my ancestors, and returned here. Soon, white men came again. Some had a notion to set up their homesteads, but none stayed for long.

We rid the land of them, myself, my ancestors, my other friends. These white men might have said they stayed here, so they could keep the homesteads they tried to claim, but really they left, and if they didn't, they died. I'm sure that was how your cousin was able to gather so vast an acreage. None of the whites around here want it any more. They know. But sometimes, they still try to get the diamonds."

"I didn't know anything about diamonds," Asa said. "That's not why I'm here."

"I am alone, mostly," she said, as though he hadn't spoken. "Sometimes my people visit. The ones who are left moved farther north, to get away from the white people. But I belong here. This land and I, we are the same."

Asa pressed his hand against a leather pouch under his shirt that held the deed. "You have a lot to say," he said.

"I knew you were coming, back in the late winter," she said quietly.

"I was 1,200 miles away. I barely even knew I was coming."

"My grandpa warned me."

"The dead one?"

"He told me much about you."

"Like what?"

"Lots of things, but mainly, that you reckon you'll take this land."

"I don't need to. It's already mine." He stopped short of adding, "So you better take your bird and your wild stories and clear out."

But she seemed to know what he was thinking.

"You don't listen very well. I told you. Other people have had a notion to take this land. They failed."

By now, he thought she might be somewhat insane, and he had to work to keep the anger out of his voice.

"Just how did my cousin die?" he said.

"He fell from the cliff, yonder. The one you almost went over," she said. "The one from which I saved you."

He remembered the small figure he saw when the lightning flashed, at the edge of the cliff.

She looked at him with her dark eyes, quietly.

Then she said, "I'm going to sleep. This rabbit is almost done. You may eat it."

Without another word, she stood and walked out of the firelight, disappearing into the darkness.

Chapter 12

Mayla was not around when he woke up the next day, and he wanted to go hunting. He saddled Buster with difficulty, due to the arm cast, and they started out of the clearing at a trot. Just as they got to a path that seemed to lead toward a creek, Buster stopped suddenly, almost unseating Asa.

"Get going, you fool," Asa said, pushing the gelding with his legs, then kicking, then slapping Buster's flank with the reins. Buster refused to move forward, and tried instead to turn around.

Finally, Asa dismounted and led the unhappy horse.

"I'm going to need you, should I get a deer," he told the horse. "So stay with me."

The horse's nervousness was contagious, and Asa felt edgy. The little hairs on his neck were standing up as a chill seemed to envelop them. Asa looked behind them, checking the trail, and Buster stopped, his ears pricked. Asa turned quickly and thought he saw a figure ducking behind a tree. Without taking his eyes from the spot, he pulled his rifle from its sheath on the saddle and held it at the ready, resting it on the cast. He and the horse walked slowly toward the spot.

When he reached the tree, he quickly stepped around it, rifle first. There was nothing there. But ahead, he thought he saw the shadow ducking among the boulders. He kept his gun out, and they continued slowly down the trail, but they didn't encounter anyone.

The trail followed a stream, and stopped at a small clearing. He tied Buster in the woods and peered out. A good-sized mule deer doe was grazing nearby. He lined his sights at a spot just below where he estimated the heart lay, knowing his rifle would jump up slightly with the shot.

Just as he started to squeeze the trigger, a person appeared out of nowhere in front of the gun. He leapt at Asa as he fired, causing Asa to jump backwards. His gun went off. The human figure, which Asa had briefly recognized as an Indian in full war regalia, vanished.

The doe bolted at the shot and disappeared into the woods. Asa hurried to the creek. He bent over it and splattered water on his face, trying to calm down. Then he heard footsteps running up behind him. He turned in time to see the same figure bearing down on him with a stone hatchet. The figure swung before Asa could protect himself, and he felt the stone weapon splitting through his skull. He heard Buster take off up the trail. Blood sprayed everywhere. He felt it pouring down his face, dripping red and thick onto his shirt. He reached for his gun, but by the time he had it ready to shoot, the figure was gone.

He leapt up, searching the trees. Oddly, now, he didn't feel the pain. He quickly reached for the creek water to wash the wound and the blood from his eyes. As he splashed his face, he was surprised to see the water ran clear through his hands. He touched his face and examined his fingers. No blood. His shirt was reasonably clean, not bloody as he thought it would be. He gingerly touched the spot where the stone weapon had struck, and found his head to be whole and normal.

Just then, he thought he heard someone nearby. He cast a quick glance around and saw a figure coming at him again. He took off, running up the trail, hearing the footsteps behind him, closing in on him.

He burst into the clearing and found Buster standing there, blowing hard. He tripped and landed on the ground next to the horse. Spinning, he searched behind him for the fearsome figure, ready to fight. There was nothing there.

Buster nuzzled his head.

He stood up and pulled off the horse's saddle and bridle. Then he heard a sound from the trail. Footsteps, and maybe something being dragged. He pointed his rifle toward the sound, resting it again on his cast. Buster pricked his ears toward it. Something was coming. He could see it through the trees. His hand shaking, he waited, holding his breath as his lungs fought for air.

Mayla appeared, pulling a dead doe with a rope. She stopped when she saw Asa's gun, and anger crossed her face. He immediately lowered the gun and sank to the ground, grasping his face in his hands for a moment. Then he sighed and stood.

"The spirits sent this little doe practically into my arms. I've gutted it, but you can butcher it."

Asa's heartbeat steadily slowed to normal. He was ashamed of himself for being afraid. He stood, walked quickly to the doe and yanked the rope out of Mayla's hand.

"It was I that sent the doe into your arms, not the spirits," he said. He found a comfortable place to work and began removing the hide from the carcass.

She looked at him quizzically.

"What did you see down there?" she asked. "Why is your face so pale?"

He turned his face toward his work, not answering.

"And is that blood on your neck and clothing?"

He looked down at his shirt, searching it for signs of the blood. He saw nothing on the shirt but dirt and sweat. He looked at her questioningly. She smiled and built up the fire for cooking.

He swore under his breath and continued his work, trying to rid his mind of the fearful images.

That afternoon, they ate venison steaks, mushrooms and boiled wild oats, then went to work salting and drying the remainder of the meat. As he worked, his cast arm troubled him, making it hard to grip the meat he cut.

"Take the cast off," Mayla suggested.

"But that will interrupt the healing," he said.

"I think it's safe to remove it."

74

"But how can it be? It's broken. You said so."

"Even so, I think it's healed."

"Well, if it's not, will you cast it up again?"

She smiled and nodded, and he quickly cut through the cast with his knife. Once released, the arm was white and wrinkled, and it felt very weak. He moved the hand gingerly, stretching his fingers. He felt up and down the arm with his other hand, prodding it for pain. Surprised, he smiled at her.

"It feels fine!" he said.

"You're a fast healer," she said, going back to work.

He continued to flex his hand, stretching the fingers, then making a fist. Less than two weeks? This was impossible. If it had really been broken, as she said, it could not have healed this well, this quickly. The anxiety he had been feeling all day swelled in him and he felt a rush of anger. He grabbed her by the upper arms and turned her roughly to face him.

"Now you see here," he snarled. "What kind of games are you playing? What are you trying to do to me? Are you trying to scare me off this land?"

She looked astonished. Seeing her innocent gaze made him feel like a fool. He got even madder.

"That arm was never broken, was it? You tricked me just so you could make me think you've got magic powers. And you did something out there to get me scared when I left this clearing, didn't you? Didn't you?"

Just then he felt a powerful blow to his upper back. He let her go and fell to the ground, rolling onto his back so he could face his attacker. The flap of huge wings blew dirt and rocks over him as the eagle returned to its branch.

"You're lucky," said Mayla, standing over him. "He could have broken your neck."

She stepped over him. "You can finish the work by yourself."

He sat up and watched her head down the trail that so terrified him. Her slender form disappeared in the dusk. He stood up, still confused, and now sore in his upper back. He was also ashamed, of his fear and for being rough with the small woman.

He lit two lanterns so he could continue preserving the meat and set his rifle nearby, just in case an animal – or something else – decided to come near.

Chapter 13

Now healed, Asa was excited to find a spot to build his home and start work. But he faced a couple of significant problems. One was that this place scared him. The enemy was not flesh and bone, but from another world, one he didn't understand and didn't know how to battle. Second, this woman was determined to stay on the land.

He chose not to think about the first problem, and instead focused on the second. He decided to give Buster a good grooming while he considered his options.

One: Forcibly remove her. This presented several difficulties, seeing as she had been kind to him, and also seeing as she might be able to control the actions of dangerous animals.

Two: Pay her to leave. Based on what she told him, this wouldn't work. But it might be worth investigating.

Three: Let her stay. But in what capacity? Could she just live up here on this mountain, while he ranched the valleys and ignored her? Or maybe offer her a position in his home as a housekeeper of some sort? She was certainly a good cook. Or – Asa felt his stomach knot up, even considering this – take her as his wife? This option was intriguing, but terrifying. He did want a wife. He felt his face get hot as he imagined touching her. What did she look like under that deerskin dress and leggings? Strong and lean, but small and soft, with smooth skin rolling over her curves? He let himself dwell on this thought for a moment before refocusing.

It was impossible. First of all, she wasn't a white woman. Second, she wasn't a normal woman of any type. In fact, as much as he hated to admit it, he was afraid of her. In addition, she made him feel helpless, and he couldn't see that being a good basis of marriage for a man, worrying that he was going to have his back broken by her pet eagle, or that a bear would attack him if they had a disagreement.

Asa sighed as he worked some twigs out of Buster's tail. He felt like a prisoner and he could not tolerate it. He had traveled all this way, proven himself to be smart and capable when faced with any other opposition, only now to find himself trapped in a tiny clearing on his own land, held captive by a crazy woman and a supernatural force he could not begin to understand.

Disgusted, he decided to head into town. He was going to proceed with locating a spot for his ranch, no matter what happened. He had a desire to see other people of his own kind, creatures he could understand – white men. He needed to learn about the availability of supplies, whether he could afford to purchase lumber or would have to cut his own and where he could get a wagon and mule team. He might have to start small and find a way to make some money and slowly work up to the ranch he imagined.

He was saddling Buster when Mayla reappeared. Remembering that she was angry at him the last time he saw her, he didn't say anything to her, but continued with the saddle, tightening the cinch and attaching Buster's breast collar.

"I need to speak to you before you go," she said.

It was as though she already knew where he was going and what his plans were. That was irritating.

"No time."

Asa slid Buster's bridle onto the horse's head.

"I've been talking to my grandfather, asking for his help."

"Have you, now? Huh."

"He told me there are but three options: You leave, you die or we marry."

"Is that what this is all about?" Asa snapped. "You are trying scare me into marrying you?"

Even as he said it, he felt ashamed, since he had, just moments ago, considered the same idea. "Well, I don't like any of those options, so there better be another."

"This is what he told me," she said, anger clouding her eyes. "I haven't finished, and I haven't given you my opinion."

He checked Buster's cinch, tightened it one more time, and mounted the horse.

"I haven't asked for it," he said.

He squeezed Buster and they started out of the clearing in the direction of town.

"Grandfather told me that marriage is not a real option," she snapped after him. "Because you have not shown any value as a potential husband."

Asa stopped Buster and turned the horse slightly so he could see her.

"Well, that's likely because I have no interest in being your husband. And the other two options aren't true options, neither, since I'm not leaving and I'm not going to die, not for a long time. In fact, you would do yourself a kindness by shoving off, yourself. I don't want to see you here when I get back. That's option number four."

"Don't you want to know my opinion?"

"No." He turned Buster again toward town, then stopped, turned again. "OK, let's hear it."

"I don't think you have any value as a potential husband, either."

Asa glared at her for a long moment, confused, angry and a little hurt, then turned and kicked Buster roughly. The horse gave a small buck in protest, then moved into a quick jog, back toward the woods they had run through in terror his first night. He evaluated his surroundings as they went, noticing that Buster seemed perfectly calm about heading back toward town. It was a clear, quiet day, and Asa, except for being irritated by the woman, was cheerful.

He guessed that the reason for his and Buster's calm demeanors was that they were heading away from the mountain. This was intolerable. He would not be afraid to stay on his own land. Something had to change, and fast.

Once in town, Asa stopped by the lumberyard to inquire about the cost of wood and was disheartened by what he was told. He looked at a new wagon and realized he could only afford to lease one, with a mule team, to start. He had a bath and a shave then headed over to the saloon for a bite of supper.

"Well, hello there Mr. Cunningham," Darwell greeted him. "Glad to see you haven't been spirited away."

"Still alive and well."

"What can I get you?"

"A plate of whatever's hot, a slice of bread and a whiskey, if you please."

Darwell served his dinner and, as Asa was eating, someone came up behind him and slapped him hard on the back, making him jump.

"Boo!" yelled a voice, which proved to belong to Cal, who took a seat next to Asa while Jake took a seat on his other side and said hello.

"Boo yourself. You could get shot doing that to a man," Asa said, but smiling.

"What, a little jumpy after staying out there for a couple of weeks?" Cal said.

"No," Asa said, a little too quickly.

Cal looked at him shrewdly, and Asa felt his ears getting hot.

"Why, Mr. Asa, look how pale you are. You look like you've seen a ghost!"

Asa was not about to admit to anything of the sort. "I did take a fall from my horse. I'm just starting to feel myself."

"I can't believe you'd fall off that horse after traveling so far on him. What happened? Something scare him?"

Asa scowled and bent over his plate, shoveling a bite of stew in his mouth before saying, "Thunderstorm."

"Thunderstorm? Why, we haven't had so much as a drop of rain for weeks. What are you talking about?" Cal continued to watch Asa closely.

Asa sighed. "I was in a thunderstorm my first night out, and it brought a branch down that scared Buster and he nearly ran off a cliff with me. I don't know what the weather was doing down here, because I wasn't down here. I was up on my land."

"Well, I reckon it seems awful strange that it would be thundering over on the mountain and dry everyplace else," Cal said. "Get me some of that stew, Darwell, and make it quick."

"I remember watching it rain across the street once, but, where I was standing, it was dry," Jake said.

"Shut up, Jake," Cal said. "Come on now Asa, pray tell, what did you see up there?"

"I saw the ghost of a white-assed heifer, and she was mooing your name," Asa said, much to Jake's delight.

"Shut up, Asa," Cal said, scowling. Then he laughed, too. "What say we have a game of cards after we eat?"

"Sounds good," Asa said.

After their meal, they picked a table and pulled a couple more ranch hands into a game. It was dusk when Asa noticed a woman passing the window, out on the sidewalk. He stared in surprise. It was Mayla.

Cal noticed his expression and turned to look.

"Oh, it's just that crazy Indian woman," he said. "H'aint you seen her? I think she spends time out on your land, as a matter of fact. She's said to be a witch."

Watching Asa's face, Cal immediately suspected a new twist to Asa's situation. He looked at him keenly over his cards.

"Yeah, I saw her. I call," Asa said, eyes on his cards. "What is she doing in town, I wonder?"

"Oh, she just sells herbs down to the store," Jake said. "Why a wild woman like that has need of money, I don't know. She eats raw meat and weeds, from what I heard."

Asa tried to concentrate on his cards, aware of Cal's prying gaze.

"Two for me," he said.

"So, you seen her up on that mountain, huh?" Cal said. "Just how much of her did you see, Mr. Asa? Come on, tell us! Did you get yourself a little honey?"

Cal slapped his lips with his hand and let out a whoop.

"You got a way of putting your nose places it doesn't belong, Cal," Asa said, anger growing.

"Yeah, Cal, shut up and play," Jake said.

Cal laughed and looked at his hand.

"Don't get mad. She's pretty. I don't blame you for taking a liking to that wild, little mare. Careful, though, she probably cast a hex on you."

Asa realized Cal was baiting him and decided to let it go. He picked up his cards and sipped his whiskey.

"Five cents," he said, pushing a coin forward.

They were joined by some other men who knew Cal and Jake, and, luckily, Cal was distracted from his taunting of Asa.

They played until after dark. Asa was winning more than he was losing. The saloon was buzzing with men's voices and the yap of a banjo, and a warm light was cast from lanterns along the walls and on the tables.

Suddenly, there was a loud bang on the window. All the men playing poker jumped and looked around. There was another bang and the saloon became quiet as folks tried to identify the sound. Some put their hands on their pistols as they gazed at the window.

Bang. It was another sharp rap on the window and Asa suddenly saw the cause. The bird! Mayla's eagle had flown against the window. It flew off for a moment, then returned, banging into the glass.

"What in the hell?" Cal said. "What is that fool bird doing?"

"What's a bird like that even doing out at night?" Jake said. "It must be sick."

"Here, I'll go shoot it," Cal said, standing and drawing his gun.

"No!" Asa said, standing also. "It's tame. Leave it alone."

Cal looked at him in surprise. Asa went out of the bar, with Cal and Jake following. The bird was perched on the saloon railing, near the spot where Buster was tied. The horse was agitated, stomping back and forth, pulling against his reins. When it saw him, the bird flapped into the air, hovering for a moment, then flew off.

"What in the hell?" Cal said again.

As they watched, the bird circled back, flying so low over them that Cal threw himself down on the wooden sidewalk.

"Tame! It's trying to kill us!"

"No, it's not. It could take you out if it wanted to, trust me."

The bird started flying away again, then circled back. Suddenly Asa understood. He quickly untied Buster and mounted. The horse was galloping before he settled in the saddle, tearing after the bird through the town.

Asa could hear Cal yelling after him, but his words were carried off by the night and the sound of Buster's hooves as they raced after the flying bird. Asa could barely see its shape against the clear night sky, but Buster apparently had no trouble seeing where the eagle went.

They galloped out of town toward a small barn just past the rendering facility, where the stripped carcasses of slaughtered livestock lay piled in a stinking heap. The eagle circled once about the barn, then flew toward it, screaming and slapping its wings against a boarded-up window. Buster stopped so quickly Asa nearly went off over the horse's head.

He looked around, not sure what to do. The rancid smell of the rendering facility was sickening. The night was silent except for his and Buster's rapid breathing. The horse tossed his head impatiently. The bird balanced awkwardly on the ledge of the window, scratching at the wooden shutter with his beak.

Then Asa thought he heard a sound, men's voices, a harsh laugh, and a moan. That moan – was it a woman's?

He didn't wait any longer. He opened the door to the barn and hurried inside. Off in a stall, he spotted a lantern and the voices grew louder. He approached quietly and was horrified by what he saw. Mayla was lying on her stomach in the stall, naked. A dirty-blond haired man was holding her wrists while a dark man kneeled over her, and another man watched, grinning under a filthy mustache.

"Stop!" Asa yelled, pulling his pistol. The men looked up, surprised.

"What's the matter?" said the one holding her wrists, the blond, about twenty-four years old. "She's just a squaw!"

"Let her go," Asa said.

The blond man released Mayla and put his hands up, while the dark one on the ground started to pull up his trousers and the mustached one stood. Asa noticed that the dark one was wearing Mayla's diamond necklace, and his fury grew. As he stood, the dark one suddenly had a gun in his hand and he fired at Asa. Asa saw the gun before the shot and dove sideways. Then he threw himself into the man's ankles and knocked him off his feet. Mayla rolled away from the men and ran out of the stall. The blond man aimed his gun at Asa, but Asa shot him first, a blow to the hip that spun the man around and he collapsed, grunting in pain.

The mustached man grabbed a shovel handle and swung it at Asa, hitting the gun out of his hand. The man swung the handle again but Asa ducked under it and leapt at the man's legs, knocking him down and feeling the man's knee bend sideways. The man yelled in pain and swung the handle wildly. The dark man then clutched Asa around the throat and tried to drag him backwards. Asa grabbed at the flaying handle and yanked it out of the mustached man's hands, slamming it against his jaw, and he went down. Asa started beating the handle on the dark man who held his throat. He gasped for air and felt like he was going to lose consciousness, but finally he got a good enough blow in on the man's head that the man released his grip.

Asa pulled himself on top of this last man and pounded his face with his fist. The dark man went unconscious, and Asa stopped hitting him. He saw with satisfaction that the man's nose was broken, his lips were bleeding and his eyes were swollen. Both he and the mustached man were unconscious. The third man, with the bullet in his hip, groaned in pain on the stall floor.

Asa yanked the necklace over the dark man's head. He stood and looked behind him for Mayla. She stood in the stall doorway next to Buster, who must have followed after Asa. She was clutching a moldy saddle blanket in front of her. In the dim lantern light, he thought he could see bruises on her cheek, and her left eye was swelling shut, the skin around it turning purple.

He stepped to her, laying his hands gently on her upper arms as he examined her face. She was as still and silent as a doe, her one clear eye wide, scared and pained. Looking at her sad expression, he was angry, and he sensed a burning shame at the knowledge that men of his kind would do this to her.

"I'm sorry," he said. "I'm sorry. I'm so sorry."

He wanted to hold her against him, but he was afraid he would scare her further. Instead, he took off his lambskin coat and draped it gently over her shoulders. He could see more bruises and scrapes on her back, arms and stomach. She wiggled into the sleeves and he clumsily buttoned it closed, his hand swelling and painful where it had been hit by the shovel handle. The coat was long enough on her small frame to cover her almost to the knees. Then he gently put the necklace over her head. She folded her arms tight and said nothing, her eyes cast downward.

Asa spun back on the men.

"God damn you!" he yelled, and he kicked the dark man sharply in the ribs. Then he turned to the blond and yanked him to his feet. The blond, whose right leg dangled uselessly, yelled in pain.

"Damn you!" Asa said, and he cracked the man's head back with a sharp blow to his chin. The man collapsed.

"You made a big mistake," Asa said, hauling him up, getting ready to strike again, but then he heard Mayla's voice.

"Stop. Asa! Stop," she said. "You might kill him."

"I don't really care if I do," he said.

Mayla looked from him to the man and then back.

"No, you can't," she said. "They are white men. The law."

It took a moment for him to realize what she meant. She didn't matter to the law, but they did.

"Well, that's a damned good reason for me to take care of this now."

"No. They might hang you."

He had been preparing to hit the man again, but now he stopped.

"This is justice."

"I agree. But it's not white man's justice."

Her expression was so scared and serious that her words finally penetrated his anger. Then he shook his head.

"No, I don't trust the law to take care of this. These men have to pay."

She stepped to him and stood very close. Her face, bruised and swollen, was solemn. She looked small and vulnerable, lost in his jacket. Behind him, one of the men stirred and moaned, then let out a stream of slurred curses.

"What should I do with them, then?" Asa asked, noticing that the two who had been knocked out were starting to revive.

"Take them to the sheriff."

So he tied their hands and put the lame one on a drag behind Buster. He tied the other two by the hands to a rope from his saddle, so they would either have to walk, or be dragged.

Meanwhile, Mayla found her clothes and dressed. He helped her onto Buster's back and walked along, leading the horse and the strange caravan.

When they got back to town, he found the sheriff just closing the jail for the night. He explained what happened, and the sheriff took a long look at Mayla and locked up the men.

Back outside, Asa took Buster's reins and they started up the street.

"Where are we going?"

"To the rooming house. You need a safe place to sleep. Or, do you need a doctor?"

"No, but they don't allow my people at the rooming house."

He looked at her, hoping she was joking, but fearing she was serious. Then he looked back at the rooming house, thinking of making a fight out of it. His anger at her treatment by the hands of the men had not yet been extinguished, and the more he learned, the more he wanted to keep fighting.

As if she could read his thoughts, she said, "There's no point. If you want to make a home here, you needn't make enemies with every person in town."

"I will if they deserve it," he said.

"Not tonight, though. Okay?"

So he set up a shelter outside of town for her, using his oiled canvas tarp and his bedroll, and built a big, bright fire to keep them warm and help them feel safe.

He encouraged her to go in and sleep, while he sat up and tended the fire and thought. After a while, she came out from the shelter and sat next to him.

"Can't sleep?"

"No."

They watched the fire and listened to the sounds of the night. It was clear and cool, and the stars were brilliant.

He took her back to the mountain the next day and stayed there for a day. They didn't speak much, just went about the necessary activities of fire-building, meal preparation, eating, taking care of Buster. After she seemed settled, he made preparations to go back to town. She sat on a rock, watching him silently.

"You going to be okay?" he asked.

"Yes. I'm safe. Here."

He nodded, got on Buster, and headed off. When he looked back, he saw her walking down the path toward the creek. The eagle circled, high overhead.

In a couple days, he rode back out with some nails, tools and other supplies. He didn't head up the mountain, but instead chose another location at its base, within view of the creek, near a spot where an earlier homesteader had built a mud-brick hut as part of his claim, under a huge ponderosa tree. Asa used small aspens and built a temporary shelter, three-sided, with a roll of waxed canvas that he could lower across the front opening. When he was satisfied that it was sturdy, he rode Buster out to explore. Anxiety gnawed at him, his frights on the mountain still in mind. But as he went, he was relieved to notice that he no longer felt that something was lurking around corners, watching and waiting.

When he headed back to camp at dusk, he was surprised to see a campfire burning brightly there.

"Now what?" he said quietly, his hand on his pistol.

But as he drew near, he saw Mayla kneeling by the fire, her russet skin glowing in the flickering light.

"You're early!" she said, nodding at the rabbits on a spit over the flames.

He removed Buster's saddle and bridle and gave the horse a handful of oats, then sat next to her at the fire. She handed him a cup of water.

As he sipped, he could feel her watching him, and he glanced at her. Her eyes were intently upon him. The one was still bruised, but no longer as swollen, and the firelight reflected brightly in their dark depth.

He picked up a stick and moved the logs around to get optimal flames. She was still watching him, so he looked back at her.

"Yes?" he said, smiling.

She glanced down in an uncharacteristic shyness.

"You saved me. From harm. Maybe death."

"I know." Angry at the memory, he jabbed at the fire.

"I couldn't save myself. I couldn't get away from them. I needed help. You helped."

"Of course I did," Asa said.

They watched the fire for a few minutes.

"Are you feeling better?" he asked, looking at the bruises by the light of the fire.

"Yes," she said, turning her face away. "I'm fine."

She sighed deeply and looked at him again.

"Before, I only saw you as someone who needed help, and nothing more," she said, hesitantly. Her nervousness made him start to feel shaky, too.

"But I was wrong. Now I see that that you actually are a warrior. You're not afraid to take on three dangerous men at once, and you can beat them. You just didn't have any reason to show me what you can do, until that night. You are like a bison. You don't mind the little flies pestering you, but should a wolf pack threaten your herd, you will fight hard and be ready to kill."

Asa was stunned. He was so unused to compliments, especially from her, that he wondered if an insult would soon follow. But it didn't. He glanced shyly at her face, trying to comprehend why she was saying this. He picked up the stick and poked the fire with energy.

"Also, you listened to the silent message of an animal."

He thought of the bird beating itself against the window.

"Well, t'wasn't really silent."

She was quiet for a moment, then she blurted, "I can share the land with you. And I believe that my grandfather will allow it, as well."

His throat suddenly seemed to close up and he swallowed hard. His mind darted to images of living with her, together, as husband and wife, of touching her, of working next to her and waking up to her pretty smile. He felt her eyes on him, and his face get hot. Maybe his thoughts had jumped ahead of her meaning.

"What do you mean, share the land? Together?"

She looked down shyly.

"I'll leave that to you. I could stay on the land and not bother you, if you want, or... ."

Her voice got so quiet with shyness that he couldn't hear what she said next, but it sounded like it might have been, "Or, I can help you build your home."

"What did you say?" he said, quiet, but excited. "I couldn't hear you."

She put her hands over her face.

"No, stop that," he said, laughing a little. "What did you say?"

She kept her hands on her face, but slid them down enough so as to peek over them. She was so close to him, her face so sweet. His hands were shaking as he gently clasped them over hers and drew them away from her face. Still holding her hands, he leaned his head down and looked in her eyes. She kept them cast down, but smiled.

He carefully kissed her lips, barely brushing them with his so as not to hurt her, then lightly kissed her nose and her bruised eye, and then her eyebrow. He wanted to crush her against his body, which was quivering like a horse's with excitement, but he was afraid if he did he would hurt or scare her, so he just held her hands, lightly like a little bird, and pressed his cheek on her forehead.

Chapter 14

"The three men who attacked Mayla served a couple of days in jail, then were released without trial," Clara wrote. "They did get a warning to get out of town. So Mayla was right about how the white man's law valued her rights."

Immersed in her recounting of the story, Clara shook her stiff hand impatiently. She kept writing.

"On the day of their wedding, Mayla presented Asa with a large, pink diamond that she had found by the cliffs near the waterfall. She had made it into a necklace for him. Many years later, after Asa and Mayla had built a successful beef and horse ranch, Asa traveled to the capital to sell some cattle. On a whim, he had the stone appraised by a jeweler. The jeweler was astonished to see the size and quality of the gem, and wanted to know where it came from. But Asa didn't want to stir up trouble, so he said he won it gambling in Missouri.

"But, I'm getting ahead of the story, Maddie," Clara wrote. "Their home was built in the shadow of that ponderosa pine, the same one I can see from my window. Asa and Mayla collected many diamonds as they worked. They each wore one on a necklace. They had a baby, William. As they grew older, and William took over more of the daily operations, Asa and Mayla tried to locate the source of the diamonds. They drew up a map of what stones they found, and where, and it became obvious that most diamonds were found around the cliffs. They never attempted an excavation, though, as Mayla stated that the land gave them diamonds, and digging for more would show a lack of appreciation for all the good they had already received.

"As you know, William married Alice Diveny and had a son. He was my father, and, he also had a son who would grow up to be your dad. Just four years after their grandson's birth, though, the family met with tragedy. Somehow, word of the diamonds leaked out, and one late, summer night, two bad men broke into their home. I have told you what happened that night, Maddie, but not that it happened because of the bad men's greed for those diamonds. I have Asa's and Mayla's necklaces here. We still don't know why the killers didn't take them. But there were a lot of strange stories about what happened to the thieves, and if any of it is true, I believe our ancestors intervened.

"I suppose I should have sold some, but it always seemed like they were part of the land, and I just couldn't bring myself to do it. But today I decided I'm going to bring some to Denver next week to sell. I need the money just now, and I think our ancestors will approve. Also, I do believe that the location of the source of the diamonds will be revealed at the right time, and maybe that will happen for you.

"So now you know why we can never sell the land to Crandall or anyone else. This land is our blood. Not only has it provided for us for generations, it contains untold wealth. And, most critically, it's protected by the spirits of our ancestors, and they do not take kindly to strangers trying to take what is ours."

Clara finished writing and put down the pen. She blew on her shaking hands. Her whole body was quivering with cold. She picked up the small stack of papers she had completed and tapped the bottom edges on the desk, so they were neat, put a staple in the corner, then folded them in thirds and put them in an envelope. She wrote "Maddie" on the front and added a fancy underline to the name, like she and her friends used to do in grammar school. She smiled and sealed it, her hands shaking near her lips, her tongue almost dry. She noticed her fingers were white and her hands a pale purple. She added some wood to the fire and prepared to make one more trip outside. She tucked the envelope in her barn coat pocket and picked up the kindling bag and cane.

Outside, the wind seemed more brutal and biting than before, blowing bits of ice sharply against her face. She bowed her head and tried to control her shaking, but it was no good.

Joe Todd appeared from the direction of the stable, wiggling and quivering.

"Oh, Joe Todd, I'm sorry. I forgot you were outside," she said, as she made her way unsteadily toward the ponderosa. Her words seemed to slur a little.

"Did you bark to come in? I didn't hear you. Well, hopefully, you snuggled up in the hay and kept warm."

She kept moving determinedly against the strong cross wind toward the tree, realizing as she went that her body was not behaving normally. She felt slow and sluggish and more unsteady than usual, stumbling through the dark night.

She finally arrived at the base of the tree. She bent down and felt the ground until she located the small rope, almost completely hidden. She yanked on it, but nothing happened. She was so weak and shaky she couldn't get the door open. She yanked again, leaning her slight weight back against the rope, and at last the ground seemed to move as dirt and pine needles slid off a small, metal door. Beneath it was a square hole some two feet deep, angling sharply under the tree trunk between the roots. Easing herself to the ground on her stomach, Clara pointed the flashlight into the hole until she located a box, fastened to the tree roots by a chain and lock. She pulled a key from a chain at her neck, opened the lock and, working hard in that awkward position, pulled the box out of the hole. A thick combination lock was one last guard, and Clara struggled to align the numbers. At last the box top opened. A gleam of light seemed to come from within, a reflection of Clara's flashlight off a small jar of crystals, mostly pink, some colorless, and all sparkling clear. She checked for the necklaces worn by Asa and Mayla, then tucked them back together in the pink, silk bag.

Clara removed the papers from the box. They were bagged in plastic, although the waterproof box was enough to protect them. She examined them quickly under her flashlight: The deed to the property, dating back to Asa's cousin, and with it, the hand-drawn map of the land. The map included notations of every spot where a diamond had been discovered.

Satisfied that everything was there, Clara tucked the envelope with Maddie's name on it on the top of the documents and carefully resealed them in the zipper-top plastic bag. She tucked the bag in the box, her breath white and freezing on her coat collar. She scrambled the combination lock, returned the box to its spot under the ponderosa and relocked the chain around it. Then she pushed herself up off her belly weakly, arranged the dirt and pine needles back over the spot, leaving just the smallest tail of rope visible. And it was only visible to someone who was looking, Clara observed.

Joe Todd hopped happily when Clara, using both the huge tree trunk and her cane, pulled herself back to her feet. She was so cold she could barely think.

She started back toward the house, but then remembered she needed more wood. She had no energy to search very far, and just picked up what small branches and twigs were easy to reach as she headed back toward the house. What she gathered wasn't enough, couldn't be enough, and she kept pausing and picking up what she could, while Joe Todd bounced excitedly around her, barking.

Finally back inside, Clara dragged the almost-empty canvas sack into the sitting room. The house was frigid, just the same as outside, but without the wind. She exhaled slowly from her mouth and watched her white breath swirl around her face.

When she got back to the fireplace, she saw that the fire was, again, out. She knew this was a problem, a bad problem, but it didn't register in her mind as an emergency. She looked for more junk mail to get the fire started, but it was all gone. So she turned to her desk and the little box of blue stationary she had used to write her note to Maddie. Sadly, she wadded the paper into loose balls and dropped them in the fireplace. She set her few twigs atop and lit the paper.

Clara's pale face was shadowed in the yellow light of the little blaze. She felt sleepy and stupid, her mouth open slightly. The fire glowed dimly, and she viewed it as though from a distance. Joe Todd curled as close to it as he could without singeing his short hair. She felt like she did after her appendix surgery, dopey. Her body was no longer shaking.

Clara was freezing to death.

This thought trickled into her dulled brain, along with thoughts that Joe Todd looked cute, and that the fire wouldn't last.

Freezing to death!

Clara suddenly became alert. There was no heat. It was late and the heat was not coming on. For some reason, down at the gas company, they had turned her heat off, and now it was after 10 p.m. and there was no way the heat was coming back on tonight.

Clara tried to assemble the course of events in her blurry brain. Fred Taylor would not have cut her off; something must have happened. And what about the check? Why didn't they keep her heat on after receiving the check? She remembered the image of Crandall driving off in his dark car, the pink envelope on his passenger seat.

Clara's mind was alive again, and she knew what had happened. Crandall did not deliver the payment. He deliberately didn't give her check to the Stony Valley Power and Gas. With her out of the way, he would be free to take her land, to build his stupid resort.

"No!" Clara whispered. This land was hers, Clara's, and Maddie's, and no one could take it from them, not by contract and not by murder.

Clara smoothed out one of the crumpled stationary sheets. Her fingers were white and her coordination was poor. She could barely hold the pen, but she scrawled:

"Maddie, Crandall has killed me. He has taken the land illegally. This is your land. Take it back. Protect it! Look at the base of the tree."

She started a second page. "Use my key. And the combination is 27-33-17-43-7."

Clara realized her note was incoherent. Her numb fingers could no longer hold the pen, and it dropped to the floor and rolled. She watched it roll and rested her cheek on the desk. She had no strength left, and with her last thoughts, she felt rage.

"Grandma Mayla, Grandpa Asa, help us. Protect us from the Crandalls, all of them. Stop them, whatever way you can, every last one. And protect this land and our sweet Maddie."

And with that, the life seeped out of Clara. She slipped off the chair, landing on her back on the floor, eyes open, mouth agape.

Abruptly, the strong wind blew the side door open. The note paper she had just written upon blew toward the fire. One of the sheets caught an edge in the flame, but then both sheets blew upward and circled, then flew out the door. One sheet blew across the lawn and vanished. But the burning sheet, with instructions to the safe, got caught in a whirlwind that caused the flame to glow bright. When the wind released it, the burning paper fluttered toward the stable, alighting against the dry, wooden wall, and catching some hay afire.

Joe Todd sniffed Clara. He licked her hand, and her taste and smell told him that her life was gone. He trotted to the open door.

The flame was growing in the wind at the stable. Joe Todd barked and ran toward Bugle's stall. The fire spread quickly. Joe Todd reached the stall and barked. The old horse, already aware of the danger, was pacing and rearing in his stall, trying to find a way out. Joe Todd leapt up at the door. Again and again he leapt, as the stable walls ignited and the fire burned near. At last he knocked the latch hook out of the eyebolt, and Bugle's stall door opened. Together, the dog and horse hustled away from the stall, toward safety.

But then, a burning beam snapped in half with a thunderous crack, and the roof collapsed upon them.

Chapter 15

"So, you have no idea where she might be, absolutely no clue?"

"Sorry, Emerson," Natalie said. "I just haven't been in touch with her. Last I knew, she was on some island near Australia, and that was years ago."

"Do you remember if she had any family?"

"Why do you need to track her down so bad, anyway?"

"Oh, you know how you get. I was going through old photos and I just got the urge to give her a call. Now it keeps bugging me until I can find her. You know."

Emerson glanced over at Courtney, who was asleep on the floor in front of the television. He didn't want to share information about her with Natalie. Courtney had told him that she and her mother had lived in Springfield, Ohio. However, she also said that, after the accident, her mother had been moved to a different hospital. Courtney didn't remember where that was, except that it was in a big city. Since there were several possibilities, including Dayton, Columbus, Cincinnati and even Indianapolis, and all the hospitals followed privacy laws, Emerson was unable to track her further.

"Didn't she have a sister?" he said.

"Yeah, a sister. She lived in Milwaukee or someplace like that."

"What's her name?"

"OK, let me think," Natalie was quiet for a moment. "Anita? No, Rita. Still Hughes, last I knew. And she was a waitress. Wait a minute! I might have her address. I think Annie stayed with her for a while. Hold on."

Emerson didn't just hold on; he held his breath. Natalie was an old college friend who had known Annie as well as any of them

99

did. He had found her online, through a quick search of a social networking site. She came back on the phone.

"Got it!" Natalie read him the address and phone number.

"Thanks, Natalie! I owe you one. Let's get together next time you're in town, OK?"

"Yeah, right. I always go to Syracuse. What a great place. It's only 3,000 miles away, and isn't it always breaking snowfall records?"

"Yeah, it does. Heh-heh. Well, the door's always open. Thanks again. Bye."

Of course, finding Rita was not that straightforward. She was no longer at the address Natalie had given him. It took several more calls and some pretty dedicated web searching, but eventually he found what, he was pretty certain, was the right number.

He left a message for her. He didn't leave any details on the message, just that he was a friend of Annie's and he had something of hers that needed to be returned. He knew it sounded weird, but he didn't really know anything about the sister, and he wasn't sure he wanted to give up all the information.

He did know he wanted to find Annie in the hope that she was healing, and would be able to take Courtney back soon. But now, there was nothing to do but wait.

He had set up a camping cot for Courtney to sleep on until he figured out what to do with her. He tucked her in and lay on his bed, hands behind his head, staring at the ceiling. With today's events – first losing the grant, then Courtney's unexpected appearance – rattling around in his mind, it was hard to fall asleep. As he lay there, he started to get a creepy feeling, as though someone was in the apartment, walking quietly toward him. He held his breath and listened, hearing the loose vinyl floor click. He grabbed his phone and turned on its flashlight, shining it around the room. Other than Courtney, who was asleep on her cot, he was alone. But still, it took a while before he could drift off to sleep.

Chapter 16

Crandall was partway through his rare steak when he noticed Toby come into the restaurant, rubbing his hands together vigorously and blowing on them. Toby was easy to recognize in his old leather hat, a droopy thing decorated with a band of braided rawhide, and his worn, sheepskin coat with big seams and yellowed wool at the collar and cuffs. Now, he was also covered with bits of ice that were still pelting the area in advance of the snow.

Toby was a methodical creature, a widower who was comfortable in a routine, and eating at Moretto's on Friday nights was one of those routines. Crandall had chosen a seat in the front where Toby couldn't help but pass him on the way to the bar, where he usually ate.

Toby spotted Crandall and nodded a hello.

"Hello, Toby," Crandall said with enthusiasm, standing and accompanying him to the bar. "Let me buy you a drink tonight. I'm celebrating!"

Toby smiled warmly. "Wonderful."

To the bartender he said, "Vodka tonic," then, to Crandall, "What's the good word?"

"Mrs. Stanton finally signed an agreement to sell me her land." Crandall smiled, and surveyed Toby shrewdly.

Toby's smile changed into a look of surprise.

"Did she?" he said, a note of concern in his voice. "Why, I wonder what ... ." He looked into Crandall's face and decided not to finish his sentence. "Well, then, good, great. That money will be a tremendous help to her. Have you got the document, then?"

Crandall patted his jacket pocket. "Right here, next to my heart."

"Well, would you like to leave it with me?" Toby said. "So I can review it for her later tonight."

"What's to review? It's the same document you already saw. Except now, it's signed." Crandall's smile didn't fade, but his eyes hardened.

"All the same, just to make sure things are in order. Clara retains me for just these occasions. I might as well earn my keep."

"Well certainly. But, you're not planning on working tonight, surely? Friday night, before a holiday weekend?"

Toby smiled. "Actually, it's either tonight or two weeks from Monday. I'll be driving south early in the morning."

"Really? Vacation?"

"Yes. I'm meeting some friends down in New Mexico for a couple of weeks. Golf."

"Oh? I'm jealous! Well, here it is then." Crandall pulled the document out of his coat. "I don't want to wait. May I stop up after dinner then?"

"Yes, good," said Toby. "Well, thank you for the drink, and," Toby paused, giving him a searching look, "congratulations."

Crandall went back to his table, satisfied. He cut a slice from his steak as he watched Toby open the document and give it a look. He looked forward to calling Kellerman, but he would wait until after visiting Toby this evening. Just in case something went wrong.

Toby's heart sank when he saw it.

"Clara Stanton" gracefully adorned the signature line on the sales agreement, with just a touch of the shakiness that had crept into Clara's handwriting as she aged.

The waitress set a basket of thick, Italian bread near his plate.

Toby was keenly aware of Crandall's scrutiny from his table, as he examined the signature.

Toby unlocked the office door and hurried to his file cabinets. He removed Clara's file and sifted through the documents.

First, the will, with "Millicent Clara Stanton," gracefully, slightly shakily, adorning the last page. He pulled out the next document, an agreement to sell her stock shares, and again noted the name, "Millicent Clara Stanton." Then he came to a photocopy of a check, a donation to a nature conservancy, made when she had been more financially stable. "Clara Stanton" was on the check.

It was just as she said. She signed important documents with her full name, but stuck with just "Clara" for everyday documents. Surely, Crandall's sales agreement would fall in the category of an important document. In fact, Toby was sure, that to Clara, that document would fall among the most important she ever signed.

If she signed it.

Toby recounted his conversation with Clara earlier that day. She was solidly opposed to selling her land. What had changed in those few short hours?

He looked at the time. 9:30. Clara might be in bed, but he had to speak to her. He dialed her number. He waited for a moment, then heard a rapid busy signal. He recognized it as indicating a problem with the connection. He dialed again and got the same sound. He wondered if the strong wind had knocked out her phone lines. He considered the possibilities. He was worried about Clara now for more than one reason. Was she all right, out there in that rattling old ranch in such bad weather? He decided to call the sheriff's office.

"Hi, this is Toby Landy. Is Doug in by any chance?" He and Sheriff Doug White Elk were longtime colleagues.

"Well, hello, Toby." It was his old classmate, Susan Hartley, who worked the sheriff's phones. "No, you just missed him. The phone has been ringing off the hook with storm calls. All the officers are out. There is ice to the north, coming just in front of the snow, the big snow, and the wind is knocking things all over the place. There are lots of accidents, lines down, falling trees. And the snow hasn't even started yet, not in earnest, anyway."

"Well, do me a favor, can you? I'm worried about Clara Stanton. I can't reach her by phone, and I just would appreciate it if someone could check on her."

"OK, sure. I'll tell them."

"Thanks a lot. You have a great weekend."

"You too. Hey, aren't you heading out of town soon?"

"Yes, that's right. I'm leaving early to get out of here ahead of the snow."

"Snow's supposed to start here for real around 3 or 4 a.m., but it is moving pretty slowly, so maybe you'll be lucky."

"Yes, well, I'm feeling lucky."

"Have a great trip."

"Thanks. I'll see you in a couple of weeks."

Toby hung up, troubled. He couldn't reach Clara, and he didn't trust Crandall or the signature on the sales agreement. He didn't think he should push the panic button yet, but it all seemed very strange.

He remembered that he had the email address of Clara's niece, Maddie. Even though Maddie was far away, Clara had told him he could still access her through e-mail although it might take time before Maddie was able to check it, since she worked in remote areas and couldn't always get web access. He located the e-mail address in Clara's file and started typing.

Hello Maddie,
Please contact me as soon as you can. There have been some important events in regard to your aunt's estate. I have some concerns, and I need to speak with you.

He included his contact information, and pressed "send."

He didn't want to sound cryptic, but he was not sure how much weight to put on his concerns yet. At any rate, he would be glad to have Maddie tuned into what was going on with her aunt, whatever it was. While he was thinking about the note and Maddie, he got down on his hands and knees and reached far under his desk. He located the hidden drawer and pulled out the only item in it, a small computer memory drive. He used this drive to back up all his files, in addition to keeping his paper versions. He crawled out and stuck it in the port in his computer, backing up his client files before he left. After a couple minutes, the backup was done and he ejected the drive, got on his hands and knees and replaced it in the drawer. He crawled back out.

He sat at his desk, looking at the sales agreement, and wondering what his next action should be. He was not comfortable with the document Crandall had given him, but he was not sure he wanted to let Crandall know that yet.

There was a knock at the door, and Rexham Crandall stepped in.

"May I?"

"Of course."

"Have you spoken to Mrs. Stanton yet?" Crandall asked, sitting in the same chair Clara had used earlier that day.

"Not yet."

"Is everything in order, then, with the agreement?"

"Let me just make a copy of it for my records." Toby stepped to his copier, feeling a nervous sweat on his brow.

"Fine," Crandall said, still watching him intently.

"So, now that Clara finally agreed to sell – which I encouraged her to do, you know – when are we going to find out what you will be building out there?" Tobey said, trying to sound cheerful. "It's got to be something exciting, based on your persistence, and this sales price."

Crandall smiled. "It is exciting, and you can be sure it will be a welcome addition to this area. A lot more useful than empty ranch land."

"Well, don't keep it a secret!"

"You'll know soon enough," Crandall said. "As soon as I tell my financiers that it's a go, I will be filing for all the necessary permits, and then everyone will know."

Toby swallowed again. "Okay."

He handed the original back to Crandall.

"So, have you had time to review it? You've seen, it's the same, except that now it's signed by Mrs. Stanton, yes?"

"Yes, it does look to be the same, except for the signature."

"So?"

Toby sighed and wiped his neck with his hand.

"Mr. Crandall, the fact is that I do have a concern."

"Oh?"

"I'm concerned about the very fact that Clara signed it. When I spoke to her earlier today, she was adamant that she would not sign, would never sign. I need to hear why she changed her mind. From her."

Crandall's face grew tight, and a look of fury crossed it. But then the fury changed to a smoldering surprise.

"Really?" He pressed his index fingers to his mouth.

"Frankly, it's strange enough for me to wonder if something serious has happened," Toby said, then added quietly, "I asked the police to check on her." He watched for Crandall's reaction.

Crandall looked at Toby for about ten seconds without moving or blinking. Toby returned the gaze calmly.

Finally, Crandall said, "I see. Well, that makes complete sense."

He stood up.

"I guess I'll have to wait until you get back from, where was it, Arizona?"

"New Mexico."

"Ah yes, New Mexico. Golf."

"Hector Longtree will be looking after my clients, but only if there is an emergency, which I wouldn't consider this."

"No, no. Well, have a wonderful time. I'll see you in a couple weeks."

With that, Crandall turned and stepped down the stairs and into the street.

The wind moaned, and little bits of ice clicked against the office window.

Toby sat at his desk for about five minutes more, looking through the document Crandall had given him and wishing he didn't feel so unsettled just before his trip. He had been planning it with his friends for about six months, but his concern for Clara was definitely removing much of the joy.

Then he thought he heard something down in the stairwell, by the front door.

"Hello?" He looked up and listened. "Mr. Crandall? Hello? Is someone there?"

He heard a noise again. It sounded like something hitting the front door. He got up and stepped into the hallway. Looking down the stairs, he saw nothing.

He took a couple of steps down the stairs, when out of the dark shadows of the landing, a figure appeared. Toby didn't even see his attacker as Crandall shoved him hard from behind. The force of the push caused Toby to fall, face first, out and away from the stairs. Then his body arched back down, almost like a diver's, landing hard on his chin, his head snapping back, neatly severing his spine at the neck. His legs flipped over his head and he continued to fall, stair after stair, until his body slammed hard against the door at the bottom.

Crandall hurried down the stairs and examined Toby with a small, disgusted frown. Gingerly, he put out an index finger, and fumbled to find a pulse at Toby's carotid artery.

Toby suddenly opened his eyes and let out a sharp, "Ah!" causing Crandall to jump back in horror. But then Toby was still.

Crandall felt for a pulse again. Nothing. He prodded Toby on the cheek, turned his face toward him, let it drop again.

Dead.

"All right, then."

Crandall checked to be sure the door was locked, then raced up the stairs and into Toby's office. Once inside, he stopped and looked around cautiously. Out of the corner of his eye, he thought he saw movement. He stood, frozen, for a moment, his eyes surveying the quiet office, his heart thumping madly.

"Seeing things," he said, and, refocusing, hurried to the desk. When he saw what was there, a grin spread over his face.

"Perfect!" He said, so excited he clapped his hands together frenetically. Clara's file was on the desk. He checked the computer to see if Toby had left himself logged on. He had. Crandall rustled quickly through Clara's will, then started perusing files on the computer. It didn't take long to find the will on the computer, and he opened it and began to delete. It only took a few minutes to alter the document. It still left everything to the wayward niece, of course, but now the will reflected changes, changes brought about by a certain, recent sale.

Now, Clara's will said she was leaving to her niece, "my entire estate, resulting from the recent sale of my land to E. Rexham Crandall Enterprises."

Crandall read it, then repeated aloud, with a smile, "To E. Rexham Crandall Enterprises."

Crandall hit "print."

"Well done, Mr. E. Rexham Crandall Enterprises."

He saved the file on the computer and carefully removed the staples binding Clara's will. He switched his new page with the existing one. Nothing else needed to change. He reassembled the package with Clara's original signature. He then noticed the "Millicent" and Toby's reaction suddenly made sense. He took a few minutes to practice the correct signature, then added it to a fresh signature page on the contract. If Crandall had known this earlier, Toby could have lived.

He thought he heard a rustling across the room. He looked up sharply, listening.

"Hello?" he called quietly, his voice husky. "Hello?"

There was no answer. Enough. He had to get out of this place. But Toby would not normally have left everything out and open like this, Crandall was sure. Why give the police any reason to think that something caused Toby to act in an unusual manner? After examining Clara's otherwise dull file, which sadly, did not contain the deed to her property, he carefully packed it together, and placed it in the proper location in Toby's file room. He closed the door and made sure it locked.

He started to shut down the computer, but, as he thought about it, he became troubled by what else might be on that hard drive that he didn't have time to read and alter. Another moment's thought, then he made a decision. Finding a pair of scissors in Toby's drawer, he went to a table lamp near a chair by the window. Unplugging the lamp, he neatly snipped the cord. Using the scissor blade, he trimmed back a bit of the protective insulation until the copper wires were exposed. He carried it back to the computer on Toby's desk. After considering the back of the computer for a moment, he plugged in the cord. He held one of the wires to the metal plate at the back of the computer near the main, electronic drive. Then, turning his head and wincing, he touched the other end to the metal receptacle where the power cable connected to the computer.

The resulting buzz and bang made Crandall jump away from the computer, dropping the cable and shielding his face with his arms. When he opened his eyes, he saw that the back of the computer was now blackened, and a small flame was burning inside it.

"What luck," he said, carefully unplugging the cable. He reconnected the bare wires to those still attached to the lamp and jammed the connection inside the lamp body, where the splice wouldn't be noticed. Then he plugged the lamp back in and turned it on.

He noticed now that the small fire in the computer had burned itself out, leaving the back a stinking, melted mess. Just to satisfy himself, he attempted for several minutes to turn the computer off and on, but it was dead. The lamp flickered. He looked at it in concern, thinking he'd wired it badly, but then all the office lights went out. The wind must have taken down a line.

He realized he had to make a decision. Initially, he had planned to leave Toby's body there, looking like an accident. But the more he thought about it, the more he realized it was ludicrous. The "accidental" deaths of two key people, just before the sale of the land to him, were too coincidental. Assuming, of course, that Clara was dead, and he had assumed that she was. He was lucky that way. Plus, they could have been overheard at the bar, and someone might remember they were meeting in Landy's office. Why hadn't he thought it out?

Acting in haste. This was not like him. He was a man who planned. He turned on his penlight and began wiping surfaces that might show his fingerprints.

Maybe, instead of leaving Toby at the bottom of the stairs, he should drive his body off the road in an icy area on the way to the airport, and make it look like a weather-related accident. He absent-mindedly gazed at an old desk photo of Toby and a woman, probably his deceased wife. He noticed something familiar about Toby. Tall, dark hair, blue eyes.

A smile crossed his face. Maybe, better still, he should make sure that Landy made it all the way to New Mexico.

Chapter 17

The ringing phone jolted Emerson awake. He stumbled across the dark room and noticed it was 2:13 a.m.

"Hello?"

"Hello. Who the hell is this?" A woman, slurring her words.

"Excuse me? Who is this?"

"That's what I'd like to know. You called me." He could hear a child crying in the background at her end. Then he heard an angry male voice, some kind of tussle, maybe, and the child's cry changed to a wail.

It dawned on Emerson that this might be the sister, Rita. Why would she call at this hour? He checked the number on his phone. Yes, it was the one he had called earlier.

"Rita? Is this Rita?"

"So, who wants to know?" She sounded very drunk. Suddenly, she yelled, "Would you both shut up?"

It was so loud, Emerson had to take the phone away from his ear. She was answered by an angry yell from the man, and the child started screaming, "Nooooooo."

"Rita Hughes?" Maybe it was the wrong Rita.

"Yeah, Rita Fucking Hughes, so what?"

"Annie's sister?"

"Yeah, Annie's fucking sister." She seemed to think this was funny, and she laughed roughly. "Who is this?"

"Uh, I'm Emerson. I went to college with her. I'm trying to, uh, find her."

"So what? Why should I care? Will you shut the fuck up?" she yelled again.

"No, you shut the fuck up," came the man's voice, closer now. There was the sound of a struggle, accompanied by a loud protest by Rita. "Who the hell are you talking to?"

"Hey! Gimme that!"

Then came the man's voice in the phone.

"Goodbye!" he yelled, and slammed down the phone. He must have missed the "off" button, though, and Emerson heard the phone clatter to the floor. He could hear more of the drunken, violent conversation, the child's wailing. He tapped his "off" button.

He sat down at the kitchen table and looked out at the dark night. Obviously, he was not going to take Courtney to stay with Rita Fucking Hughes.

Chapter 18

Crandall had to work quickly. First, get the body to Landy's car without being seen. He quickly donned Toby's sheepskin coat and droopy leather hat, finding the car keys in Toby's coat, and started toward the stairs.

As he crossed the landing, he thought he saw movement in the shadow, and he jumped sideways, almost losing his balance on the top stair. It had seemed like something was coming at him through the dark, just as he had swiftly approached Toby, just a little while ago. But there was nothing there.

"That would be wonderful, if they found us both at the bottom of the stairs," he murmured as he quickly trotted down the long flight. At the bottom, he stepped over Toby's body and checked to see that the street was still empty, which it was. He stepped over the body again and made his way through the dark hallway to the back door. It opened onto a small alley.

The cold wind made it hard to breathe, and little pellets of ice hit his face. He found Landy's car and pulled it up to the alley door. He quickly dragged the body through the hall and hoisted it into the trunk. Some people whooped and laughed in the apartment above Toby's office, causing Crandall to freeze in fear. But no one looked out the window, that he could see. He went back upstairs, checked the office to make sure everything was in place, picked up Landy's briefcase and went back down to the car, climbing casually behind the wheel.

As he turned on to the main street, he saw the ambulance going by. Its lights and siren were off, so it must have just finished a run. The driver waved to Crandall, whose face was half hidden by the hat and fleece collar. He waved back, as Landy, and headed toward Landy's house down Red Rock Lane. He pulled in the garage, which had an automatic door, and went in the house.

Everything Landy needed for his trip was waiting by the door. He was fully packed, and the hotel reservation and was sitting on top of his suitcase. Crandall exchanged his clothes for some of Landy's, stashing his own in the suitcase. He would need them, eventually.

But the one loose end that he was leaving behind had been nagging at him. He kept imagining some infuriating, kind neighbor stopping by to check on Clara Stanton, just in time to keep her alive. He knew he had to go by Clara's house, just to be sure. But what if she was still alive? Well, he would just decide what to do at that point. He had just murdered one person. He probably should have done the same to Clara, he realized now, and then he wouldn't be worrying about this. But, at the time that he left her basement, he didn't know that he would have actively caused someone else's death within a few hours. Somehow, it seemed much simpler now.

He took Landy's suitcase and travel documents, went back to the car, and headed out of town. It was 4 a.m. and the snow was getting serious. It came in small, fiercely blowing flakes. He saw Jason Childers, the mail carrier, coming out of the diner to start his rounds. He smiled at Crandall and waved. Crandall waved back.

Perfect. Witnesses everywhere he went that could verify that Landy left town, early as expected, getting ahead of the weather.

As much as he just wanted to get on the highway, he took the pass toward Clara's. The road wasn't covered yet, which was good, since it was scary, even on a good day. In about twenty minutes, he arrived at the end of her drive. He peered down the driveway, his heart pounding fast, despite his trying to stay calm. The house was dark. If nothing else, that hell dog would be around, waiting to throw its nasty little self at him.

Crandall felt a sense of anticipation, mingled with dread at what he might find.

He made his way down the driveway, the tires of Toby's car creaking on the fresh snow. He stopped by the front door and waited. He opened the car window a crack, listening. No barking, but now he smelled smoke. It was too dark to spot its source, with sunrise still a couple hours off.

No barking. That was odd.

He slipped out of the car and shut the door gently, so it made only a muffled click. The cold was shocking, and the wind stole his breath, causing him to gasp. He clamped Toby's hat on his head with his hand and went to the window. The front hall was dark, but she wouldn't be there, anyway. Pulling the penlight from his pocket, he used it to make his way to the side of the house. That's when the strong smell of smoke hit him fully, and he saw the dying red embers of what once was the stable. He stared at the heap of smoldering rubble, unable to comprehend what had happened here. It had been a bad fire, and it had gone unnoticed. If the wind hadn't been blowing so hard away from the house, it, too, would surely have gone up.

He shone his light on the house and saw that the side door was wide open. A worm of fear tickled up his neck. He stepped toward it quietly, even though any noise he made was carried away on the howling wind. When he was inside, the sound of the storm was abruptly muffled, so the house seemed silent. He guided his light up in front of him. It showed him the furniture of a sitting room. Then, as the light roved toward the fireplace, past the sofa, he saw two thin legs.

His heart pounded. He took a step.

"Hello?" he called quietly, keeping his light fixed on the legs.

He stepped again, moving slowly toward the figure. As he got past the sofa, there she was. Sprawled on her back, not peaceful, Clara looked stricken, even furious. Her green eyes were open and staring off at the fireplace, and her mouth stretched down in a gaping frown.

Crandall stepped back and turned around. He closed his eyes and took a deep breath. He turned back. He yelled in shock.

The eyes were now fixed on him.

"Mrs. Stanton?" His breath fogged around his face in the cold.

She didn't move. He stepped toward her and knelt down. He pulled off his glove, but shielded his fingers from her skin with Toby's cuff, feeling for a pulse at her neck. Once he touched her skin, though, he knew he did not have to go further. Her body was cold and waxy, nothing more than meat in a freezer.

The eyes, though.

That must have been his imagination.

He stood and, shining the light one more time at the pale face, he left the room quickly, expecting the dog to appear out of nowhere at any moment.

Just one more detail. Putting his gloves on, he hurried into the basement. In the tiny, bright circle made by the penlight, he found the furnace switch, and turned it back on. He thought he heard a step on the stairs, and shone the light in that direction, his heart starting to pound harder, while he tried to quiet it so he could listen for footsteps. But there was nothing there.

To his surprise, the furnace didn't come on. He clicked the switch back off, and then on. Nothing. Strange. He tiptoed up the stairs, found a hallway light switch and flipped it off, then on. Nothing.

He realized it then. All the power was off, not just the furnace. The storm had killed the electricity to Clara's home. When he realized what that meant, he choked back a nervous laugh. The old coot would have died anyway. He had just hurried it along, maybe by hours, but maybe only by minutes, maybe seconds. She had managed to waste his time, again. This wasn't really even a murder, he thought. He considered this for a moment. Could he actually remove this killing from his conscience? His mind flicked back to Toby, regret nagging at him for a moment. Then he shook it off. Toby still would have held everything up, because of that signature. One way or the other, both deaths were necessary. But from that moment on, he absolved himself of Clara's murder.

He looked cautiously in both directions before hurrying toward the front door. He couldn't resist one more look at Clara's body. He wished he hadn't. He was sure her mouth had been open before. Now it was clamped tight. Instead of looking vacant, the eyes were angry, glaring right at him.

He must not have been looking carefully when he first saw her. He must have been too nervous to really see how her face looked, where her eyes were pointing. Still, he had been pretty sure she had not been facing that way when he came in.

He decided he better get out of there, and fast. He closed the door quietly behind him. The wind was bitter, pushing him as he went. He got in the car, turned it around and started back up the driveway. He glanced in his rear-view at the house and jumped. He was sure he saw a figure in the window. He stopped the car and turned fully around in the seat. No, there was nothing.

He started driving. He glanced in the rear-view again and yelled in shock. In the mirror, he saw Clara Stanton in his back seat, glaring at him with her icy green eyes. He stopped and turned around again. There was nothing there.

"Get a grip, Rex," he said. Being up all night, stressed to the core. He must be hallucinating.

He put the radio on. Country Western music twanged from the speakers. Naturally, just Toby's style. He didn't change the station, though. From here on, he was Toby.

Driving was difficult, even on the highway. The snow, light and dry, blew all over the highway, making it hard to stay on track. About fifty miles from Stony Valley, he detoured off the highway onto a park service road. He had to do this soon, since he didn't have much darkness left, and it would be fading gradually to light during that next hour.

The road he chose was barricaded with two sawhorses and a "No Entry" sign, which he drove around. In less than a mile, he found a narrower drive, also barricaded. This dirt road was edged on either side with brush and trees, so it was impossible to drive around the barricade. He got out and moved it. The snow seemed to slice at his face like little shards of glass, beating sideways in the wind. He pulled in, then got back out and replaced the barricade, and drove about three miles on the rocky and pocked surface. There, the trees grew thick, and he pulled over. He yanked Toby's body out of the trunk.

He found a tow rope in the trunk and tied it roughly under Toby's armpits and around his shoulders. He yanked a towel off Toby's golf bag and pulled out the pitching wedge. He tucked these items on Toby's body, and started to drag it into the woods. Toby weighed a good 200 pounds, and the rough ground made walking hard. He deliberately had not chosen a trail but went straight into the thickest growth he could get through. After going about 70 yards, he put the towel over Toby's face and took the pitching wedge to his teeth. It was harder than expected to break them, but a step he considered worth taking. He pounded that face with sickening thuds until the teeth were broken or knocked clean out. He scattered the resulting mess with his shoes, then started dragging the body again, the bloody towel still draped over Toby's pulpy face.

A man less driven with the belief that this must work, that he must succeed, would not have gotten far. But Rexham Crandall would not let the thought of failure at any level and in any place trouble him for even a millisecond. Failure was not an option, and he yanked that heavy body, as patiently as a draft horse, for fifteen minutes across rocks, tree branches and other forest debris. Ice now coated everything.

He stopped when he saw, in the first pink light of dawn, a spot where a large tree had fallen over. It had pulled its roots from the ground, leaving a deep hole. Into this, he dumped Toby's body.

Without pausing to catch his breath – even though he was gasping – he tossed logs, leaves and other debris from the forest floor on top of the body. When it was fully covered and out of sight, he paused only long enough to examine the effect of his work. No trace of Toby's body was visible.

This cold would not last. In a few months, the body would be nothing but bone. It would gradually just sink deeper into the root hole and disappear forever. It would never be found. But even if it were, his bet was that there would be no record of Toby's DNA anywhere. Why would there be? He had led a nice, quiet, legal life.

Crandall headed back to his car. The snow was falling so heavily now that his tracks were almost covered already, and he was glad he had taken the chance of leaving the car lights on, because without them, he would have been lost for the last few hundred yards, in the snow.

He backed out of the service road, removing and replacing the barricade again. When he emerged onto the main road, there was no traffic. The sun was just rising, but the highway was virtually empty, as this huge storm did what it could to bring human activity to a standstill.

He turned the car south.

"New Mexico, here I come."

Chapter 19

Maddie inserted a hypodermic needle carefully into the medial artery on the little cat's forearm. She withdrew fifteen milliliters of blood, removed the vial, attached a second, and withdrew another fifteen. She yanked a small sample of fur from the grayish brown coat and dropped it in a jar, then set the limp body on her scale. The male cat weighed 10.25 kilograms. She checked its teeth, eyes and ears, making notations all the while. She worked quickly, not wanting the rare, wild cat to remain unconscious much longer.

In a few minutes, she made her last note and then injected a liquid into the cat's bloodstream. She nestled it under some brush on the rocks and stepped away, perching in a squat nearby. A strand of her long, honey-colored hair clung to her sweaty face and she pushed it behind her ear, watching the cat as it sat up groggily and gradually became more aware of its surroundings. Then, as if remembering that something bad just happened, it leapt away over the rocky ground. Maddie smiled and checked her tracking device and saw with satisfaction that cat number MS10 was heading north at a quick clip.

She heard movement behind her and turned quietly, growing still, hand on her pistol. A dark man stepped into the clearing. He looked her up and down, his eyes alighting on her tidy hips, waist and breasts, then back up to her face, which was smeared with reddish dust that streaked from one high cheekbone to the other, stuck to her sunscreen.

"And what will you do with that pistol, senorita?" he said, a grin spreading across his dark face.

They stared at each other for a moment, neither moving.

"I'll use it to whip your butt for scaring me like that."

He laughed. "Oh, don't be so cruel!"

He stepped toward her, palms out in a placatory gesture, smiling warmly. She fixed a hard look at him, a challenge in her slightly sloping eyes, which sparkled an amazing greenish gold. When she stood this way, stern and strong, he thought he could see the drop of Native American blood she carried, despite her deep golden hair and the spray of freckles on her thin nose. Then she smiled, her cool glare melting in the sunlight, and he silently admired her beauty. But then she abruptly turned her full attention to her laptop screen, back to business.

"Number Ten is heading north," she said.

"Good. Let's get down to base. We have good news, so we should all celebrate. The study has been approved for an additional grant. $300,000! Fiesta tonight!"

"No! Really?" She said. "That's fantastic!" She smiled, showing mostly straight teeth, except for one rogue canine that protruded slightly. It made her smile unique, and he adored that tooth.

The grant meant they could continue their work to protect the Andean cat. She threw her arms up in the air and leapt at him. He caught her in an embrace and after a moment, bent to kiss her lips. His kiss was passionate, but she cut it short and gently pushed him away.

"Let's go tell the others," she said, noticing the disappointment in his brown eyes. She ran a playful finger quickly along the short, black beard that decorated his long chin, conciliatorily. "Come on, help me pack up."

She squatted to pack her laptop and the tiny satellite dish used to track the collared cats.

He remained standing, still looking downhearted by the way she quickly ended the kiss, his eyes forlorn under his low, long eyebrows. Then he sighed and bent to help her pack the rest of the equipment.

"You know, we are so close now. That money might be just what we need to really make a difference," Maddie said as they worked, her voice happy, trying to get things back to normal after their awkward, silent exchange.

"Maddie!" She heard her name, called urgently.

She sat up abruptly, a stricken look on her face. She knew that voice.

"What is it?" Eduardo asked.

"Shhh."

They both listened.

"Maddie!" She heard it again. She looked at him sharply, but he just looked back at her with a questioning gaze. Here, in the Patagonian mountains near Chile, it was always smart to listen for trouble, but he obviously wasn't hearing this thin call.

"Maddie!"

She stood as recognition slowly dawned upon her. She definitely knew that voice.

"Maddie, help! We're in trouble!"

She took a couple of steps. It didn't seem to come from any direction, but to be carried in on the wind. Eduardo stood also, watching her with concern.

"What's wrong?"

"Maddie, help! I'm so cold!"

"Aunt Clara?" Maddie said, almost whispering. "Is that you?"

It didn't make any sense. Her Aunt Clara was 5,000 miles away, at home in Stony Valley.

"Maddie, I need you!"

Maddie took a few steps, then a few more. Then she broke into a run.

"Wait!" Eduardo gathered the remaining equipment, then ran after her. Her slender figure was bounding along the path they had followed to this spot, her T-shirt clinging to her sweaty back.

"Maddie, what is it? What's wrong?"

"My aunt! She's in trouble!"

Maddie continued running. Again she heard Clara's voice, calling her name through the trees like a breeze.

"Maddie!"

She reached base camp at a run and tripped over a sleeping bag airing out in the late afternoon sun. Her stumble caused her to almost somersault into the group of researchers, gathered there to prepare dinner.

"Nice entrance," said Meg, an intern, slouched over her laptop.

"Who has a phone? I need a phone!"

"We all have phones," Meg said. "But none of them work up here, as you well know."

"I need to talk to my aunt."

Maddie got up and paced, thinking. Clara didn't have a computer, but someone in Stony Valley did. Toby Landy! The lawyer. She could contact him.

"What about Internet?" she said to Meg. "Any luck?"

"Nope, sorry," said Meg, her large gray eyes guardedly concerned. "You know that. You have to go down to Punto Guardino to make any kind of contact with the states."

"Punto Guardino?" Maddie knew she was right. It was a five-day trip, much of it walking.

"What am I going to do?" Maddie ran her hands up her face and into her sweaty hair.

Eduardo burst into the camp, avoiding the sleeping bag and hurrying to Maddie.

"Are you OK?"

Maddie didn't answer. She stood still, her face pointed upward as though she were listening to voices in the treetops.

"What are you doing?" Meg said. "You look kind of scary."

Maddie didn't hear Clara's voice any longer, but the urgent feeling still remained. If her aunt was in trouble, Maddie needed to try to reach her. Clara was her last relative on her father's side, and she had helped to raise Maddie. Clara had given her a home while Maddie's professor parents spent so much of their vacation time on overseas archeology excavations in places that were not safe for a little girl. Actually, it turned out those places were not always safe for people of any age. When Maddie's parents vanished during a dig in a remote dessert in Afganistan and were presumed dead, it was to Clara's home that Maddie went during college holidays. Clara was one of the most important people in her world, and now Maddie wanted to get to a phone. However, she was also starting to realize how weird this situation was, and how she was acting. Maddie looked at the concern in Eduardo's dark eyes. She looked over at Meg, who also appeared worried. The others, too, were watching.

She sighed. She knew it seemed crazy.

"It's my aunt," she said finally. "I think she's in trouble."

"Your aunt?" Meg said in disbelief. "The one out west someplace? How could you possibly know she's in trouble?"

"I heard her. She was calling me. She told me she was in trouble, that WE are in trouble, and that she was cold."

"Hey, now," said Eduardo, surprised, scolding.

"You know, I've heard of people who start, like, hallucinating out here after they eat a certain mushroom," Meg said. "It's called the Copelandia, I think. It has, like, almost the same effect as peyote buttons, but it doesn't make you throw up."

Eduardo looked at Maddie. "Did you eat any mushrooms?" he said.

"No! Jesus Christ!" Maddie turned her back on them and pushed a strand of hair off her forehead. "I heard her."

Eduardo took a step toward her. Meg, cocking one cycbrow skeptically, made a "Hmm," noise and turned back to her laptop.

Maddie allowed Eduardo to take her hands as he searched her face.

"You scared me back there," he said. "Maybe you're working too hard."

His handsome, angular face with its neatly trimmed beard softened with worry, his eyes gentle. She took a deep breath. The urgency she felt was passing, but what remained was a nagging feeling that she had to get to a phone and call her aunt.

"Sorry," she said to Eduardo, and cast her eyes around the group to include them. "I can't explain it."

"Well, if you are okay now, let's celebrate!"

Happily, he announced to the others that tonight they would celebrate the winning of the new grant, so everyone should bring whatever they could to the fiesta. He mentioned that they were due new supplies soon, and with that reminder, all kinds of delicacies emerged from the nylon tents. Canned salmon, olives, and chicken breast appeared. Beef jerky was offered. Sealed, foil containers of corn tortilla batter were opened, and a fire baked the mixture into solid form, to which they added canned beans, beef and chicken. Bottles of whiskey and tequila appeared. Someone pulled out a small bag of marijuana, and another turned up some reggae in his laptop, so it resonated across the black mountains.

They ate, drank and danced in the cool darkness. When the night slipped toward morning, members of the research team began to quietly disappear into their tents, either alone or in pairs, content in the night's revelry. Maddie stared into the fire as it burned low, the coals soothing, orange and white. Eduardo sat attentively next to her, strumming a small, four-stringed instrument, a *cavaquinho*. He was wearing a light, stretchy, long-sleeved tee-shirt that helped keep off mosquitos but also flattered the strong, round muscles on his chest and shoulders and his flat stomach.

Although she had gone through the motions of celebration, she couldn't shake the frightening feeling she had about her aunt, nor forget the terrified voice that had called her name.

"Well, I guess I'll turn in," she said to Eduardo.

"I'll walk you to your tent."

He helped her up and held her elbow lightly as they crossed the clearing. The night was clear and starry and cold, away from the fire. They could hear murmured conversations coming from the tents of some of their colleagues who had formed couples – some already established, and some probably just for the night. In one tent, they could see a silhouette of two people sitting together, backlit by a small lantern. From another came the sounds of lovemaking.

Maddie grew increasingly uncomfortable as she walked next to Eduardo, dreading the awkward conversation she knew they would soon have. As expected, at her small, single tent, he moved his face near hers.

"Can I have a kiss goodnight?" he asked.

She sighed inwardly. She had been planning for this moment.

"Eduardo, I don't want a romantic relationship with anyone out here," she blurted. "I'm here for the cats." She had meant it to come out much better than it did.

"OK, well, a kiss does not mean a marriage."

"No, but a kiss is a step I'm not willing to take."

"Have I done something?" He was poised, hiding the hurt.

"Look, there's nothing wrong with you." She cringed inwardly, hating her bad choice of words. "I mean, you are fantastic. You're smart and handsome and smart, and, but, no."

"You are not very encouraging."

"Good." She tried to say it lightly, but, again, it sounded a little harsh. "And goodnight."

"Alas," he said, disappointed, but with a little smile. "But I'll be nearby if you need anything. Anything." He wagged his eyebrows in a comical, exaggerated way.

"You're a good friend," she said firmly, but also smiling to try to soften, well, everything.

"A good friend?" he said, a scolding look on his handsome face. "Well, if that's the best I can be, I'll take it. For now."

"Good night." She slipped under her tent flap, glad to be alone.

As she changed into the sweatpants and a long-sleeved tee-shirt she used as pajamas, she tried to understand what had happened earlier, her aunt's voice in the breeze. Was it real? Was it imaginary? She had never experienced anything like that before, and she couldn't stop worrying about her aunt.

Chapter 20

The day of Emerson's appointment at the Office of Children and Family Services arrived. He was going to talk to them about foster care. He had decided he couldn't possibly keep her. He was down to his last few hundred dollars, and there was a real possibility that, instead of just eating fast food, he would be serving it soon. But really, not even the fast food joints were hanging out "help wanted" signs. Times were tough; jobs were scarce, even terrible ones.

They had to take a bus to the government building because his car was temporarily disabled, due to a failed fuel pump. When they arrived at the Office of Children and Family Services, Emerson's stomach was churning. He was hopeful that foster care would be the right move, but his gut told him otherwise. He and Courtney sat in the waiting room for quite a while after he checked in. The furniture was hard plastic, the floor strewn with dirty toys. Several crusty-nostrilled children played among them, while worn-out women sat looking vacantly into space. They barely seemed to notice the children's activities. A large woman with reddish brown skin and short cropped, curly black hair, worked at a desk, a fingerprint-spotted window between her and the waiting room, which smelled of diapers. Courtney sat close to him on the green plastic bench.

"What are we doing here?" she whispered.

"Trying to get some help, like I told you."

"Why do we need help?"

"We just do."

"You can come in now," the woman in the office said, not leaving her desk or looking up.

Emerson looked at her apprehensively and she raised her head and nodded at him sternly.

He got up. Courtney started to come.

"No, sweetie, you stay here."

"I want to come."

"You will be able to see us through that window, right there," he said.

He went in and waved at Courtney, who sat, stricken, on the bench.

"Please have a seat," the woman said. Her desk nameplate, barely visible under piles of paper and file folders, said "Mrs. Jackson."

"What brings you here today?" she said, with the crispy manner of an impatient woman who had heard and seen a lot.

"The girl, Courtney," he nodded toward Courtney. "She, uh, well, her mother kind of had her delivered to me."

"Delivered?"

"She left a note," he fumbled around in his pocket, found it and handed it to Mrs. Jackson. She read it thoroughly, then looked up at him without emotion.

"So?"

"So, I ... I can't really keep her," he stammered under her icy glare. "First off, I don't even know if I'm really her father."

Mrs. Jackson looked at Courtney, then back at Emerson and raised her eyebrows in a skeptical way. The resemblance was obvious, he knew.

"And, even if I am, I have no way to care for her. I'm a researcher, and our worked just got canceled."

Mrs. Jackson said nothing.

"That means I have no way of taking care of her. There is no money coming in."

"Well?"

"So I wanted to see what I need to do to get her placed safely with a foster family."

"Oh, I see." Mrs. Jackson said with surprising sweetness. "You want to give up your daughter to some nice family that makes sure she gets everything she needs to be healthy and happy, just like her real parents?"

"Yeah." Emerson felt his face grow red.

"Well, let me tell you something," No sweetness now. "We are talking about a child here, not a puppy that you can just drop off at the pound. The only way you can make sure she gets all those things is if you take her home and give them to her."

Emerson stared dumbly, shocked.

"I might not be her father," he mumbled.

She looked like she wanted to snap at him again, but then she seemed to make an effort to soften her tone. "I can help you learn how to sign up for assistance, food stamps, housing aid. Don't feel like you need to put her in care, just because you're overwhelmed. That's only natural."

Emerson sat watching her for a moment. She returned his gaze, unyielding.

"And the only way you could look more alike is if you were twins."

He gazed out at Courtney. She had tucked up her feet on the bench and was watching him with anxiety.

"You can go to the next office down the hall to sign up for assistance," Mrs. Jackson said, handing him a sheet of paper listing state services for parents and children. Her expression softened. "They even hold classes for first-time parents. You can do this, honey. I know you can."

Emerson still could not find words. He gazed at the paper without focusing, then back at Mrs. Jackson.

"And if, after you check into those programs, you still think you want her to go into foster care, here are the forms to get started. And this booklet on voluntary foster care. OK? Now, you think about that and stop next door. You'll be surprised what they have to help you."

He mumbled a thanks and left the office. He held out his hand for Courtney, and she jumped up and took it. A feeling of great relief seemed to envelop them both as they walked down the hall. He realized he didn't want to put her in foster care. Maybe Mrs. Jackson could tell that. He was just going to have to find Annie, or, better yet, maybe she would get well enough to come claim Courtney. But now he had to focus on how to pay for food and his apartment.

Chapter 21

The frantic little honking signal Maddie heard didn't mean a busy line, but that the phone hadn't connected properly. She sighed and hung up, then started touching numbers again.

This time there was a long silence after she hit the last button. But then, she heard ringing.

Five thousand miles away, the disconnected telephone rang. A few feet away, Clara's body still lay frozen. The ringing continued, six rings, seven.

No longer sparkling green, Clara's dead eyes were frosty white. A mist surrounded her. Eight, nine, ten rings. Clara's eyes turned slowly toward the phone.

Maddie plugged her ear with a finger, hunching close to the phone as she strained to hear the ringing. It was so far away, but it sounded even farther, like it was coming from someplace in the atmosphere. Then she heard a voice on the phone.

"Maddie? Maddie! I need you! Help me!"

Clara's voice seemed so distant, so odd. It must be the phone lines.

"Aunt Clara? What's wrong?"

"Maddie! I need you! Please come! Maddie, it's cold. It's so cold."

"Aunt Clara? Aunt Clara?!"

Maddie listened hard, but now there was no sound from the other end.

"Aunt Clara!? Are you there?"

She waited a moment, but a recorded voice abruptly interrupted, telling her in Spanish that she needed to hang up if she wanted to place a call.

Maddie awoke and realized she had been crying in her sleep. Then the memory of the nightmare crept into her consciousness.

She wiggled out of her sleeping bag, wrapped herself in her coat and quietly unzipped the door. The first breath of the cold, dry morning air burned her nose and lungs as she left the warmth of the tent. She walked away from the little village of colorful tents, then sat by herself, gazing across the sparse, dormant field, glowing golden as the sun squeezed up over the blue-gray silhouette of the snow-capped Andes. She wondered if the cold air and all that distant snow had influenced her nightmare about Aunt Clara.

She wanted to make sure her aunt was OK. But she also felt the time-based pressure of her work. This area was slated for oil and gas development, and her team's grant was specifically designed to study the Andean cat in this area prior to the start of development, scheduled for the end of August. It was important to learn all they could now to ensure the creature's protection during and after the development. Interrupting the study now, to travel all the way back to the states, well, that would greatly hurt the study, her colleagues, her reputation as a scientist, and possibly the cat, itself. It would take a good month out of her work, and there was such little time. These next four months would give them the information they needed to help the government and the oil company put safeguards in place to protect the cat.

She watched the subtle colors of the landscape brighten as the sun finished its ascent over the highest peak and inched upward in the huge sky. Her greenish-golden eyes caught movement in the shrubs, a couple hundred yards away, and she automatically focused on it. It was a guanaco, a small, llama-like creature, grazing along the edges of the field, its cinnamon-colored hair catching the sunlight and glowing warmly. She watched the pretty creature and the rest of its herd that strolled into sight behind it. She knew she had to finish her work here before going back to the States. It was important, impacting more than just herself and her aunt, and it had been the main focus of her world for the last three years, the final work that would lead to her PhD.

But she would get word to Clara. Their supplies were due today. She would put a message to Clara on a USB drive and ask the delivery man to send it to Clara's lawyer when he got back to town. If she paid him enough, he would also check her email for a response before making the trip back up the mountain with supplies the next time. Once she made the decision, she would stick to it. But she knew it would be a hard fight against the nagging of her conscience.

And she was right, because the frightening, heart-wrenching image of her frozen aunt would visit her dreams until that day, five months later, in September, when she would board a plane for home. She dreaded what she would find when she arrived.

Chapter 22

Crandall's colitis hadn't bothered him for weeks. Usually stress of any kind, even when caused by happy events, such as today's, brought on a bout of the painful, bloody condition. But as he signed and received the documents making Crandall Enterprises full owner of the land he had so long been seeking, he felt superb.

Hector Longtree, the lawyer who had taken over Toby's clientele, was relatively new to Stony Valley, and to practicing law, and posed little obstacle for Crandall. He did make the expected inquiries after Toby's disappearance, but ultimately seemed glad to be able to close out some of the nagging details that Toby had left behind.

"One last document here, Mr. Crandall," Longtree said, pushing some papers across the table to Crandall's lawyer, Alex. Alex also happened to be Crandall's nephew. Crandall liked to keep his business in the family. Since his own son had proven himself to be a completely incompetent disappointment, he had to turn to his nephew. He thought of his nephew as a sly creature whom he had to watch at all times, but that was to be expected, and it was better than trusting an outsider.

Alex reviewed the document, recognized it, and slid it to Crandall with a nod. Crandall signed it without bothering to read it and looked up. The sun was setting through the window behind Longtree, and for a terrible moment, Crandall thought he could see two people seated on either side of him. He blinked.

Sitting next to Longtree were the shapes of Clara Stanton and Toby Landy.

"Ah!" He said in surprise, making both Longtree and Alex jump and look up sharply.

"What?" said Alex.

At once, the images seemed to fade away into the long shadowy light cast by the setting sun.

"It's nothing," Crandall said, uncertain. "Nothing. I thought, I just thought I saw something."

"Don't startle me like that," Alex snapped, peevishly. "So, that's it then."

He passed the last sheet back to Longtree.

"That's it," said Longtree. "Congratulations, Mr. Crandall. I hope your endeavor turns out to be a profitable one for you, and for our area."

Still distracted, Crandall looked around the room nervously. "Yes, I'm sure it will. Thank you, Longtree."

Everyone stood and shook hands.

"When will we start to see some activity out there?" Longtree asked, as he and Alex quickly assembled the stacks of papers and tucked them into their hard briefcases.

"Very soon," Crandall said, glancing at the window. It was clear. "We actually are already underway on the first parcel we purchased, on the northeast side, getting the utility lines started. And with this formality complete, we'll start some of the facilities that are somewhat distant from the central resort. As for the main structures, the hotel and casino, I have had the permits reviewed already, so their approval won't take long. I think we'll see construction start on the hotel late next month. The hotel should open in the fall, and the casino next year."

"Wow," said Longtree, standing by the door. "No grass growing under your feet."

Crandall smiled slightly and nodded to Longtree, then left the room, followed by Alex.

"So, that was well done," Alex said, when they got to the car.

Crandall turned on him sharply.

"Don't be using tones like that with me again," he said to his nephew.

"What are you talking about?"

"'Don't startle me like that,'" Crandall imitated his nephew insultingly.

"Well, you made me jump a mile," Alex said.

"That doesn't mean you can be insolent."

Alex eyed him with concern.

"I'm sorry. I didn't mean anything by it," he said, his tone melting from sharp to deferential. "Uncle. Sir."

Crandall turned and strode to his car, Alex following anxiously.

"I'll expect to see you tomorrow morning, so we can get on with this damn thing. You have everything ready, correct?"

"Yes, it's all but finalized. Just a couple more signatures, some fund transfers, and we'll be breaking ground."

"Don't be late."

Crandall got in his car and slammed the door.

"No sir. I won't be," Alex said, watching the car drive away. Then he added, "You miserable prick. Oh, excuse me, I mean Uncle Miserable Prick. Sir."

Chapter 23

Emerson took Courtney with him to meet Gary at the lab. They had to clean it out. It was a depressing activity, but made slightly better by Gary's constant prattle, so familiar to Emerson that it brought comfort, although it sometimes tottered into the inane. After a while, both he and Courtney became worn out by it, and once they got back to the apartment, she flopped on her cot, a book in her hands.

Emerson checked his e-mail. He saw a new message from Natalie, Annie Hughes' old friend. It said, simply:

"Hi Emerson. After you called the other day, I have been doing some searching. Today, I found this."

Attached to the e-mail was an Internet link. He clicked on it to find a short death notice in the Columbus Daily Press about the death of Annie Hughes, the victim of a hit-and-run driver who had never been identified. Emerson groaned and covered his face with his large hands.

"What's wrong?" Courtney asked.

He slid his fingers down until they were just covering his mouth and chin, and he looked at Courtney.

How would he tell her? And when? She was looking at him with concern, and he looked back, wide-eyed, over his fingers.

Not now. He couldn't do it now.

Sorrow for the child bubbled up inside him, linked to his terror of knowing that, now, there was no possible hope of reuniting Courtney with her mother. She was his. She had no one else.

Emerson paced. He had some options, of course. He could start pounding the pavement for a job. He could write a new grant application, but it would take months to get an answer. And how would he feed himself and Courtney until the grant came through, if one did? He could fill out the food stamp application, apply for a professorship somewhere, maybe even catch a summer course. But teaching one summer course wouldn't pay the bills, and getting a job as a professor was not a given, and it was several months before something like that could start, anyway.

Realistically, he knew he had only one, guaranteed option for making a good salary, fast, but it was one he had passionately avoided. Going this route would definitely secure a comfortable living for Courtney, and that was what was important now. As for him, well, the choice filled him with dread.

He sighed deeply and punched the number on his phone.

"Yes?" Two thousand miles away, E. Rexham Crandall answered his cell.

"Dad? It's me."

"Emerson! My son the bug doctor. To what do I owe the honor of this call? Not stuck in a swamp or being eaten alive by one of your little lab subjects, are you?"

"No," Emerson said, feeling utterly miserable, and automatically correcting his father in his head. He wasn't a doctor. He had a master's, no more. He skipped even asking how his father was doing, and went right to it. "Something has come up, and I'm wondering, well, I was just hoping that, uh, maybe your offer of that, um, job is still good?"

Stunned silence from the other end.

"Dad?"

"Emerson, I'm speechless. Don't tell me you are tired of playing with your little arachnids and are finally ready to join me in the real world?"

The triumphant glee in his father's tone caused Emerson's fist to ball up. He tapped it against his forehead and leaned into the wall. He sighed and swallowed. He didn't play with arachnids. He played with *geometridae*.

"Yeah, I guess that's what I'm telling you."

"Great news!" Crandall exclaimed, jubilantly triumphant. "How soon can you be here?"

Emerson swallowed again. It would only get worse from here.

"I'll, uh, I'll have to check the bus schedule."

"The bus schedule?" Crandall snapped in surprise. "You are in bad shape, aren't you?"

Emerson was silent.

"Don't you have a car?"

"Yes. I have a car."

"Oh, but not one that can get you here from New York?"

"Right."

"So, what happened? Bottom fall out of the bug market?" Crandall didn't try to hide his glee.

"Something like that," said Emerson, miserable.

"I'm so glad I paid for that $45,000 degree."

"You only paid $30,000," said Emerson, then wished he hadn't. His father could still make him react like a churlish boy.

"Oh, that's right. Just most of it."

When Emerson didn't say anything, Crandall said, "So, what does the trip by bus take, about two days? Maybe three?"

"Probably."

"And do you actually sleep on the bus? That must be terribly uncomfortable."

Emerson sighed. His father was not going to let him off lightly.

"It'll be OK," he mumbled.

"Oh, well, I'll see you in a few days, then." His father's tone was light. "You can call me when you get to Stony Valley. No, wait, let me help. Call me from the capital, and I'll pick you up from there."

Emerson waited, silent. Crandall let the pause drag on. They were both stubbornly delaying the inevitable outcome.

141

"I suppose I could speed up your trip a little by purchasing you a plane ticket."

Finally, Emerson thought, gritting his teeth. The first of many handouts he would be accepting from his father, who would make sure each came with many strings attached. He might as well get used to it.

"Yes, you could. Except I need two tickets." Before his father could ask for an explanation, Emerson said hurriedly, "You can have them sent to this cell number, and thanks, Dad. Thanks a lot. OK, then. See you soon. Bye." He hung up and sat down heavily on the couch.

To what misery had he just committed himself?

Chapter 24

Emerson parked the car in a dirt lot and looked through the windshield at the construction site. Two huge backhoes were ripping the ground for the foundation, dropping scoops of yellow soil and rocks in waiting dump trucks.

"Are we there?" Courtney said.

"Yup."

She looked through the windshield, too. "Is that where the resort will be?"

"Mm-hmm. The hotel part of it, anyway."

"What other parts will there be?"

"Condos, apartments. Um, let's see. A casino, airstrip, mountain cabins."

"A swimming pool?"

"Lots of swimming pools. A, what's it called? Something for horse shows."

"There will be horses?"

"Mmm-hmmm."

"Can I have a horse?"

"Maybe. I don't really know yet."

"When will you know?"

"Once I figure out what I've gotten us into."

"Can I at least ride a horse until then?"

"Yeah, I think so. Probably."

They were still gazing out the windshield at the busy construction site.

"Is your father up there?"

His heart beat rapidly.

"I think so."

"Are we getting out?"

"Yeah."

"When?"

He spotted his father standing at the edge of the central building foundation, looking down imperiously into the pit of workers. Emerson's stomach tightened. He sighed, trying to calm down.

"When, Daddy?"

"Now."

They both opened their doors and he met her on her side, offering his hand, which she took. They started up a rough, dirt road toward Crandall. His father had been talking to another man, looking at a large document, maybe a blueprint. Emerson could tell by his body language that the other man didn't like Crandall, but they seemed to reach an agreement and the man went away, leaving Crandall standing alone, watching the work.

Then he noticed something. Or someone? A figure appeared near his father. Emerson had not seen this person approach. It was just there, suddenly. Also, the figure was not clear; it was a dark, smoky silhouette, and it moved toward his father without walking, but rather, it glided. Emerson and Courtney kept walking but slowed down, both peering intently at the figure.

At that moment, a strong wind blew up, swirling around them briskly, chilling them and rushing toward his father. The gust of wind reached his father at the same time as the figure. The figure spread out like someone raising his hands and grew large, as though it were stretching to three times the size of a normal man. It lunged at his father and, through the swirling red dust kicked up by the eddy of wind, Emerson saw his father lose his balance over the high foundation wall. Crandall teetered precariously, fighting to maintain his balance on the ledge that jutted thirty feet above the foundation floor.

Courtney screamed.

Just then another man appeared behind Crandall, apparently having climbed up from the other side. He grabbed

Crandall's coat and helped steady him. Crandall regained his balance and then spotted Emerson. He strode down to greet him.

"Emerson!" he said, shaking Emerson's hand.

"Hi." Emerson cast an uneasy glance back up at the foundation.

"So, you found it."

"Yes."

"And who is this little person that had to fly across the country with you?" Crandall eyed Courtney without warmth.

"She's your granddaughter."

Crandall gave Emerson a look of disgusted alarm.

"Really? How charming. Wait here a minute, child."

He took a hawk-like hold of Emerson's arm and pulled him a few yards away.

"What the hell have you done?" he said.

Emerson quietly filled his father in on how Courtney happened to be with him.

"Typical," his father said. "Sloppy. Loose ends. And is this why you are here now, because you knocked up some girl and you're groveling for a job?"

"We're a little beyond the knocked-up part."

"And have you tried to find the mother?"

"Look in Columbus. She might be buried there."

"She's yours? Definitely?"

"For Pete's sake, Dad. Look at her."

Crandall turned and gave Courtney a long, appraising look. She was chasing a butterfly that had flown over the construction site.

"Well, I guess I should thank her for scaring you to your senses and bringing you here so you can start to do some real work. And earn some real money." He pulled Emerson back to the girl.

"And what is your name?"

"Courtney." She reached for Emerson's hand.

"This is your grandfather, Courtney."

"I know."

"Courtney, be polite," said Emerson gently.

"I don't know what to call him, though," she whispered.

Emerson and Crandall looked at each other, each with his eyebrows raised.

"Who was that dark man who pushed you?" Courtney asked Crandall.

"Dark man? Do you mean Chilson, the masonry foreman? He didn't push me. He helped me."

"No, the one who was there first, the one who pushed you."

Emerson looked at her in mute surprise. So, he hadn't imagined it.

"No one pushed me. A gust of wind nearly sent me over the edge, though."

"But, I saw him!"

"That's enough," Emerson said, as his father gave him a cross look that seemed to accuse him of creating a lunatic.

"Come on." Crandall started walking. "I'll show you where you'll be staying. It's a trailer, nothing fancy. But perfectly situated for my new project manager."

He clapped Emerson on the back.

The wind blew strongly as they walked. Emerson noticed without interest a piece of crumbled blue paper blowing across the lot toward them. Courtney saw it too and chased it. She caught up with it and examined it closely.

"Put that down," Crandall snapped. "It's dirty."

She trotted over to Emerson.

"Look Daddy, it's somebody's letter."

Emerson started to squint at the writing as Courtney held it out. Without looking at it, Crandall abruptly swatted it from Courtney's hand. The paper blew quickly away in the brisk wind and disappeared over the foundation wall.

"Hey!" Courtney said.

"I don't know what your daddy has taught you." Crandall said "daddy" with a particular sneer. "But Crandalls don't pick-up other people's garbage."

"But it might have been a secret message," Courtney appealed to her father.

"Leave it, sweetie."

Crandall took Emerson's arm, guiding him toward what looked to be the start of a large area of landscaping at the front of the resort. He pointed out a small trailer nestled there among bags of cedar chips and fertilizer.

"The first thing you'll have to do is find a nanny. A construction site is no place for a child."

They had dinner in Stony Valley's only fine-dining restaurant, Moretto's. Emerson ordered steak, as did Crandall, and Courtney ordered fried chicken strips.

Crandall asked for a bottle of red and now he held up his glass.

"To Crandall Enterprises and the start of an extraordinary venture."

Emerson tried to smile. He clinked glasses with his father.

"Raise your glass, kiddo, it's a toast," he said to Courtney. She did.

"It doesn't look like toast," she giggled.

"It's a different kind of toast," Emerson said.

"We'll get you started right away. You'll need some steel-toed boots. You can pick up a pair at the sporting goods store down the street in the morning. Expense them. Then you can start on the hotel site."

"What exactly will I be doing?"

"You'll be the site foreman, making sure that construction proceeds quickly, that the workers are following the rules, resolve any questions about the way things are going. Our plan is to have the hotel open for guests by the end of September, with a grand opening in October. The casino will be finished by next August, weather permitting."

"You do realize I have no experience doing this?" Emerson said.

"It doesn't matter," Crandall waved it away. "It's just common sense. Just be the boss and let me know if there are problems."

Salads arrived and they dug in. Crandall chewed vigorously and peered at Emerson, who tried not to squirm under his father's scrutiny.

"The contractor is top-notch, name of O'Mara. He'll ask you to make decisions on things that aren't answered in the plans. But if you get questions you can't answer, I'll always be available," Crandall said. "I'll be around quite a bit at first, but I need to start focusing on the apartments and condos going up, near the cliffs. And I need to get the rest of the operations going."

"Operations?" Emerson said, vaguely.

Crandall gave him a withering look.

"You really are a biology major, aren't you? I mean building the legal team and the financial details, especially, but also doing the marketing. I'll be heading the marketing, and my brother will be taking care of the financials, of course. I wouldn't trust anyone else to do that. He'll be doing it from Manhattan for now, until I can get him out here. I really detest letting anyone outside the family do that type of work. My motto always has been to keep what's important in the family. Your grandfather taught me that."

Emerson had a fleeting memory of his grandfather spanking him after Emerson accidentally crushed the flowers his grandfather had just planted around a flag pole.

"That's why I want to be sure about the girl," Crandall added quietly.

"Don't worry about it."

"What about me?" said Courtney.

"Nothing," Emerson said. "Your grandpa is being silly."

"You can't really trust anyone else," his father was saying. "Your family will have your back, in the end. No matter what other crap they put you through."

The steak and chicken arrived. Emerson checked that Courtney had what she needed and then dug in ravenously. He hadn't had a steak since, well, since he could even remember. This one was rare – he had wanted it medium, but his father overruled him – and charred, salted and buttered on the outside, topped with mushrooms, red on the inside and absolutely delicious.

His father watched him with amusement.

"You bug people do eat once in a while, yes?"

Emerson chewed and nodded.

"Rare all right, then?"

Emerson nodded and swallowed, wiped his mouth with the cloth napkin and politely said, "Yes, it's delicious. Thanks."

"Well, don't let me interrupt you. You had quite a rhythm going there. Are you practicing for a speed-eating event?"

Courtney watched her father carefully, caught the smile he had trouble hiding, and giggled.

"Speed-eating champion!" she said.

They had their first look at their new home a little later, the foreman's trailer. Stepping up into the front door brought them into a small office, with a desk at the window that faced the construction site, already equipped with a laptop, site plans, and a folder of what turned out to be a stack of invoices. A doorway into the next room bore a sign saying, "No boots past this point." On the other side, they found a diminutive kitchen and living room combination. The kitchen held a small table and chairs, and the carpeted living room hosted a couple of comfy chairs and a tidy loveseat, surrounding a wall-mounted TV. In the back were two tiny bedrooms, big enough for one twin bed each, only, with drawers built-in underneath, and a bathroom with tub and shower.

"This is so cool," Courtney said when she first saw it. But she was tired, Emerson noticed. After a little while, the trailer seemed to take on a creepy feeling, out there in the middle of a desolate construction site, with dark shapes and strange sounds in the night. Before long, Courtney had what Emerson recognized as a full-fledge meltdown, caused by grief and exhaustion, and she sobbed for her mother. She wouldn't let him touch her at first, but wept by herself on one of the living room chairs.

As he watched her sadly, he thought of his own mother. He only had a few memories of her, but he kept them alive by remembering every detail. She was sitting in the dark summer grass in a yellow blouse, gently holding a dandelion he had handed her, her gray eyes full of love as she gazed at him. Her face held a real smile, the rare one she showed only when she was feeling truly happy. He remembered doubting the quality of his gift, since the dandelion already seemed to be wilting, and he had not managed to pluck quite enough stem, so she was really just holding the blossom, but her smile gave him hope, made him proud.

She was gone, too. First she left. Then she died. He couldn't tell Courtney how deeply he understood her sorrow.

Finally, Courtney accepted some hot cocoa and an offer to watch the cartoon channel, then sniffled herself to sleep, next to him on the sofa.

Emerson wasn't so lucky. All night long, he had the feeling that someone was watching him. Once, he thought he saw a face at the window.

Sleep was hard to come by, on that spot where Clara Stanton's house once stood.

On a dark road nearby, Emerson's cousin Alex was heading back from the resort site. He had just dropped off some papers at the trailer Crandall was using as an office, and was done for the night. He had the radio up and was singing with it as he careened along the curvy, cliff-side roads that he had come to know so well. Just as he swung around a blind curve, he saw a small, bright shape on the road ahead. He stopped singing and swerved on the narrow road, just missing a little white and tan dog. The car careened to the left, then to the right as Alex turned the wheel madly, trying to get it under control. His spinning tires sent stones tumbling off the cliff.

Finally, he steadied the car. He let out his breath in a short chuckle of relief. That had been too close.

Then he saw the horse.

Black and white and bony, it stood across the narrow road. Alex yelled and turned the wheel again, this time flying into the berm. He couldn't correct the turn in time, and the car sailed over the cliff, falling sixty feet before it hit, nose first, crumpling like an accordion on the switchback road below.

The horse and dog watched from the cliff overhead before disappearing like mist.

The next morning, Emerson and Courtney went back into town for some groceries and work boots.

His father had given him a company credit card, and, in addition to the boots, he used it to buy new jeans and T-shirts. Courtney had outgrown the sparse clothing she had brought in her little knapsack when she had arrived at his door, so he decided to use the card to get her some new clothes as well.

He had never bought clothing for a child before, and he was grateful to accept the help of the saleswoman, a thin woman of around thirty-five with purple lipstick and brown curls. She easily fitted Courtney with jeans, shorts, shirts and sneakers.

"Should I have work boots, too, Daddy?"

"Well," Emerson thought about it. "I don't really want you on the construction site, kiddo. But you might need them out there, anyway, just for hiking or climbing around. So, yeah, I guess so."

"What construction site is that?" asked the saleswoman.

"Oh, I'm working out at the new resort site," Emerson said, feeling like an impostor. "Have you heard of it? The Crandall?"

Her smile faded. "That place? Oh, wow. You be careful out there."

"Why?"

"Oh, it's probably stupid. But some people think the Crandall is cursed."

"What's a curse?" Courtney said immediately. "Daddy, what's that mean, 'cursed?'"

"Why would anyone say anything like that?" Emerson said, annoyed.

"Well, Mrs. Stanton, the nice old lady who lived out there, she died in her home right after she signed the sales agreement," said the saleswoman. "And her horse and dog burned to death in a barn fire that same night."

Courtney gasped.

"And then her lawyer went on a trip to New Mexico, and he never came back." She wiggled a boot onto Courtney's right foot, then the left. "The police looked into it and everything. Try those out, honey."

Courtney obediently got up and jumped up and down.

"There are a lot of weird stories about that place," she said, leaning into Emerson, a knowing look on her tanned face.

Courtney had stopped jumping and was staring at the saleswoman, her mouth open, eyes wide.

"Run down there and back," Emerson told Courtney. "Make sure they don't rub."

When she had trotted off, he said, "What did the police find?"

"Not a thing," she said, obviously relishing delivering this gossip to fresh ears. "And you know what? They never found the lawyer. Not him or his body. They found his car at the hotel where he was meeting his friends, but no sign of him. Nothing. Just, gone."

"Right, well, I don't want anyone having nightmares tonight." He nodded toward Courtney, but, after his bad night, included himself in the thought.

"Oops! Right," she said. "How do those feel then, honey?"

"Good," Courtney said.

"That's a wrap, then," said Emerson. "Let's go."

"Thank you both, and you have a good day," said the saleswoman as Courtney trotted toward the checkout counter, still wearing the leather boots as well as her new jeans and shirt. They had left their old clothes in a garbage bin near the restrooms. The sales woman put her hand on Emerson's upper arm, stopping him briefly.

"Just be careful out there," she said. "OK?"

"Yeah, sure," Emerson said. "Hey, I need to get her enrolled in school for next fall. Any idea where I should go?"

She told him where to find the school district headquarters. It was a small town, and a nice day, so they walked. Partway down the block, Emerson had the feeling they were being watched. He looked around and thought he noticed the dark shape of a man in an upstairs office window, staring down at them. But, as he watched, the image faded away. It must have been a reflection, or some trick of the sunlight.

It didn't mean anything to him at the time, but he was passing under the office of Toby Landy.

Chapter 25

By late August, the basic structure of the main resort was up, and, while the internal details were still under construction, Crandall moved into an office on the second floor. Because the resort was high up the hill, he could overlook the whole project from there.

Emerson stopped up one Monday, ostensibly to ask his father whether the latest load of beams they had received were of the right safety rating. Really, however, he had been bothered by the repeated rumors he had been hearing from locals about the resort — the clothing store clerk being the first but not the last – and he finally decided to ask his father about it.

But when he stepped into the office, he saw Crandall there with someone Emerson recognized, someone who made him want to turn and run. His father spotted him before he could escape.

"Emerson! Just in time! Come say hello to your Aunt Irma."

A stout, black-haired woman with pale skin and red lips moved toward him, swaying like a cobra.

"Emerson!" She looked him up and down. "So tall and handsome. You have grown up."

She ran her long fingernails down his chest and, to his dismay, brushed his groin. She made it seem like an accident, but he knew her too well.

"Oh, yes," she winked. "You're a big boy now." She grinned, her teeth looking sharp and yellow against the red lips.

He flushed.

"So terrible about your cousin Alex," she went on. "He wasn't as smart as you, but at least he chose a profession in which he could make some money."

Alex, the lawyer, had been the only one of his cousins for whom Emerson held some affection, and he was shocked and saddened by the auto accident that had killed him in March. The funeral was held back East, so Emerson stayed at the construction site while his father attended the services. He regretted not being there but didn't mind avoiding his other relatives who showed up in force. Unfortunately, Irma was one of those he dodged with vigor. And now, here she was, leering at him.

"My sister's here to start hiring hotel staff," Crandall said. "She's going to manage the personnel in the main building."

Irma leered at Emerson, bringing back unsettling memories. He didn't want to work anywhere near his aunt.

"Great," he said.

"Well, I'll just find my office and start my plans," she said. She let her hand trail across Emerson's chest again as she left. "I may need your help later, Emerson, so don't wander off."

After she closed the door behind her, Emerson said, "I can't believe you hired her."

"What? Oh, honestly. She's an excellent businesswoman."

Uncomfortable memories of his aunt flicked through Emerson's mind like a slide show. Most of them revolved around her being a bully. When he was a child, she had been one of the first people to teach him that not all grown-ups could be trusted.

"She's sick."

"Oh, you're exaggerating. So what did you need?"

"Those beams that just came in, I don't think they have the right load rating. I think they are too low."

"Oh? What are they?"

"They are thirty pounds per square foot and I ordered forty."

"Oh, yes. I asked Chilson to change that order, because the cost of steel is going through the roof."

"But, is it still strong enough?"

"It's fine." Crandall sat at his desk and started reading a long, legal-looking document.

Emerson watched his father with concern. His father glanced up at him, then back at the document.

"Was there anything else?"

Emerson took a breath, feeling his ears getting red.

"Did you know anything about the old lady who died out here, after she sold you her land?"

Crandall looked at Emerson, then put down the document and stood, turning to look out the window.

"Yes, a shame. Nice old bird."

"And her lawyer?"

"Very unfortunate. He hasn't shown up yet, has he?"

Emerson stared at his father's back. What was up with his father's ultra-casual attitude?

"The old lady, she has a niece, or she did have," Crandall said, still with an uncharacteristically light tone. "I sometimes wonder if she might show up someday and cause us some minor trouble."

"Why? Why would she cause us trouble?"

"Well, it was not easy to convince Clara Stanton to sell. I had to literally do everything I could think of to get that sale." Crandall stopped talking, turned to glance at Emerson again. Emerson was very still, watching him closely. Was he hiding discomfort?

"The niece might put her nose in it," Crandall went on. "Who knows? Anyway, last I knew she was in South American someplace."

His father still gazed out the window. Emerson watched him anxiously.

"Does she have any reason for causing us trouble? I mean, I'm saying, there was nothing strange about the deal, right?"

"Strange? Well, it was all legal, but it certainly was strange that she died right then, and then her lawyer. The whole mess just caused a bit of a delay. But, the niece, well, you just never know what people will do when they go and get emotional about things like family land."

There was a loud crash in the corner, causing both men to jump. A bronze statue from the top shelf of the bookcase had hit the floor.

"That shelf is brand new," Crandall said, walking over to examine it. "If it collapsed, someone is in trouble."

He tapped the shelf and wiggled it. The shelf was firmly set in its correct place. Crandall and Emerson looked at each other in surprised silence.

"Do things like that keep happening to you?" Emerson whispered.

"Things like what?" Crandall stood straight and glared at Emerson, as though daring him to go there. "Things like what? So, a statue fell. It probably wasn't set there correctly in the first place."

Emerson looked around his father's immaculately neat and tidy office. Everything in the place was set correctly.

"So, I have been meaning to ask you," his father said. "Did you ever think to get a DNA test on the girl?"

Emerson gave his father a long look, recognizing how quickly his father had skipped away from the questions Emerson had come to discuss, away from the strange fact that a statue had fallen by itself, and onto a subject that was almost certain to completely distract and engage his son. He wanted to just skip this conversation and leave, but he had to remember that his father was also his employer, and this job was paying him very well.

Still, he couldn't stop from saying. "Really? You bring this up now? Well, OK, to answer: No."

"I think you should."

In recent years, Emerson had found that using his imagination at times like these helped him maintain a sense of objectivity, and this prevented him from engaging with his father with the childish fury that his father was still capable of mustering in him. He now imagined himself popping his father in the nose. He smiled at the image.

"Well, I don't. All you have to do is look at her to see she looks just like me. And just like you, for that matter."

"Looks can be deceiving. And you have always been so gullible." It was as though his father recognized Emerson's change of approach and kept baiting him.

"We don't need it."

"I'll pay for it."

"What's the point?"

"I would like to know if she is your actual daughter or if she is the daughter of some other poor schlep that botanist happened to be screwing the same time she was screwing you."

Pop! Right to the nose. Emerson smiled again. "I'm not worried about it." He noticed some activity outside and joined his father at the window.

"I would really like to know if she is actually my granddaughter. It could be important."

"Why? What are you talking about?"

"Well, she could have a lot riding on being a real Crandall. I like to keep our business in the family."

He felt the anger pushing through his facade, and so focused intently on the activity outside. His father was an expert at knowing just where to poke to aggravate him.

"Well, consider her family," he said. Then he added. "I am checking with the state to see if there is anything I need to do to make sure it's legal, so no matter what, she's your granddaughter."

A large truck with a boom lift had pulled into the construction site. Several workers jumped out, donning hard hats as one climbed into a hefty nylon harness. It looked like the work crew was preparing to cut down the huge, ponderosa tree that dominated the location.

"I like that tree," Emerson murmured. He suddenly felt strange. A cool chill fluttered through his body. He shut his eyes for a moment, trying to fight off the uncomfortable feeling. Still, the cold filled his body. The short hairs on his neck and arms stood on end. His scalp tingled. When he opened his eyes, he had only one thought: The tree must stand.

He turned to his father. "Stop them!"

Crandall was about to continue trying to convince Emerson to get the DNA test. But he noticed, with concern, when his son shut his eyes, and that he had grown pale and looked ill.

"What's wrong?"

"Stop them!"

There was something strange about Emerson's face. His eyes seemed to be changing. It looked as though they were turning from their normal deep blue to a greenish gold color. His nose and mouth seemed to be changing shape, growing shorter. And his hair, it was getting lighter, turning from almost black to a rich brown. Not taking his eyes away from his son, Crandall moved closer to see if it was a reflection from the light, peering at Emerson uneasily.

"That tree needs to stay!"

Crandall glanced out the window and saw the crew at the base of the tree, then looked back at Emerson. He jumped back. It was not Emerson, but a stranger, a broad middle-aged man with greenish-gold eyes and a square face.

"Stop them!" the man demanded.

Crandall jumped back, pressing himself against the wall, terrified. The man strode out the door.

"What in holy hell?" Crandall whispered to himself, staring at the door. Then he went to the window and saw Emerson enter the yard below. It was definitely Emerson now, and he was hurrying toward the tree, through piles of rolled landscaping cloth, around gravel and over steel beams. Crandall thought what he saw must have been his imagination and now watched his son with growing annoyance.

"That crazy fool. He's going to get hurt." Crandall headed after his son, grabbing his hardhat on the way out the door.

Emerson reached the tree.

"Watch out!" yelled a man near a bulldozer, who had been preparing chains for the tree.

"Do not take down this tree." Emerson had no idea why he was doing this, but he knew he had to. He tried to sound less hysterical and more commanding. "This tree should stay as part of the landscaping."

The workmen watched him skeptically. The foreman said, "But we have to build a walkway on this spot. It's on the plans. Anyway, this tree is old. It's probably rotted out inside. If it goes down, it could hit the building."

Crandall reached Emerson. "What is going on?"

"This tree is staying," Emerson said. "We'll just have to build the walkway around it."

The workmen looked at Emerson, Crandall, each other, the foreman, waiting for a decision.

"That's final," Emerson said, mustering all the authority he could.

The foreman looked at Crandall. Crandall glanced at Emerson and, once more, thought he saw the shadow of someone else in his son's features.

"OK. The tree stays," Crandall said.

Emerson nodded sharply at his father, and it seemed to Crandall that a dark shadow pulled away from Emerson and vanished like smoke. He watched the spot where it had been uneasily for a moment.

"Let's get out of here so they can work," Crandall said to his son, keeping his composure in front of the workers, despite what he had seen.

Emerson walked off toward his trailer, the workers exchanging glances behind his back.

"Include the damned thing in the landscaping for now," Crandall told the foreman quietly. "You can always take it out later if you have to."

Crandall went back to his office. He sat as his desk and went through everything he had just seen, or thought he had seen. Was he going crazy? He felt normal, but he had to believe he had just had some kind of hallucination. And what about that statue falling? He went over to the shelf and picked up the heavy bronze buffalo. Emerson had witnessed its falling, too, so it wasn't all his imagination.

He thought back on the other strange things he had been experiencing. Since the day he checked Clara's frozen body, he had been seeing things. Shadows and objects moved on their own. He occasionally thought he saw Clara, appearing and watching him with a fury that chilled him. And then there was this man, the one he saw in Emerson. He thought he might have seen him in a nightmare, together with an Indian woman.

He shook his head. He didn't believe in ghosts. He blamed this on stress. He might need to go see his doctor and get something for anxiety. He didn't like feeling like he was always being watched, like there might be something lurking in the corners. There must be something he could take.

Still, if he didn't know such things were impossible, he would think that the Crandall was haunted.

Chapter 26

Maddie landed at the international airport in the capital at 4:47 a.m. By the time she got through the gate and rented a car, it was 5:30. Now that she was finally here, the last two hours on the road to her aunt's would seem unbearably long. Her failure to reach Clara or her lawyer, the unsettling note from Toby, it all made her exhausted brain feel stressed, bordering on frantic. But she found her rental car in the lot and headed out on the dark interstate toward Stony Valley.

When she finally reached the outskirts of town, she recognized the beautiful view near the ranch and let out a big sigh. Finally, she would see Aunt Clara. Then she noticed a new billboard, glaring against the natural environment.

"Future Home of the Crandall Resort," the sign announced. It was illustrated with a large, lush hotel, resort cabins, a casino, and waterfall to a lake. The lake pictured was definitely the same one that was on her aunt's property, the only one like that in the area.

She was scrutinizing the sign as she drove when a steer trotted out from behind it, right into her path. She hit the brakes and swerved. The rental car spun neatly around the beast, never hitting it, and collided sharply with the billboard. The billboard shuddered, then creaked. Maddie, who had slammed her forehead on the steering wheel, looked up with dizzy apprehension. The board started to topple. Maddie unhooked her safety belt and dove out of the car. She rolled across the road and scrambled to her feet. The steer trotted after her, and they both were barely clear when the billboard collapsed, first hitting the rental car, then tilting and landing hard on the road, sending up a huge cloud of red dust.

Maddie rolled onto her back in the dirt and propped herself up on her elbows, gasping. The steer came over and sniffed her head.

"Thanks a lot," she said to it. "Good thing I bought the rental insurance."

The steer let out a loud bawl.

Maddie yanked her bag out of the rubble, threw it over her shoulder and started up the road. The steer followed along behind. After about 25 minutes, she arrived at what was once her aunt's driveway. She stopped and stared. The property was transformed. A lushly lined, gated drive led up to an enormous, luxurious resort. A fountain in front of it was not yet filled with water. On the surrounding cliffs, the skeletons of more buildings were sprouting.

Maddie put her hands on the gate and stared in stunned disbelief. The steer, which had ambled along with her, now grazed on the shrub near the fence. Ignoring the "No trespassing" sign, Maddie climbed up the gate and dropped down on the other side.

She looked around, confused, amazed. If she hadn't recognized the towering ponderosa tree, she might have thought she was in the wrong location. She stumbled through the unfinished garden pathways to the huge pine. She put her palms against its rough trunk and looked up into its awesome height. She felt completely disoriented and also angry. What had happened here?

Emerson had been watching from his trailer when Maddie and the steer had appeared at the gate. At first, it was the movement that caught his eye, and then he was surprised to see the agile young woman climb over the gate.

Courtney was making her way through a bowl of frosted wheat cereal. The coffee maker was slowly gurgling out a pot of coffee.

"Stay here, kiddo," Emerson said.

"Where are you going?"

"Just out to the garden. I'll be right back."

"I want to come!"

Courtney had become increasingly afraid of being alone in the months they had been there. Emerson didn't blame her. This was sometimes a scary place.

"No. There's someone out there. I need to see who it is."

"Be careful, Daddy!"

Emerson slipped out into the garden, heading toward the ponderosa. He decided to stay somewhat concealed, at least until he could get a better look at the unusual intruder. He caught glimpses of her through the newly planted hedges. She looked fit and tanned, with long, golden-blond hair. She was wearing shorts and light hiking boots. As he got close, he lost sight of her. He peeked out from the shrubs toward the ponderosa. She was nowhere to be seen.

If he had looked to his right, he would have seen two golden green eyes peering intently at him from the long, decorative grass.

"Why are you trying to sneak up on me?" said a soft voice.

He jumped and spun that way. "I'm not! I wasn't. I just wanted to, to see what you were doing."

She was standing, her hand resting on a hunting knife sheathed at her hip.

"Who are you?" she said.

"I'm the site manager," he said, remembering that she was the one who wasn't supposed to be there, not him. "Who are you? Can't you read? You're trespassing. And you can leave that knife where it is."

She gave him an appraising look.

"I guess you're right," she said.

He thought he had been insulted, somehow. He looked her up and down in return. Her tan legs were lean and strong, her shoulders finely muscled. She seemed to have no extra fat and was even a little too thin, with a striking, angular face with high cheekbones, freckles flecking her nose. Finally, he noticed her hard expression.

"So, what are you doing here?" he said.

"That's a good question." She moved back out in the clearing, looked up at the ponderosa, then searched the garden, her gaze landing on the resort building. "I didn't think I would be trespassing coming here. But, if it weren't for that ponderosa, I would think I was in the wrong place."

Emerson watched her with admiration. She was so comfortable in her lovely body that he felt awkward and clumsy by comparison. But when her words sunk in, he started to have a suspicion as to who she was. Was this the potential trouble his father had mentioned?

"Yup, it's my family's property. Has been since the Civil War," she said, almost to herself. Then she looked back at Emerson. "I'm not sure what's happened since I left. Something sure did. I'm looking for my aunt."

Emerson felt a sweat break out on his forehead. All the rumors he had heard about this land came back to him, about the strange death of Clara Stanton and the missing lawyer. His father was strict about visitors staying off the site, and he would especially want this one gone. He would want Emerson to call security and have her escorted off the grounds.

"I, uh, I'd like to talk to you," Emerson said, feeling his face blaze red, realizing then that he didn't even know what he wanted to talk about. "Would you like to come into my trailer for a cup of coffee or, uh, chocolate milk?"

She looked skeptically at him, then cast an appraising look at the trailer. It was partly hidden by the lush landscaping. He realized that, from her perspective, it could definitely look like a serial killer's hideout.

"My daughter's in there, and I promised I wouldn't leave her for long. She's seven. Otherwise, we could stay out here. I can go get her, but I do have coffee in there, if you want a cup."

"Oh."

165

He saw her anxiety start to diminish, and he smiled at her, trying to look non-threatening. She gave him a small smile, and he saw, for the first time, that she looked exhausted. He really didn't want her to think he was creepy.

"I'm Emerson Crandall," he said, offering his hand.

She shook it, a good handshake. "Maddie. I guess I could use a cup of coffee. Lead the way."

As he approached the trailer, he saw Courtney's little face watching from the window. He opened the flimsy aluminum door and led Maddie through the office to the kitchen.

"Courtney, this is Maddie Stanton."

"Hi," Courtney said, looking at Maddie with unabashed curiosity.

"Here, have a seat. The coffee's almost done." The trailer suddenly looked very small.

"You can sit here," Courtney said to her. "I'm done." She got up and carried her bowl to the sink, then plopped down on one of the living room chairs.

Maddie looked around at the little home with interest. "What is this? Why are you living here?"

"I, uh, I'm the construction supervisor here," he said. "For this project." He nodded toward the window.

She raised her eyebrow skeptically.

"It's true," he said, feeling silly. He sat down at the table and sighed. An image of his lab back in Syracuse flickered through his mind, then whisked away.

"My daddy runs the hotel construction project," Courtney said.

"That's what they tell me." He smiled, then looked at Maddie to see if she was at all impressed. She just looked like she was waiting for the punchline.

"You don't really look like a construction supervisor," Maddie said.

"What do I look like, an entomologist?" He smiled, wondering how she would respond to this odd question.

She raised her eyebrows in surprise. "Now that you mention it, yes. I've worked with plenty of entomologists, and you look like one."

"Well, actually, I am an entomologist."

"That's a person who studies insects," Courtney offered, spinning her chair around and around.

The coffee maker gurgled and clicked.

"What's an entomologist doing running a construction site?" Maddic said distractedly, now looking out the window at the hotel.

"My research got canceled at the same time my father started this project, so I came to work for him." He tried to muster enthusiasm, failed, sounding both miserable and phony. "This is his project."

She turned her attention back, giving him a hard look. "Your father?"

The coffee maker belched loudly and then was silent, and he got up and poured two cups of coffee. He placed one in front of her and sat back down.

"Yeah. He bought this place, from your aunt, I think it was." It came out with a bit of a stammer.

"So, that's how you knew my family name." She sipped her black coffee, looking down into the cup. After a moment, she looked back up, still wearing an unfriendly expression. "What do you know about this sale?"

"Not much." It came out too quickly, and she noticed.

"Not much? What then?"

She looked and sounded angry. He shook his head slightly, watching her with apprehension.

"Well, Mr. Crandall. Crandall, yes?"

He nodded.

"Well, Mr. Crandall. I don't know where my aunt is." She was seething now, choosing every word carefully, speaking slowly. "Last I knew, she lived right here. Right on this very spot, in fact, in her ranch house. It was right here. And she loved this land. And she told me many times, over many years, that she would never sell it. So I'd like to know about this sale. But mainly, I want to find my aunt. Do you happen to know just where in hell she is?"

He stared at her, non-plussed. He had no idea how to answer. He could tell his wide-eyed expression looked guilty and probably stupid from her viewpoint.

She drained her coffee and smacked the mug down sharply on the tabletop.

"Woah! Didn't that burn?" he said in alarm.

"Well?"

"Isn't that the lady who died?" Courtney said.

Uh-oh, he thought, watching Maddie with apprehension.

"What?" She looked at Courtney, then Emerson.

"Hush, Courtney," he said, still watching Maddie, then, quietly, "I thought you would have known. I'm so sorry."

Her eyes narrowed. "I don't believe you."

"That's m-my understanding, that she p-passed away a while back," he said. He pressed his lips together, not trusting himself to say anything else.

Through her furious glare, he noticed tears welling up in her eyes. She wiped them impatiently, fighting them back.

"Listen, I really don't think I'm the one who should be telling you this, and I'm really sorry to shock you, and that you learned it this way. I, we, we just didn't know."

"I agree," she snapped. If she didn't like him before, he could tell she really didn't like him now. "To be honest, I suspected something like this." Tears rolled down her cheeks, and she ignored them. "But I need to find out everything. It's completely wrong to me. Because I don't think my aunt would have sold this land to anyone for any price, and ...." She stopped suddenly. Then she said, "I don't want to talk to you about this. You're the last person I'll be talking to about it, you and your father."

He handed out a napkin. She looked like she wanted to spit on it for a moment, then wiped her cheeks on her the shoulders of her shirt and started toward the door. Emerson watched, mutely, as she yanked it open. A loud clap of thunder suddenly shook the trailer, making everyone duck for a moment.

Maddie recovered quickly. "I'll find out what happened. If I do talk to you again, don't be surprised if it's in front of a judge."

There was a flash and another thunder clap, and she went out, slamming the door. The latch didn't catch, and the door swung open, just as the rain started.

"Why is she mad at us, Daddy?"

"She's just upset, kiddo. Stay here."

He hurried out after Maddie. It was as dark as dusk, now, and the rain was heavy, making it hard to see.

"Miss Stanton? Maddie! Wait!" He ran toward the front entrance. In a flash of lightning, he saw her dropping down off the gate, onto the other side.

"Maddie! Wait! I'll give you a ride!"

She didn't stop. The thunder pounded.

"It's too dangerous!"

"Daddy? Daddy?"

He turned back. Courtney had come along the path after him, and they both were already soaked in the deluge.

"Come on."

He scooped up Courtney and ran to his car, plopping her in the back seat. He drove down the drive, opened the electronic gate with a remote control, and started down the road. It was so dark he could barely make out where the shoulder was, since it had not yet been paved or painted. His and Courtney's wet bodies caused the windshield to fog up and he turn on the defrost, full blast.

In a flash of lightning, he saw her up ahead. He drove up alongside her and pushed a button to open the passenger window.

"Miss Stanton, please get in! It's too dangerous out here."

She ignored him and broke into a jog. She was drenched, her T-shirt clinging to her lithe body.

"What's the matter with her, Daddy?"

He drove next to Maddie. "Please! Get in. I'll drive you wherever you want to go!" He had to shout to be heard over the pounding rain.

In the next flash of lightning, he could see a steer in the road up ahead. As he watched, the lightning streaked and hit the animal directly. The beast was suddenly bright with blazing light. He could feel an electric charge and the hair on his arms and neck stood straight up and his scalp tingled. He, Maddie and Courtney all screamed at once. Then the animal toppled over, smoking, in the road.

The next thing he knew, Maddie was in the passenger seat, dripping wet and gasping.

He hit the accelerator, swerved around the steer and headed out to the main road as fast as he dared drive.

Courtney cried in the back seat, grief stricken for the animal. Emerson reached back with one arm and gave her leg a gentle squeeze.

"It'll be alright, kiddo," he said, feeling around until he found an old blanket he had stashed behind the driver's seat. He yanked it over the seat and dropped it on Maddie. She tucked it around herself without thanks and stared dully ahead through the windshield.

Not long after reaching the main road, they saw the wrecked car and sign. Emerson paused by it, peering through the rain to see if anyone might be in the car. Then a thought occurred to him.

"Yours?" he said.

Maddie nodded, not looking at it or him.

He drove on toward town. For a while, the only sound was the rain on the car, the fading rumbles of thunder, and Courtney sniffling in the back seat.

After a while, Courtney said, "Is that cow dead?"

"Yes,"

"How do you know?"

He was concentrating on the dark drive, aware that he needed to be extra careful with these two important people's safety in his hands, and conscious of the beautiful woman next to him, soaking wet under the blanket. He could smell her sweet, earthy scent.

"How do you know, Daddy?"

"It couldn't have survived being struck by lightning like that." He felt sorry for the cow. Nonetheless, he imagined making a joke about smoked beef for dinner, but forced himself to match the prevailing, serious mood in the car.

"But are you sure? Can we go back and check? Maybe it's still alive. Maybe it needs our help."

"We'll check when we go home."

"Where are we going?"

That was a good question. Emerson glanced at Maddie, who was still looking straight ahead, strands of her long hair plastered against her cheek and neck.

"Are you staying in town?"

"Just drop me off in downtown. I'm going to see the lawyer," she added, with a bit of a snarl in her tone.

If she meant her aunt's lawyer, well, he wasn't about to surprise her with any more bad news. Houses started appearing sparsely as they neared town, then some small businesses. He turned down the main street.

"Tell me when," he said.

In the middle of the block, she said, "Here."

171

He didn't see a parking spot, so he just stopped in the street. She shoved off the blanket, yanked up her bag and got out. She looked at him with contempt for a moment through the open door, small in her wet clothes.

"Thanks." She slammed the door and headed toward the sidewalk.

Now that her back was turned, he unabashedly watched her lovely body move gracefully away. He sighed and drove on, looking for a place to turn the car around.

"Where is she going, daddy?"

"I don't know. Are you warm enough back there, kiddo?"

"Yes."

"OK, let's go home."

Chapter 27

Maddie found that Toby's office was locked and dark. The insurance agent downstairs directed Maddie to Hector Longtree, and Maddie called Longtree's office, making an appointment for a little later that day. She used the wait time to grab breakfast and, using her phone, search the Internet for information about her aunt's death and the Crandall resort. She found her aunt's obituary and plenty of news about the Crandall. The Crandall also had its own web page, so she was able to get a good understanding of the scale of the project going up on her aunt's land. She also spotted coverage of Toby's disappearance.

Hector Longtree had a broad, square face with deep creases on either side of his mouth. About forty and slightly chubby, he wore glasses, a white shirt, blue-striped tie, and a friendly smile.

"Please make yourself comfortable," he said, shaking Maddie's hand and beckoning to a seat. "Would you like a coffee?"

"No, thanks."

"You're Clara Stanton's niece, right? Cunningham?" When she murmured "yes," he said, "I was hoping I would get to meet you. I'm guessing you have some questions?"

"I was in Patagonia. I didn't have any way to reach her," Maddie blurted. It came out sounding as an excuse. "I didn't know. I'm just getting caught up, and it seems very strange, her death, Mr. Landy's disappearance, the Crandall going up out there. I mean, Jesus."

"I know. It was a weird set of circumstances."

"Were you the one who handled the sale, after, I mean?"

"Yes."

"Well, what the heck? Was everything OK? What did the police say? Was there an autopsy?"

Hector look at her a moment, eyebrows up. Then he said, "Let me get everything. I think, all those questions you have, I had too. We can look at it and talk."

He went through a door behind his desk, then reappeared after a minute with three fat file folders. "Here. We'll work here." He plopped them down at a round table near the window, and opened a file. "We'll start with her will."

When she left Longtree's office, Maddie knew that Clara's death had, at first, been treated as natural, but once Longtree alerted police that Toby Landy had vanished and the land had been sold, all in rapid succession, an autopsy was performed. Longtree had requested a delay on finalizing the land sale and probate of Clara's will until the autopsy was done, and until the police had determined that Toby would not be found easily, if at all. During his review, Longtree had determined that the sale looked legal, and that the price Crandall was paying for the land far exceeded its value, based on appraisals and sales of similar properties in the area. After the autopsy showed that Clara's death was likely cause by freezing – and she wasn't the only one who died in that storm — Longtree closed the sale. Just over five million dollars was deposited in Clara's account.

"Even after income and inheritance taxes, you're a millionaire," he told Maddie.

"Except," Maddie had said, a mix of sorrow and anger building in her, making her tone harsh, "she never would have sold the land. She told me that, many times. She never would have."

Hector looked at her for a few seconds, considering the options. "Probate can be reopened," he said. "Do you have anything in writing from her? We would need some proof, something definite that would make a judge take notice."

Maddie thought about it. "She might have mentioned it in a letter, something like that?"

"It would have to be recent, and it would have to be written in a way that would not allow for consideration of the fact that, well," he looked at her cautiously. "Did you know that she was almost destitute when she passed?"

"What?" Maddie was shocked.

"It's true," Hector said gently. "She hadn't paid her bills for months. I think she was in trouble and she knew it. She might have finally decided to sell, to help herself. I do know Toby had been encouraging her to do it, that he thought it was an excellent deal for her. She must have finally decided it was the best thing to do."

Maddie felt tears burning her eyes. She stood abruptly, not wanting him to see her cry.

"I appreciate your time, and the work you did." She hurried out of the office.

"Maddie?" He called after her in alarm. "You don't have to go!"

She hurried passed his assistant, out to the street, walking, then jogging. Her aunt had been destitute and she didn't know it. She turned down a side street, not noticing where she was going, flooded with guilt and sorrow. She could have helped her aunt. She could have come as soon as she had that terrible feeling, that worry that had started that day when she was tagging that cat. Why had she stayed there instead of coming here? How could she have put that project above her Aunt, who would have done anything for her, who practically raised her? Now Clara was dead — frozen to death. And she might have been able to prevent it.

She stepped into the delivery doorway of a small apartment house, then sunk down against it, sobbing.

Chapter 28

When Emerson walked through the lobby later that day, he saw it was filled with an assortment of waiting men and women, looking uncomfortable in slacks, skirts, jackets. He could tell this was the first group of local interviewees, all hoping to get a job at the big new resort in town. They turned toward him hopefully, then looked away when they realized he wasn't there for them.

Then he saw his aunt appear in a doorway to the left, walking with a man who looked vaguely familiar. Emerson tried to duck out, but she spotted him and called his name loudly, gaining the attention of everyone in the lobby.

"Emerson!"

He felt his face grow red and tried to just wave and keep walking.

"Oh no, you don't," she said, coming up next to him and grabbing his elbow. "Emerson! Give aunty a kiss."

To his horror, she reached up and grabbed him by the head, pressing her dry, red lips against his. She tasted of coffee, cigarettes, bourbon.

"Cut it out." Emerson jerked back, wiping his mouth.

"Now, now. Do you remember your little cousin, Raffie?"

He looked more closely at the man following Irma. He was short, pasty and pudgy with a pencil mustache and a goatee that tried, unsuccessfully, to hide his complete absence of a chin. He had the same deep blue eyes and dark hair of the Crandalls, but lacked the lanky angularity characteristic of Crandall and Emerson. And Courtney.

Emerson experienced a couple of quick, unpleasant memories of Raffie as a little boy, the pale, whiny cousin with the heart problem. He remembered Raffie crying, Raffie being fairly inept at any of their normal activities, always running to Irma and whining, and Irma alternatingly telling them either to include Raffie or to not allow him to get overexcited because of his heart. That was just an impossible balance for young boys to achieve. Then there was that time Emerson had stopped Raffie from attempting to cut off the neighbor's dog's tail with a pair of pinking shears.

"Oh, yeah. Sure," Emerson said as he shook Raffie's soft, moist hand. He had to stop himself from wiping his hand on his pants. Raffie mustered a snarly little smile.

"Raffie is now the Crandall's head chef," Irma said. "Did you know he was a chef, Emerson?"

"No." Emerson suppressed images of dog parts being served under glass. "Well, that's great. Welcome."

He wondered if he would ever be able to enjoy a meal at the resort now.

"Off you go, Raffie, to your new empire."

Irma turned him in the direction of the kitchen and sent him off with a little shove.

"And you, you great handsome boy!" she said to Emerson, leaning close to his face. "You must come to my office so we can catch up."

"Oh, sorry, I have to go see my father. I'm ...."

"No, no. I think you have been avoiding me. You can spare a few minutes for your dear aunty."

She rested her arm around his waist as she guided him toward the office she was apparently using to conduct interviews. As they walked, her hand dropped and squeezed his backside briefly, then went back to his waist. He clasped her arm, removed it from his waist and stopped walking, glaring at her.

"What?" she said, all innocence. Then she smiled and tried to take his arm. He pulled it away and stood up straight, frowning down at her, a foot taller than she. He could squish her into the rug like a roach.

"Oh don't be such an old grouch. I'm just happy to see you. Come in here."

She shut the door.

"So how are you Emerson? Rex's not working you too hard, is he?"

She stood too close.

"No. It's going great. Just great."

"Wonderful. You have so much potential." She placed her hand on his chest and he removed it. She barked out a laugh. "And you don't miss playing in the dirt with all those little creepy crawlies, do you?"

"No," he lied.

"Of course not. Leave the little boy jobs for the little boys." She pressed on his chest again. "Oooh, and the muscles of a real man, too!"

He grabbed her hand and stepped backward. "You really need to keep your hands off me."

He imagined snapping her fingers like dry sticks. She chuckled and didn't attempt to pull her hand away. He dropped it.

"Not afraid to fight back anymore?" she said huskily. "Well, I like it rough."

She leaned toward him with her tongue out, as though she were going to lick his face. He stepped away, disgusted. She had done this kind of thing to him since he was a teenager. He really wanted to hold her by her neck against the wall. It would be so easy, one hand on her throat, one over her big mouth. But then he thought of Courtney. He couldn't let anything keep him from being able to take care of her, and strangling his father's only sister might possibly cost him his job. Still, he took a moment to imagine her dangling there, her feet dancing, her eyes popping out like a cartoon character's. He smiled. Irma, apparently expecting more anger from him, looked a little disappointed.

"Well, it was super good to see you," he said, keeping the smile and making his voice sugary sweet. "I'd love to stay and catch up on all the fantastic, illegal things I'm sure you've been doing for the last fifteen years, but, gotta go."

"Oh, what a big, important business man you are." She said this as though she were talking to a baby. She put a cigarette between her lips and moved a lighter toward it.

"Yeah, well, see you later," he said. But then he paused, reached out one long arm and plucked the cigarette from her papery lips. Holding the cigarette up where she could see it, he crushed it in his hand, then let it fall on the carpet.

"This is a smoke-free facility." He smiled.

He heard her laughing derisively as he shut the door behind him, gratefully closing out the sound and sight of her. He dashed up the stairs to the next level, where most of the offices, conference rooms and the lavish ballroom were situated, richly decorated in red, cocoa brown and gold.

He knocked on his father's door and realized his father was already talking.

"Come," his father called.

Emerson walked in.

"No, damn it. I'm telling you no. We required the contractor to carry worker's compensation insurance. Did he have it? Did he?"

This was very familiar to Emerson. His father was rolling over the top of someone. He looked out the window at the beautiful gardens, growing in lushly, ringing the ponderosa tree that he had, so unaccountably, fought to save. Emerson shook his head slightly at the memory. Weird.

"And we have a copy of the certificate? Well, good. That's enough. We did our part. Let the insurance company do what it has to do."

There was a pause, while the person on the other end of the line said something. Crandall interrupted.

"Look, I'm sorry for her, I really am, but this happens every day, all over the world. I can't take care of everyone. That's what the insurance was for. That's why we required them to have it, and we did what we are required to do. She will get the benefits, and it will be plenty. Now, if you don't mind, I have got to get back to doing my job, which is making sure this place is making money by Thanksgiving."

Emerson noticed a large web outside the window, strung between the glass, a tree limb and one of the cement lion heads that lined the ledge. To his delight, he spotted the spider, which was nestled next to the window. He reached in his pocket and pulled out a small magnifying glass and peered at the creature. It was a beautiful, female, banded *argiope*.

"Look, you have been doing this stuff for a long time. Don't bring this kind of chicken shit to me anymore. You know what to do. Now, what is the status of the airstrip? No! Not that! I know that already! Arh!"

Emerson looked around briefly, in time to see Crandall throw the cell phone on the carpet, then looked quickly back at the spider, eyebrows raised. He heard his father retrieve the phone.

"Look, I have to go. I'm up to my elbows here. I'll stop out later." Crandall clicked off the phone.

"What an imbecile!" Crandall stomped over next to Emerson. "What are you looking at?"

"An orb spider."

"Well, cut it out." Crandall bent down and scowled closely at the spider. It seemed to Emerson that it tucked in its legs a little.

"Get your mind off the damned bugs. If you were farther along, I wouldn't have to be talking to these idiots. It's time for you to come inside and start running things in here for me. I have got to start focusing on the biggest ticket items we have going, and right now that's the airstrip and the casino. I need you to move in here and start making sure this place is running right."

His father was highly agitated. The smart thing for Emerson to do would be to keep quiet and ride it out. Crandall was pacing. He stopped and looked out the window for a moment.

"Hmmh," he said with a derisive snort. "Emerson's tree."

He turned sharply to Emerson and looked him up and down. Emerson braced himself.

"Look at you. You look like a college student who just rolled out of bed. Tuck in your shirt. What's the matter with you? Don't you know who you are? Well, you need to carry yourself that way, like you run this place. If you would get your head out of your ass and you mind off the goddamned orb spiders."

Emerson tucked in his shirt. These displays of fury still frightened him, almost as much as they did when he was a kid. He forced his mind elsewhere, trying to find some humor in it.

"Actually, I specialize in *geometridae*, not *araneidae*," he said quietly.

His father glared at him as he picked up his cell phone and pressed a couple of numbers.

"OK, not funny," Emerson said.

"Yes, it's me. Get up here right now. I need you to measure Emerson for some clothes. Yes, of course a suit." He clicked off the phone.

"You have your tailor on speed dial?" Emerson said.

"Once he's done, I want you to go get a haircut. You come out of there looking like a page out of a men's fashion magazine. It's time you started looking the part."

Emerson ran his hand through his dark hair. It had gotten a little shaggy.

"I want you to start working with me directly a couple hours every day."

"What about finishing the construction?"

"Yes. Finish that. It's almost done, though, so this is a good transition point. I'll get O'Mara to take care of it at the condos.

You're too valuable to be doing that now, and those condos might be a bear, up on the cliffs like that. Better leave that to him. You don't want a headache."

Emerson's head was actually already aching a little. His father had calmed down though.

"Now, what was it that brought you up here?"

"Oh. I ...." He looked at his father appraisingly. This did not seem like a good time to bring this up.

"Yes? What? Wait, hold on a minute." His father called another number.

"Hi," he said. "Listen, we may get some media attention. No, not the good kind. One of our contractors had a worker clipped by a truck that was backing up. No, he didn't make it. I need you to write a release, just in case, and give me a couple statements, too. Make it look like I have a heart." His father smiled slightly. "Yes, I know it's difficult, but I know you can do it. OK, thanks."

He clicked off the phone and sighed.

"That's terrible," Emerson said.

"Yes. So what was it you wanted?"

Here we go, he thought. "You know that girl you mentioned, Clara Stanton's niece?"

He suddenly had his father's full attention.

"What about her?" he said.

"She was here this morning."

"What?" Crandall looked angry again.

"She came into the garden. I stopped her and, uh, got her out of here."

"What was she doing here? What did she say?"

"She was confused, to see all this. She was expecting the family farm."

"What did you do?"

"I got her off the place, like I said."

He didn't think his father would like to hear that he had given her coffee and driven her to town.

"Well, if you see her again, you call security. That girl has no reason to be here. Her aunt sold me this land and that's the end of the story. If she keeps bothering us, I'll have her thrown in jail."

"She seemed to think, well ...." Emerson swallowed hard and tried again. "She didn't know that her aunt was dead. She also said she didn't believe her aunt would have sold the land."

That was it. His father exploded.

"So what? People die all the time. What is she trying to do? Make a case of it? Is she? Is she?" His face was so close that Emerson could feel his breath.

"I don't know," he said, backing away. "She thinks it's all suspicious, though."

"Damn it!"

"Dad, was there anything about that deal I should know? What happened?"

His father swung around so fast that Emerson ducked back. Crandall swiped all documents off the desk, together with his pen holder, desk phone and computer monitor. It all hit the floor with a crash and he faced Emerson furiously. Emerson felt his heart starting to speed up. His father's tantrums used to bring on anxiety attacks, and he was afraid one was starting, now. He knew he should stop talking, but he couldn't.

"Why are so many people talking about this place like something really bad happened?"

"Why? Why? Because they're fools who have nothing better to talk about. And she's a fool who wants someone to blame!" His father glared at him. Nope, I'm not backing down this time, Dad, Emerson thought. He stood up straight and looked steadily into his father's furious eyes.

Surprise flickered across Crandall's face, then he almost smiled. He stepped closer to his son, put one hand on his shoulder and said quietly, "You need to know. There are people like that all over this world, Emerson, people who want to drag us down, and you and I just need to clear them out of the way so they don't pull us into their hell."

"What are you telling me?"

There was a knock at the door.

"'Clear them out of the way?'" Emerson said.

His father leaned closer and grasped the back of Emerson's head, pressing his cheek roughly near his ear and saying quietly, "If you want the answer, ask the real question."

Another knock. His father let go of Emerson and stood back.

"Come!" he called, still looking at Emerson.

The tailor came in, nodded to Emerson, glanced at the mess on the floor next to the desk and looked inquiringly at Crandall.

"Well, there he is, get to work," snapped Crandall. "This is Milton Kramer. He's the best. He's setting up a tailor shop down on retail. My son, Emerson."

"Pleased to meet you," the tailor said as he opened his case, took out a handheld electronic device of some sort, punched a few keys, stepped over the broken monitor and approached Emerson with a measuring tape.

"Arms at your side," he said, and started measuring. Emerson kept his eyes on Crandall.

"Starting tomorrow morning, be here at 8, no 8:30," Crandall said to Emerson. "Plan on spending the mornings here. You can finish up the other work during the afternoons. I'll have the office ready for you next to mine."

Crandall strode toward the door, stopped to look at himself in the wall mirror, smoothed his hair, straightened his tie, and looked at Emerson's reflection, holding their eye contact for a couple seconds. Then he stepped into the hallway, shutting the door with a sharp snap.

Emerson stood mutely, repositioning himself slightly when requested by the tailor. He still looked at the door. His father's wild tantrums used to work on Emerson, completely ending all conversation as Emerson crumpled into self-protection mode. But not this time. This time he had held on, barely, and he thought he had noticed his father's surprised respect. But what happened next had unnerved him again. Emerson didn't know if he was brave enough to ask the real question.

Crandall headed toward his sister's office, anxiety mingling with his anger. He didn't think Emerson had the nerve to ask him directly if he had killed Clara Stanton and Toby Landy. But what if he did answer Crandall's challenge and ask? Part of Crandall longed to tell him the truth, to show his son that he meant what he said about clearing away people who got in his way. But what would Emerson do? Would he go soft and try to go immediately to the police? Or, could Crandall count on his loyalty, and then, joined with a renewed determination by this shared secret, could they then continue on as an unstoppable force together, bound for greatness, wealth and fame?

Crandall preferred to be prepared, so he would have to decide what his answer would be.

Chapter 29

"Right this way," Irma said to the next applicant as she held the office door for the girl and followed her in, admiring her shapely, youthful bottom and legs.

"Have a seat."

Irma indicated a chair and sat at the desk across from it. She quickly read the application, then looked back up at Angelica. She said nothing for a moment, but smiled at the girl. The girl smiled back, a big, nervous, white-toothed smile, outlined in deep purplish red lipstick.

"Lovely," Irma said. "You have a lovely smile."

"Thank you."

"A smile like that would look very nice at our front desk, or in our restaurant."

"I would like that, ma'am."

"But, unfortunately, you don't appear to have any experience as a hotel clerk or a waitress."

"No ma'am. But I am a very good employee and I would learn very quickly."

"What do you do that makes you a good employee?" Irma's eyes trailed to Angelica's blouse, then slowly back up to her face.

"Well, I'm on time, even early. And I don't take time off. I don't get sick. I want to make a good living for myself and my son, so I am very serious about getting a job here."

"Do you think you could make a good living on a housekeeper's salary?"

"A housekeeper?"

"Yes, of course."

"Well, I was really hoping to work at the front desk, or maybe as a waitress, like you said."

"Yes, well, as I also said, you don't have any experience doing those jobs, so I wouldn't be able to start you there. I would have to start you as a housekeeper, and see how you do. If you do a good job, and don't miss time, and come early, as you said, and if you show the right kind of behaviors, are willing to, uh, learn new skills." Irma looked the girl up and down again, making sure Angelica noticed the look. "Then you might be eligible for a promotion."

Angelica's brown eyes were guarded.

"I am very good to employees who are good at their jobs, and do what I ask them to do. If you do a good job in housekeeping, who knows where you could go from there? What do you say?"

Struggling to hide her disappointment, Angelica said, "Well, OK then. Yes, I'll do it."

Irma stood and reached both hands out to the girl. Angelica took them, hesitantly.

"Congratulations." Irma pulled Angelica closer.

"You have a great future here," Irma said. "All you have to do is start at the bottom and work your way up."

She turned Angelica around, resting an arm across her shoulders, and guided her to the door.

"Just take a left down the hall and tell Jeremy that you're our newest housekeeper. Give him this. He will give you your work schedule."

"Alright. Thank you."

She headed off down the hall, wobbling on her high heels.

"Luscious," Irma murmured.

She went back out into the lobby to look for the next candidate. There weren't too many left this late in the day. She noticed a young man sitting quietly in a wooden chair near what soon would be the grill room. He was wearing clean blue jeans, a neat, button-down shirt, a tan cowboy hat and boots. He glanced up and they made eye contact for a moment. She felt a tingle.

"Yee-haw!" she said to herself. "Who are you, cowboy?"

She was riveted by his strong and handsome face, his quiet manner. She was about to beckon him in for the interview when she heard her name being called. Jeremy, twenty-three, thin, bespectacled, a new grad with a hospitality management degree, hurried toward her.

"Sorry, but I'm not sure which person you hired for what job," he said, looking nervous. "I'm mixed up among these last few women."

She took the applications from him, irritated, and put the papers in order. "The top two are maids. The third one is a waitress and the last one is in the laundry."

"OK. That's what I thought. Thanks." He hurried back toward his office.

Irma turned back to summon the cowboy. He was no longer sitting in the chair. She looked around the lobby but did not see him. She walked into the entrance of the restaurant, but it was empty except for a man who was bringing in the centerpieces.

Disappointed, she went back out in the lobby, tapped another young man on the shoulder and asked him to follow her.

"The rest of you," she called to the other applicants who were looking at her hopefully. "This will be my last interview for today. I will finish interviewing for the open positions tomorrow morning, starting at 8 sharp."

Chapter 30

Raffie was stirring a bubbling sauce, watching it closely, picking up the spoon and letting the smooth brown substance dribble thickly back into the pot. It was critically close to being perfect, and in danger of going too far. He smelled it and stirred, waiting for the right moment to remove it from the heat.

Suddenly something hit him from behind. He was thrust forward and the spoon flew out of his hands. He spun around to find one of the new dishwashers cowering back, a large box of dish detergent in his hands.

"I'm s-s-sorry!" the young man said, sheer terror on his face. "I slipped and thought I was going to drop the box."

In that second, a hiss told Raffie that his sauce had just boiled over. He turned back to the stove. The brown fluid was frothing over the edge of the pan.

"You idiot!" He picked up the pot and shook it at the man. "It's ruined!"

"I'm sorry!"

Raffie threw the pot on the floor. Sauce sprayed up in a hot, brown fountain. The dishwasher covered his face and cried out.

"Clean it up!" Raffie stormed out of the crowded kitchen and to his office. All the kitchen employees froze as he went past.

His mother would hear about this one. She was the one who hired the incompetent boy.

"Imbecile!" he shouted at the door, knowing everyone in the kitchen could hear him.

He picked up the desk phone and threw it against the door. It broke into pieces with a satisfying clatter. He picked up a book and threw that at the door. To his shock, the book stopped in mid-air. It hovered there for a moment, then abruptly flew back at him. He was too shocked to duck, and it hit him right in the head. He was horrified. He then noticed another book on a shelf near the door was starting to quiver. He watched it, stricken, his heart starting a rapid, uneven flutter. The book lifted off the shelf and he screamed. The book hurled itself at him, as though thrown by an unseen stranger. It hit Raffie in the chest and he ran to the door, trying to open it. The knob wouldn't turn. He started shaking the door.

"Get me out of here! Help! Get me out of here!"

It felt as though someone was behind him in the office, but he was afraid to look. His heart was tightening and he pulled a nitro tablet out of his pocket, slipped it under his tongue and pounded on the door.

"Open this door! I'm trapped!"

He could feel the presence coming up behind him. He turned slowly around and saw the two books hovering in the air on either side of his head. He tried to duck, but it was too late. Both books clapped together against his head like cymbals. He screamed and dropped to the ground, clutching his head in pain. He felt the door start to move.

"Mr. Raffie? What's wrong? Are you against the door? I can't open it. You need to move."

Raffie flopped over on the floor, sobbing, allowing the door to open. The dishwasher was standing there, looking at Raffie with alarm. Raffie stood up, shoved the young man out of his way and ran out of the kitchen.

The dishwasher looked around the office curiously. Except for the broken phone and the two books lying on the floor, all seemed normal. He picked up the books and set them back on the shelf.

He wasn't sure he was going to like this job.

Raffie sobbed in his mother's office. He had just told her what happened. She was watching him with a perplexed look.

"Books don't fly around by themselves, darling," she said.

"These did," he yelled with the fury of a four-year-old in full tantrum.

"OK, fine. I think you were just upset that the baboon spilled your sauce. Your heart feels OK now?"

Raffie nodded.

"That's a good boy. Now, I hired your cousin Derrick to start working with you as a chef-in-training."

Raffie looked up in horror, his previous fears forgotten. "You what?"

"I hired Derrick to come help you, and you can teach him how to cook."

"Mother, I went to school for four years to learn to cook, then I apprenticed at some of the finest restaurants in Europe. If Derrick wants to be a chef, he should do the same thing."

"Well, he's kind of skipping the school and coming right to the apprentice part."

"Impossible."

"Well, give him something to do, and teach him to make a hard-boiled egg or a peanut butter sandwich now and then. He just got out of jail and he is having a hard time getting a job, the poor lamb."

"Terrific. What was he in jail for?"

"Something minor, robbery or burglary or something. Nothing to worry about. Nothing that could affect his work here."

"Oh, no, a robber won't find anything to steal in a resort that caters to the richest people in the world."

"He won't do anything like that, darling. We're family. He knows we're giving him a chance. He'll be a good worker for you, you watch."

"I can't wait."

"Now run along back to your kitchen. I'm busy."

Raffie went down the long, quiet hallway toward the kitchen. He felt as if someone was watching him, but when he looked around, there was no one there. He reached the kitchen and sighed, looking behind him again. Then he pushed the door open slowly and looked around. Everything looked normal. He stepped back in and started mixing a new batch of sauce. But he kept looking behind him and over his shoulder, and the sauce did not come out quite right. In the end, he thought it tasted a little like blood.

Chapter 31

Maddie had looked through everything. She had spoken to the local police from Stony Valley, and the state police for both Colorado and New Mexico. She met with the coroner. Then she went back to Longtree.

"Hey, Maddie," he said warmly. "How ya' doing?"

"Better, I guess. Just wondering, did you ever look for a back-up of Toby's files, just to see if, maybe, there was anything, just, I don't know, odd?"

"I did look," he said. "All I can say is that it's a good thing Toby kept good, old-fashioned paper records of everything because his hard drive was corrupt."

"Corrupt?"

"Yup. The computer wouldn't even start. We think it got zapped during that storm when the transformer was hit by lightning."

"No surge protector?"

"He had one, sure, but that was a pretty big zap. You have to realize how big a storm that was. It wasn't just snow. There was a huge thunder and lightning storm before the snow started. Plains City was hit by a tornado, eight miles north. The whole area lost power at one point or another during it, and half the town got zapped. It wrecked a lot of electronics. Anyway, I tried to have his system restored, but it was beyond hope."

"Didn't he use an online backup?"

"Nope. Most do, but not Toby."

Maddie stood up and paced.

"No external drive? No USB or disks?"

"Nothing I could locate."

"Argh." She made fists and brought them down on the windowsill. "It's so frustrating."

"Did you find anything from her, like we talked about?"

"No," Maddie said, sinking in a chair, miserable. "I sent for my box of old letters, but there was nothing in there that could help."

"That's too bad."

She stood up again. "I have to find something. The more I think about it, the more I'm sure that my aunt and Toby Landy were killed to get them out of the way of that damned Crandall."

"Pretty strong words," Longtree leaned back and looked out the window. "But you're not the first one to think that."

She looked out the window, too, in the direction of her aunt's land. "I don't know how, but I'm going to prove it."

After their meeting, she went across the street to get a cup of coffee. While she waited, a young man came in and ordered coffee and a muffin.

"Hey!" said another customer to him, a man about the same age, early twenties. "How's it going?"

They shook hands.

"Good! I just found out I got that job up at the Crandall."

Maddie now turned to watch and listen, not hiding her interest.

"Yeah? Hey, congrats! Bartending?"

"Yeah."

"Fantastic. That should be some pretty good dough-re-me. They're supposed to get some pretty fancy customers up there."

"How about you?"

"Still in the running. I'm supposed to hear by tomorrow."

"Good luck."

Maddie's coffee was ready. She held the warm paper cup with both hands, mulling what she heard. It sounded like some people were happy about the Crandall. In thinking about it, it must mean a lot of jobs in this area, first with the construction, then, all those positions in the hotel, the casino, the restaurants, all the other parts of it.

That gave her an idea.

Irma was tasked with hiring for the main hotel, but Crandall was still in charge of it in other parts of the resort, at least for the management level. That included the equestrian facilities. Since these were located some distance away from the main hotel, they were not on Clara's land, and he was able to start their construction earlier than some of the other features. Like the rest of the resort, the horse facilities would be world-class, with two indoor arenas and four outdoor, including a stadium jumping ring, as well as a cross-country course and polo grounds. Crandall didn't know anything about horses, but his advanced marketing had shown him that a significant percentage of the guests he wanted to attract would be drawn by this facility, and their presence would help set the tone for the resort's reputation, more than making up for the expense. He had to hire a well-respected equestrian professional to manage it, and that person was Karla Ostholt.

Born in Germany, practically raised on the back of a horse and short-listed for the Olympics early in her career, Karla eventually had moved to the States, running her own successful training barn for twenty years. She had just sold it and gone into semi-retirement when Crandall heard of her, and convinced her to join the Crandall. Of course, he left the hiring of stable hands to Karla.

That's when Karla hired Maddie.

Sure, Maddie needed a job, since she wasn't about to touch Aunt Clara's money until she knew the truth, and since her doctoral degree wasn't going to do a darn thing for her in Stony Valley. But more important, being at the Crandall would give her access to more of the information — whatever it was — that could help her expose this whole Crandall operation. When she realized the Crandall was hiring locals like crazy, she started watching its website for the right opening. Then the stable hand position popped up, and she immediately submitted her application. She had paid her way through college by working at a horse training facility, and she was a good barn worker and rider. Plus, working in the stable would get her up there, but probably keep her out of the direct line of vision of any of the Crandalls. She applied using her full name, Katherine Madeline Cunningham, and told Karla that she went by Kathy. She was pretty sure, should he see the name on an employee roster somewhere, neither Crandall nor Emerson would make the connection of Kathy Cunningham to Maddie Stanton. That local misconception that she bore the same last name as her aunt would come in handy now. She got the job, and it came with a bonus — an inexpensive apartment above the stable.

She just had to make sure that Emerson never actually saw her.

In addition to the top-quality competition facility, the resort would keep a few reliable horses to give guests lessons and trail rides, so the first horses coming in were simple, safe, beginners' mounts. They were a collection of older horses and ponies with good feet and good brains that had already packed kids around for many years. Maddie helped Karla pick them out and trailer them to the resort, and was now responsible for their daily upkeep and exercise.

She was certain that, if she saw Emerson, she would be fired, but the stables were far from the hotel, and had their own entrance. And he was probably busy, doing whatever it was a project manager-entomologist did, so she felt pretty certain that she could avoid him.

But one day, after just a couple weeks of work, she walked past the end of the arena with a wheelbarrow to get some stall bedding, and she was shocked to see the little girl, Courtney, on an appaloosa pony, getting a riding lesson from Karla. Maddie stopped short and searched the edge of the arena, spotting Emerson. He leaned against the rail, watching the lesson.

Maddie put her ball cap low over her eyes and hurried out of sight. She was certain that he had noticed her, but was counting on his thinking she was just some employee. There would be no reason for him to think for a second it was her. She abandoned her task of cleaning the stall and instead grabbed her favorite horse, Bop, quickly saddled and bridled him and hurried him out on a trail. That way, if Emerson had an inkling it was her, he would have no way of getting close enough to confirm it.

After about an hour, she headed back. Courtney and Emerson were gone. She found Karla in the barn office and asked her about the little girl.

Karla was going through a pile of invoices.

"She's Crandall's granddaughter. Her father wanted her to start lessons."

"You gave her one yourself? Lucky kid!"

"Yes. What the heck? I couldn't really refuse them, right? And I don't have a trainer yet."

Karla looked up at Maddie with an idea in her expression.

"Hey, can you give her lessons?"

"Uhhhh."

"She is a rank beginner, so it's just basic horsemanship, some walk-trot lessons, maybe a trail ride on Cocoa after she's had some practice."

"I'm not really experienced in giving lessons."

"Oh, it's not hard, especially since she is just starting out."

"Well, would it be OK if you keep working with her until she is a little more solid? Then maybe I can take over, after she is, you know, walking and trotting and cantering, and maybe taking a few jumps."

"Are you crazy? That will take a year of steady work, probably longer."

"OK, that sounds about right. Well, see you later." Maddie hurried out, pretending not to notice Karla's perplexed expression.

She actually would have enjoyed giving beginner lessons, but couldn't risk it. At least, not with Courtney Crandall.

Derrick stood watching the honey-haired woman as she rode in an outdoor arena. In her tank top, her slender body moving with the horse's gait, she was mesmerizing. His mind was skipping around to all the things he would like to do with her.

She stopped the horse and dismounted, adjusted her stirrups and the saddle girth, then led the horse through the gate. He was leaning against the door jamb of the barn, and he grinned at her as she approached.

"Hello," he said.

For a moment her eyes got big, as if she recognized him. She stopped walking, peering at him. Then her expression relaxed a bit, and she kept leading the horse into the barn. She didn't look friendly, but not hostile either.

"Hello," she said, walking past him. She slipped off the horse's bridle, replaced it with a halter and tied the horse in the aisle. Then she took off the saddle and started to brush the horse's back.

He sauntered over.

"Pretty horse."

"He's not too bad," she said. "Excuse me."

He moved out of her way slowly.

"You looked great riding him."

"Thanks."

"Do you ride here often?"

She looked at him over the horse's back. Any friendliness she had shown before was now gone.

"May I ask the reason for your visit?"

"Oh, sure. I'm starting work up at the hotel today. I just got here so I thought I would look around a little bit. It has a lot of pretty sights, but you're the prettiest one of all."

She sighed and scowled. "Well, hotel staff are not allowed in the stables, so you should probably head back up there."

"Real friendly. I'm Derrick. What's your name?"

She came around on his side of the horse. She was holding a riding crop.

"I am not very friendly, and you are bothering me. Now please leave the stables or I will call the hotel."

He had seen it a million times. Hotties like her thought they were too good, trying to boss him around. He smiled at her, a deliberately dirty smile.

"Alright. Just trying to be friendly, that's all."

She glared at him, her mouth set in a tight line.

"Oh, yeah, you're not friendly, right?"

"I'm busy."

"Alright. Well, maybe I'll catch you one of these days when you're not so busy and you can take me for a ride."

"Not likely."

He smiled that smile again and walked out of the stable.

Maddie watched him go, then went to the barn door to make sure he was gone. He was sauntering up a trail to the hotel, not even taking the road.

Maddie didn't like him one bit. He gave her a very uneasy feeling, and she had learned she needed to trust her uneasy feelings. First of all, she had thought from a distance that he was Emerson, which unraveled her for a moment. Even when she realized he wasn't, she still saw a resemblance, but it was all off. He should have been handsome with his dark hair, blue eyes and well-defined features, but there was something crude and harsh in his face. It was as though someone had taken Emerson and twisted him up, turning him ugly and angry. Still, she was fairly sure she had just had another encounter with a Crandall.

Derrick considered circling back to watch her from the woods, but he decided to go on to the hotel and start his shift. He snorted. Working for his cousin, Raffie. How had he fallen this far? But still, it could be good, working at this big playground for the rich and famous. Maybe he could meet someone, get into the real game. None of this little crap he had been pulling off. This crowd probably had tricks he never even thought of before. And he was just the man to help them.

A few hours later, Derrick was wearing a clean white uniform and washing the dishes of the rich and famous. When Raffie had told him he was going to be a busboy, Derrick almost punched him, but Raffie then explained it was the first step in becoming a chef, and he would start to teach him some basic food preparation on quiet days. Derrick wasn't sure he believed him, but the explanation satisfied him for now.

Raffie, the pudgy, soft boy that Derrick knew, ran the kitchen with a furious tyranny that actually impressed Derrick, and also amused him. Not that he would put up with being pushed around by his younger cousin, but Raffie did seem to have found his niche, and he was ruling it in the despotic manner typical of their clan. Say what you would about them, his family had a way of getting what they wanted.

Emerson had the results of his paternity test. He had finally had his and Courtney's DNA tested, not because his father demanded it, but because a lawyer had recommended it, for a good reason. Since the circumstances behind Courtney coming into

Emerson's life were so odd, there was a chance someone might show up, claiming to be her father, or someone in Courtney's mother's family might try to take her.

He brought the envelope containing the test results, unopened, to his father's office. His father was sitting across a table from a dapper, middle-aged man with a brushy mustache. They were looking at blue prints.

"Come in," his father said. "This is John Hundert. He designed the Seashell Royale Casino in Dubai, among others. He's our man. My son, Emerson. Join us. We're just finishing."

Emerson shook Hundert's hand, then sat with them at the table, not paying any attention as they finished their discussion. When Hundert left, Emerson's heart started pounding as he prepared for this conversation.

"What's up?" His father said, scrutinizing his face. "You're pale."

Emerson dropped the envelope on the table.

"What is it?"

"The DNA test."

Crandall's eyes lit up. "And?"

"I haven't opened it yet."

His father reached for it, but Emerson clamped his long hand over the envelope.

"How dramatic," his father said. He looked keenly at Emerson's expression again, and Emerson could tell that he knew what was coming. Crandall sat back and stared at him steadily, a small smile on his lips, eyes ablaze. "Well?"

"Did you murder Clara Stanton and Toby Landy?"

His father's expression didn't change. He looked at Emerson, the rage boiling in his eyes behind that little smile. It seemed to Emerson that his father was appraising him. Emerson looked back, not moving, his hand still on the envelope.

Ten seconds passed. Fifteen. Crandall's phone rang. Somewhere in the hotel, a man yelled and a woman laughed.

Then Crandall said, "No."

Now, it was Emerson who let the seconds tick by, looking steadily into his father's eyes. It was the answer he wanted, but he didn't feel relieved. Should he ask again, pressure his father for a different answer, or should he accept it, and go on, despite his suspicion? Finally, he took his hand off the envelope. His father reached for it, opened it and read. He looked up at Emerson, his hardened face betraying a rare sense of wonder.

"I'm a grandfather," he said.

Crandall looked at his son, but his eyes seemed distant. Then, quietly, he said, "I wish your mother were here to share this."

Emerson was shocked, so rarely did his father mention her. Their sorrow filled the space between them, connecting their hearts for one, brief moment. Then Emerson held out his hand and his father returned the lab results to him. Tucking the envelope in his breast pocket, Emerson stood, searched his father's eyes one more time, then left.

Crandall got up and walked to the window, looking down over the swimming pool filled with guests, laughing, splashing, yelling.

He had a feeling that Emerson would try again. Crandall sighed. He was fairly certain that, if he told the truth, Emerson would try to do something drastic.

That would be unfortunate.

Chapter 32

Irma walked down the dark hallway toward her office. The hotel was starting to hum. The restaurants were fully operating, and some of the first guests were coming in to try the food. Mostly locals so far. The more desirable clientele wouldn't start visiting until the facilities were complete and the grand opening was held. But a few of them were already coming in to check things out. For instance, a tech millionaire from Silicon Valley had stayed for a few days, and ended up putting a down payment on a condo. And an oilman from Alabama had checked the place out, promising to come back for skiing, when it was ready.

She was walking in a hall decorated in rust and brown, with sconces every few feet. It had a warm, muted feel. Irma admired the carefully chosen, narrow tables that were placed against the walls, bearing expensive-looking vases, bouquets and bronze-colored sculptures, depicting cowboys on bucking horses, Indians in full headdress, elk and grizzly bear. Then she noticed a movement at the end of the hall. She looked up, surprised. She didn't think there was anyone else in this part of the building. But, surely, that was the shape of a person in the shadows near the stairwell. Near-sighted, but too vain to wear glasses, she squinted to focus better. The form seemed to gradually take shape, and she realized it was the handsome cowboy she had seen a few weeks ago, while she was interviewing. She smiled and started walking toward him. He was watching her steadily, a small smile on his lips.

"Hello?" Irma called.

Just then a housekeeper stepped out of the employee lounge, right in front of Irma. She saw Irma and her face fell into frightened surprise.

"Miss Irma!" She was one of the young women hired last week, no more than 18, and delicious to Irma. Nonetheless, Irma was annoyed.

"What are you doing down here?" Irma snapped. "Get back to work."

"Yes, ma'am. Sorry. I was just taking my break."

Irma looked back at the doorway where the cowboy had been waiting. He was gone. Irma frowned. She reached the doorway and tried the knob. It was an ice room, and it was empty, except for the ice machine, humming away. She opened the door to the stairway and listened for the possibility of booted feet making their way up or down. Silence.

Irma sighed. This cowboy was attractive, but the mystery-man thing was getting a little old.

And why was she feeling a little afraid?

Emerson had worried, from the moment he had called his father from his Syracuse apartment, back in March, that he would hate working for his father, no matter what it paid. Now, with his own office on the second floor, surrounded by expensive things, making an obscene salary, eating well and able to provide Courtney with everything she needed, he sadly knew that he had been right. Even though he was trying to accept that his father had told him the truth, he hated the job. He was surrounded by his father's family, a group of people from whom he had, until recently, steadily distanced himself as soon as he was able to leave home. Other than being related, they had little in common, which is how he wanted it. The fact was, he was afraid of his father, and his aunt disgusted him. Raffie was just repulsive. And his father had just told him that his other cousin, Derrick, the son of Rexham's brother, was now working in the kitchen, and this was not good at all. Derrick was a felon, and he used to be very rough on Emerson when they were forced together as children.

Unfortunately, with Courtney at his side, he needed a good income. Working for his father provided not just an income, but more than he had ever imagined making, three times what he would have made if he'd found a job as a professor.

And hadn't Crandall immediately welcomed him and given him a fantastic chance at a job for which he wasn't qualified at all, and wasn't Crandall doing his best to teach Emerson how to rule this world in his own style, repugnant though Emerson found it? And, after the initial friction caused by questions about his paternity, now that his father knew she was a "real" Crandall, his father had started lavishing Courtney with gifts and acting like she was the most important thing on the planet, whenever he happened to see her.

Still, Emerson thought of all this as temporary, just until he could find something he liked more that would provide decent income. He didn't share that with his father, of course.

When he had seen Irma and Raffie, and now, with the arrival of Derrick, Emerson's internal alarm was sounding. They were not good people, and he resolved to never allow them a clear path to Courtney without planting himself directly in their way. Almost worse than this, however, was the nagging fear, the fear he was finding it easier to look the other way when Crandall and the rest of the family did things that were not acceptable in normal society. What did that make him? He didn't want his little girl brought up that way, thinking it was OK to run over the top of people with no regard for their feelings. Or for the law.

He had asked his father the question that had stretched between them, but his father's entire demeanor during it left him feeling there was more to that story. It was as if his father had only answered "no" on a technicality of some sort and that he knew a lot more than he was saying. Maybe it was to protect himself, maybe Emerson, probably both. But he knew he couldn't let this go, and yet, he dreaded having to bring it up again. It was hard enough the first time. And if his father told him anything other than "no," what would Emerson do?

Emerson stared out his office window and sighed. For now, he needed to keep Courtney far away from Auntie Irma and Cousin Derrick. Good grief.

He had a view of one of the outdoor pools from here, the only one that was open so far. There were several guests splashing around, or lounging in the sun.

If he didn't have Courtney, he might have gone off and joined a research group somewhere in the wilds — the same way Maddie had — lived off the barest possible necessities, studied invasive species, gotten his PhD. But now, he wouldn't trade being Courtney's father for anything.

To make matters worse, he couldn't get Maddie out of his mind. Their brief encounter buzzed around in his memory, and he went over and over it, remembering what she said, how she looked, how she started suspicious, then softened, then became hard as those rocky cliffs. He was fascinated by a woman who apparently detested him, and if his father knew he was dwelling on her, he might toss Emerson back out in the cold.

But he was sure if Maddie would get to know him, she would like him. Really, how many people in the world shared their type of specialized interests and education? He was sure she would quickly see, given a chance, that he was nothing like his father. But, to be honest, why would she see that? From her perspective, he must just be a carbon copy of his father. And now, with his businesslike haircut and custom-fit suits, he even looked more like him than ever.

His attention was suddenly caught by a slender, honey-haired woman who had just arisen from one of the lounge chairs. Bedecked in a pale green bikini, she stretched and pulled off her sunglasses. He tried to focus on her, but she was a little too far for him to be sure. Was that her? It looked like her. But what would Maddie be doing lounging by the pool? It was impossible. But still, he decided he better go check.

He was in the habit of taking the stairs instead of the elevator. He was aware that he had added a few pounds, surrounded by the food that Raffie prepared, which, despite his misgivings at first, turned out to be excellent. He was trying to keep his weight under control through exercise. He was up to one-hundred push-ups a day and had added a pull-up bar to the bathroom threshold in his suite.

As he was trotting down the stairs, he thought he heard someone else using them, about a floor up. That was unusual. He paused at one of the landings, listening. The stairwell was silent. Emerson started going, and he heard the footsteps start again. Maybe it was an echo? He stopped again. This time, he heard the footsteps come to a stop. They sounded much closer than he had expected. He felt a chill go up his neck. He took a couple more experimental stairs and immediately heard the steps start up. They sounded like they were coming up right behind him. He turned around and saw nothing. He went back up the stairs to peer up to the next landing.

"Hello?"

He stood quietly, listening and watching.

"Hello?"

There was silence. He turned around to head down the stairs and yelled. In front of him, he saw the shape of a person. It appeared as a black shadow, directly in front of him. The shadow moved toward him with a *whoosh,* seeming to go right through him. This caused him to lose his balance and he stepped backward and slipped on the stair. He realized he was falling, so he twisted himself in the air so he wouldn't go head first. As a result, he bumped and rolled down to the next landing, skidding on his back and shoulders. When he landed, he lay still for a moment, mentally checking himself over.

He was sore, but nothing major seemed broken; except, his left wrist might have a mild sprain. He got up cautiously, then, with a glance behind him up and down the stairs, he hurried out of the stairwell and into the comforting warm colors of the main floor hallway.

What was that, he thought frantically as he hustled past the guest rooms. What in hell was that? He was starting to experience more of this type of thing, and it had gotten to a point where he either had to decide it was real or that there was something wrong with his brain.

He was shaking and in pain. He relived the sight and sound of the dark shadow appearing, then rushing through him, not trusting his own senses, searching for an explanation. He kept looking back over his shoulder at the stairwell while he could, but then the hallway turned and it was out of sight. When he arrived in the lobby, he saw with relief that it was filled with people, going about their business. A pair of well-dressed tourists were checking in. The concierge was happily giving directions to a couple who were dressed for a hike. Derrick was skulking around near the restaurant, dressed as a busboy and checking out the women in the lobby. Emerson pretended he didn't see him.

He remembered his mission: Was Maddie by the pool?

He strode quickly through the expansive lobby. This particular pool was situated off one of the side entrances, and at its edges climbed the lush gardens that spread toward the front gate, where his temporary trailer used to sit. He stepped out onto the deck and was engulfed in sunshine and the smells of chlorine, garden vegetation, cocoa butter and the tangy scent of human skin in sunlight. About a hundred yards away, his tree towered over everything. He liked this spot. And now, there were many beautiful bodies splashing around, lazing on the lounge chairs and sipping drinks under the umbrellas by the bar.

He stood near the bar and scanned the women, looking for the one with the golden hair he had spotted from his window. To his surprise, he found her just a couple of seats away, sitting at the bar. Her back was to him, and she still looked like Maddie.

Could it be?

The bartender set a drink on the bar in front of her. It looked to be a seltzer with lime. She turned to pick it up and, at the very moment she noticed him examining her, he realized she was not Maddie. She was a lovely woman, about the same age as Maddie, but other than that and her hair, the resemblance ended. This woman had a darker complexion, dark brown eyes, bigger lips. Beautiful, yes, but she just wasn't Maddie.

She looked at Emerson's suit and back at his face and she must have liked something, because she smiled at him and said, "Aren't you a little overdressed?"

Filled with disappointment, but not wanting to be rude, Emerson said, "Oh, well, yes, I'm actually working here, uh, upstairs that is, but I just thought I'd come out and see, uh, how things are going out here." He waved his hand, indicating the pool area.

She looked at him appraisingly.

"You work here? What, in the office?"

"Well, no. Yes. I mean, I manage the resort." It still sounded strange to say this, always felt like a farce.

"Really?" She now seemed immensely interested, and she suddenly seemed to be putting out some kind of charge that caught his interest. "You don't happen to be Emerson Crandall, do you?"

This surprised him. He had not yet seen the latest edition of *Western Entrepreneur* magazine, in which both he and his father had been named dual "bachelors of the month."

"I do," he said. "I mean, I am, yes."

"Well, I am very happy to meet you," she said. She moved over the two bar stools between them in a silky, catlike way.

"I'm Rachel Characetti. This is my first time visiting your resort and I think it is just fantastic."

She smiled at him and blinked a couple times. Emerson was surprised. He had never in his life experienced this kind of instant attention from a beautiful woman that he would have normally considered to be entirely out of his league — at least, when he was a poor, scruffy-haired entomological researcher in a T-shirt and jeans. He actually doubted that he was reading her correctly.

"Well, thanks," he stammered. "I'm glad you like it."

"And I was hoping to meet you so I could tell you so, and now, here you are." She smiled again.

He smiled back.

"Here I am," he said.

Emerson couldn't believe it. The last time he was this close to a beautiful woman, he seemed to have engendered nothing in her but aggressive fury — from Maddie. This woman wasn't Maddie, no, but she was really beautiful, and, unlike Maddie, this woman actually seemed to like him. And, at the moment, she seemed to be churning with sexual energy that was definitely being aimed at him. This was just too good to walk away.

"So, where are you from?" he said, leaning back onto the bar and smiling.

His scare on the stairs was completely forgotten, for the moment.

Chapter 33

September was almost done now, and Maddie was depressed that she had made no progress. At least, in all this time, she had managed to avoid Emerson at the barn, despite Courtney's continuing to take lessons there. It wasn't difficult. Once she knew the girl's lesson schedule, Tuesdays and Thursdays at noon, she took one of the horses out on the trail for a couple hours, just before they arrived. When she got back, the girl, and her father, were gone.

That Tuesday, however, Karla apparently decided to take Courtney out for her first trail ride. Maddie was already out, riding on a thoroughbred mare that had once raced under the name Mind That Minnie Ma, but who was now simply called Minnie. She caught glimpses of Karla and Courtney meandering along the trail below her, Karla on a big, bay quarter horse named Winston and Courtney on her usual mount, Cocoa, an appaloosa that was as safe a child's pony as could be found. Karla and Courtney turned right at the trail fork and headed out along the rocky cliffs overlooking the mesa. It was a pretty ride along a dusty, red stone path, the golden mesa below, the craggy blue mountains in the distance, and the aspens that lined their way just starting to show signs of their brilliant, autumn yellow. Maddie's route took her along the same direction, but up a higher, rockier trail. She had a good view of them from her spot.

It was a beautiful day. Maddie kept an eye on the other riders with mild wariness and curiosity. She was pleased to see that Courtney had progressed well and that she was practicing good riding form on the pony even on the trail, a time when a lot of riders just relaxed. Of course, she was just a beginner, and so it was all about practicing good form. The two riders and horses were almost silhouettes in the glare of the bright sun overhead.

Then, out of the corner of her eye, Maddie thought she saw some movement. She turned to focus on it, and for just a fleeting moment, she thought she saw another horse, riderless, galloping toward Courtney and Karla. But then the image disappeared like a mirage. Maddie kept looking there, however, and she thought she saw a churning of the air, a dusty, shimmering motion, moving at the same speed as the illusionary horse had been. It was closing on the two riders. Suddenly, it was on them and Cocoa leapt sideways and started running, the dusty, shimmering cloud right behind him, almost pushing him along in front of it. In the split second before she acted, Maddie thought she could almost see the outline of a horse in the swirling, translucent cloud. She heard Courtney scream as her pony raced away, out of control. Maddie urged Minnie to run, and the thoroughbred needed little encouragement. Within moments, Minnie was in full race stride, thundering along the trail after the crazed pony. She closed on Cocoa and Courtney quickly, but Maddie saw with horror that the unmarked route the pony was taking was heading straight toward a ledge. Overhead, the sky was darkening as a storm rolled in, out of nowhere. Lightning blazed and thunder cracked, causing her horse to charge even harder.

In a moment, she was next to Courtney, their horses pounding along, the unaccountable haze still flanking the pony.

"Courtney, take my hand! Take my hand."

Courtney looked at her in terror, afraid to take her hands off the pony's mane, where she clung, the reins flopping against the pony's neck.

With her reins in her left hand, Maddie used that same hand to hold tight to her own horse's mane and, braced there, she leaned out across Courtney and grabbed her around the back, both their horses still running blindly toward the cliff. She got a good grip on Courtney and yanked hard, pulling the girl off balance. Courtney started to fall off the pony just as they neared the edge of the cliff. Maddie sat back hard on her horse and pulled her to the left so that she stopped quickly. Maddie still had a hold on Courtney, not enough to keep her from falling, but enough to guide her to a controlled landing on the ground.

Cocoa did not stop, though, and his momentum sent him straight out over the edge of the cliff. He continued out in the air for almost a stride, then vanished over the rocky ledge.

Thunder roared overhead, and huge raindrops pounded them, out of the dark sky. She could hear Karla's horse coming up the trail at a run.

Before she could dismount, Maddie saw the translucent, shimmering cloud that had chased Cocoa over the cliff now forming into the shape of a horse again. As she watched, it became more solid. It reared and pawed the air above Courtney, and Maddie could clearly see it was a mostly white paint, with a few round, black spots.

"Bugle!" Maddie said in astonishment. She dismounted from her horse and dropped to Courtney's side. The spotted horse still reared above Courtney, as though to stomp its hooves down upon her.

"Bugle! No!" Maddie yelled, not even knowing why she was saying it. She put her arms around the sobbing girl. As she did, the spotted horse stopped rearing. It put its front feet down and snorted, then reached its nose toward Maddie. She thought she could feel its hot breath on her, through the dark, cold rain as the lightning flashed again. She felt it nuzzle her hair, just like Bugle used to do. Then, as she watched, still holding Courtney, the spotted horse turned and calmly walked toward the edge of the cliff. But, instead of falling after the pony, it seemed to walk out on the air, becoming less distinct as it went, gradually fading away until, in another flash of lightning, it was gone.

Maddie turned her attention back to Courtney, who was sobbing.

"Is she alright?" Karla yelled against the wind. The storm was quickly blowing away overhead, moving swiftly across the mesa.

"I think so. Courtney? Are you hurt?"

Courtney shook her head, tears still pouring down her cheeks. "Cocoa! Oh, Cocoa!"

Courtney tried to get up and go to the cliff.

"No, honey, no, no!" Maddie said. "I'll find him. You go with Karla now."

Karla dismounted and helped Courtney up. The girl was still sobbing and crying out, "Cocoa!" in anguish as Karla took her hand.

Karla checked her over, looking for breaks or sprains. Once satisfied, she said, "Let's go, Courtney. We'll just walk back with Winston."

She gave Maddie a horrified look without Courtney seeing, shaking her head, as if to say, "What just happened?"

Maddie shook her head back at Karla, frowning.

"I'll stay here and look," she said.

Karla and Courtney headed back toward the barn, leading Winston. As the last drops of rain fell, the sky cleared overhead and the sun came back out. Maddie hurried to the edge of the cliff and looked over, her stomach in knots. She could see Cocoa at the bottom of the cliff, lying on his side with his nose pointed out in front of him. He had dropped about sixty feet down, and there was no doubt he was dead. She got back on Minnie and took the fastest route down that she could, a switch-back trail off to the east, about a quarter mile long.

Once at the bottom, she could see that, indeed, Cocoa was dead.

"Poor little pony," she said.

Minnie sniffed the pony's body and hung her head by his side as Maddie stroked the pony's already cooling neck. After a few minutes, she remounted Minnie and they walked slowly back toward the barn. But as she approached, she saw Emerson's car outside the barn office, so she turned Minnie around and headed up to a pasture on the northern edge of the stable area, one that was out of sight of the barn. There, she stripped off the saddle and bridle and let

Minnie go in the pasture, giving her a chance to rest and graze after their frightening ride. She could see the barn from here, but not be seen.

It seemed like Emerson's car was there for a long time. As she watched the barn absently, she went through the recent events. She knew what she had seen, but as she continued to try to make sense of it, she started doubting herself and questioning it, trying to figure out a way she could have imagined seeing the ghostly image of Bugle. Even if she did take what she saw as fact, which she had trouble doing, Bugle would never have acted like that. That ghostly spotted horse had driven the pony right over the cliff. Bugle always took care of Maddie when she was a little girl and never tried to do anything that would hurt her. Still, when she had felt the ghostly image touch her hair, it felt the same way as when Bugle used to nuzzle her.

Finally, she saw Karla come out and search the horizon for Maddie, followed by Emerson and Courtney. After Emerson helped Courtney into the passenger side, he stood and scanned the area. Maddie knew he was searching for her, and she ducked farther down behind a large, round bale of hay, peering out from behind it cautiously.

He had changed since she saw him last. His hair was short and businesslike, not hanging in unkempt waves. He had put on some weight, but it filled out his formerly thin frame nicely. Instead of an untucked T-shirt and baggy jeans, he wore slacks and a baby blue golf shirt that showed his wide shoulders to a good advantage.

After looking back and forth for a moment, he got in the car and pulled out of the stable parking lot.

Karla then emerged on the all-terrain vehicle, starting out in the direction of the trail where the nightmare had occurred. Maddie, realizing she was going to look for her, stepped out and waved her arms. Karla headed up the hill toward the pasture, pulling up next to Maddie.

"Here you are! I was afraid you were hurt! What are you doing up here?"

"I just wanted to give Minnie a chance to rest and calm down after ... ," she trailed off

"Cocoa?"

"Dead."

"I thought so," Karla said grimly. "I don't know what came over him to run like that. He has never bolted on the trail like that."

Karla, normally the epitome of a tough horse woman, had tears on her cheek.

"We nearly lost the girl," she said.

"I know."

"Thank God for you," Karla said, gazing out toward the cliffs. She turned back to Maddie.

"Thank you," she said.

Maddie didn't know what to say and just shrugged and shook her head slightly.

"What happened out there?" Karla said, still looking toward the trails.

Maddie searched Karla's face.

"Did you see anything?" Maddie said. "Anything that might have, uh, spooked Cocoa?"

"No, I didn't see or hear anything," Karla said. "But something sure did. Winston jumped at the same time as the pony, but he didn't try to run off like that. It was just a normal spook, like something had surprised him. I can't believe that pony took off like that."

So, Karla hadn't seen the ghostly horse. Maddie was starting to wonder if she had seen it, herself.

"Mr. Crandall stayed for a little while, hoping to thank you," Karla said. "After he made sure that Courtney was OK, of course."

"That's not necessary," Maddie said. "Anybody would have done it."

"I didn't do it," Karla said quietly.

"Well, you would have. I just had a head start, and I was a lot closer."

"Mmm," Karla said. "Come on, let's bring this red horse to the barn. She deserves some extra hay, ya'?"

"I'll say."

She collected the mare, leading her back to the gate.

"That Emerson Crandall is quite the looker," Karla said as they walked down the hill, Minnie behind them.

Maddie didn't say anything.

"Did you see that he and his father were named 'Bachelors of the Month' in some business magazine? It has all the female staff up at the hotel quite giddy, I hear. Some of the male staff, too."

"Barf," Maddie said.

"I notice you manage to make yourself pretty scarce when he's around," Karla said, glancing at Maddie.

"I don't like authority figures," she said lightly.

"Emerson? Boss' son, yeah. But he's a nice guy. Different from his father."

"I bet."

"He is, and he sure adores that little girl. You should get to know him."

"You get to know him. I'll throw rice at your wedding. I'm not interested in him."

"I would if I weren't thirty years too old. And you don't even know him."

"Let's leave it that way, huh?"

"Alright already," Karla said. "I just think you would like each other, if you gave it a chance."

They had reached the stable.

"Hand me that halter, will you? And don't try to fix me up with Emerson Crandall. I'm not in the market."

"Why not?"

"I have other things to keep me busy." And nothing good can come out of a Crandall, she thought, slipping the halter over Minnie's head.

"OK, OK. I'll be in the office if you need anything."

Could Courtney have recognized her, and would she identify her to Emerson? They had seen each other just the one day, and it had been more than a month back. No, Maddie decided. Courtney wouldn't have expected her there, plus she had her hair up, and was wearing a riding helmet. In the terror of the event, she was certain that Courtney would not have known who Maddie was, even if she was able to recognize her in normal circumstances, which was unlikely. She felt fairly certain that her anonymity from the Crandalls was still secure.

Emerson was sure that Courtney was not hurt, but he drove up to the resort nurse's office, where the nurse checked her over and pronounced her sound. Courtney had cried herself out by then, more from sorrow for the pony than the terror of the events that led up to Cocoa's fall. Emerson, who knew nothing more about horses than what he observed during Courtney's lessons, had secretly decided that Courtney would never get on another one again. But Courtney was already exclaiming about how she stayed on the pony even though it had run really fast, and it definitely did not sound like she had any intention of stopping riding.

"It was lucky for me that Maddie was there to pull me off Cocoa, wasn't it, Daddy?"

They were driving back toward their end of the hotel. The name surprised Emerson and he felt fleetingly wistful.

"You mean Kathy."

"That wasn't Kathy. That was Maddie," Courtney said, looking out the window of the passenger side.

"No, it was Kathy. Karla told us."

"Well, I don't know Kathy, because I never saw her at the barn," Courtney said.

"OK, then."

"But I know Maddie, because she had coffee with us and then we drove her to town and that cow got hit by lightning."

Emerson was interested. "That was Maddie that day, but Karla said it was Kathy, the barn girl, who helped you today. I think you're mixing them up."

"I think it's Maddie, and that's why she never comes to the barn when we're there, because she doesn't like you."

Emerson looked at the road and wondered about this, but he didn't know what to make of it. Just hearing Maddie's name caused a strong physical reaction in him. He sighed. He was meeting Rachel for dinner, and he needed to catch a shower and drop Courtney off with Mrs. Gamino, the night office manager who adored Courtney and said she loved to babysit her.

He was driving a little too quickly on the curving roads around the resort. He came around a bend and there, in the road, was a little tan and white dog. Courtney screamed and he swerved. He could feel first the front tire, then the rear, bump up over the dog just before the car spun out of control on the gravel and hit the large boulders that lined the road. It made a terrible, grinding crash. He and Courtney jolted forward in their seat belts and then back.

"You hit a dog!" Courtney said.

"Are you OK?"

She threw off her seat belt and darted out of the car. With the driver's side up against the rocks, he climbed out the passenger side, after her. She was standing in the road, looking both ways for the dog.

"He must have run away," she said in surprise.

"I thought I hit it," he said.

"You did."

He looked back at the car. Its front end was bent every which way and it was definitely not drivable.

"Well, we were lucky," he said. "That's twice for you today. This is your lucky day."

"I don't feel very lucky," she said.

"We might as well walk from here."

He pulled out his phone and called the resort, alerting his father's assistant to the wreck and asking him to take care of it. Then he called Rachel to tell her he was running a little late.

As they walked the ten minutes to the hotel, he started thinking about the strange things that were happening to them and wondering what the hell was going on. It was as though something unseen was always around them, just out of sight, menacing them. The feeling had started that night back in March, in his squalid little Syracuse apartment. It was strange to think of what was happening out here at that same time. His father was working on the resort plans, buying this land from the locals, negotiating with Mrs. Stanton.

Emerson felt a cold tingle run up his back. That was when the books started falling, when dark shadows started appearing in his periphery, when an ominous darkness started to lurk at the edges of his world. It started at the same time as Clara Stanton had died.

He stopped walking. The thought gripped him. He looked all around him, slowly, as if, now that he made a connection, he expected something horrible to appear before him.

"What?" Courtney said, stopping a few steps ahead and looking back at him.

He stepped forward and caught her hand, grasping it tightly, still looking around. His gaze stopped on the giant pine.

"What?" Courtney whispered, catching his mood, looking at the tree.

"Hey kiddo," he said. "I'll race you."

And they ran, pretending it was for fun, but feeling like something was reaching for their heels.

Chapter 34

Crandall was driving along the dark mesa road, going to check the progress on the luxury condos. They had been blasting out the rock the previous weeks, but now, building had started and the frames of the homes were going up. The blasting had restarted farther south for the townhouses.

He could see the construction lights from the main highway, so he knew there was some activity out there. As he drove, he remembered how many times he had looked over the mesa and pictured those luxury condos sprouting up there like boulders, and now, here they were, emerging out of the rust and ochre cliffs. The framing was made of steel, but to Crandall, it looked like gold.

He pulled into the construction site. A few safety spotlights lit bits of the area, and he spotted some workers down at the south end. Piles of steel girders, coils of cable and stacks of lumber made the area hard to walk through, and wooden mats had been laid to keep people and equipment out of the mud.

Crandall walked quietly along the wood platform to the main buildings, admiring the progress as he went. Then he thought he saw some movement out to his right, inside one of the skeletal structures. He stopped walking and turned that way, peering through the darkness. He saw it again. It looked like a person, walking very slowly along the newly installed rafters, in the direction that would take them out over the cliffs for the best view of the mesa.

"Hello?" Crandall called out, then waited. He just had the one quick glimpse of the person walking away from him, and now saw no one.

"Hello?" Crandall started walking quietly in that direction. Where had that idiot gone? It was not easy walking along these slippery boards, and as he got closer to where he had seen the person, he realized he would need to start walking along the girders himself.

"Hello? Come out here, now!" he yelled, then listened. He thought he heard some quiet steps. They were above him, now. He let his eyes move slowly up the structure and, there it was. He saw the small form, walking slowly along the second story framework of the building. He reached for his phone, but realized he had left it back in the car.

"Hey!" he yelled. "You there! Get down here right now. You're going to get yourself killed!"

He tried to focus on the small figure, which seemed to cast the slightest glow. It reminded him of someone he had seen before, but whom?

A chill slithered up his back. He remembered. The small, almost shuffling steps, the stooped figure.

No. Impossible.

Crandall stood watching, his eyes big, but then the figure seemed to vanish into the dark.

"Oh, for God's sake, man. Pull yourself together," he muttered, stubbornly denying what he was seeing, as he had for several months. "You'll have a lawsuit if this fool falls and breaks his neck."

He saw the ladder to the next floor in the dim lights and carefully climbed up. He was wearing his smooth, leather-soled office shoes and they were not ideal for this kind of activity. He thought he caught site of the small figure again.

"Hey! You! Stop!" he yelled. He walked carefully along the girders. They were about two feet wide, ample space, but he felt high up, and a jolt of vertigo made him lose his balance for a moment. He caught himself and continued walking. There she was, walking slowly along the beam, using a cane, seemingly oblivious to the height and danger. His heart was pounding, and, almost mesmerized by this uncanny sight, he followed along the top of the wall, heading toward the overlook that would be the foundation of large, sweeping porches and glass-enclosed patios.

"Stop!" he yelled. The little figure walked behind a beam and disappeared from view. He followed, balancing carefully, and found himself on a beam overlooking the whole valley, and a drop of about 200 feet. Trying not to look down, he swallowed hard, attempting to get rid of the feeling that his stomach had moved up into the back of his throat.

"Hello?" he said, hesitantly. Where was she? Had she fallen?

He stepped a little further out, looking around. It was time to stop climbing around out here, get back to the car and call site security.

He didn't see the dark figure standing behind a beam until he had passed it. He then felt a terrible cold, like something evil was standing on that beam, and he turned slowly around. Then the figure moved and he saw an American Indian woman in a leather dress and leggings step toward him, raising her hands in a sweeping motion. A giant bird seemed to fly from her, straight at his face, talons bared.

Crandall jumped backward involuntarily. His shoe missed its footing and he fell off the side of the beam, landing on his belly, but slipping. He managed to cling to the other side of the beam desperately with both hands, and he hung on painfully, trying to hoist himself back up.

"Help!" he yelled as loudly as he could. "Help!"

He heard steps above him and saw the figure of the hunched-over person that had first drawn him here. She was walking slowly along the beam from which he hung.

"Help!" he yelled again.

As she drew near, he again noticed the strange glow that seemed to come from her. Then he realized that he could see the beams behind her, right through her body. She continued moving slowly near him and, when she was almost close enough to step on his hands, she looked down at him and smiled.

It was a sweet, unassuming smile, and it was on the face of Clara Stanton. As he watched in horror, though, the smile became wide, ugly, malicious, and she raised her small foot as though to stomp his hand. Crandall yelled, squeezing his eyes shut, mentally bracing himself for crushing pain. Yet, instead, her foot passed right through his hand with a cold chill.

He opened his eyes. The figure was gone.

"Help!" Crandall yelled, trying to swing his feet up on the beam again. He realized that his hands still felt cold. In fact, they were freezing with cold. They felt so cold, it seemed like they were hardening onto the beam like ice, like they would snap off at the wrists. He felt he was going to lose his grip any moment and plunge to his death below.

"Help!"

He heard the sound of footsteps again and saw a dark shadow approaching from inside the building structure. These footsteps sounded heavy, and as they approached, he saw big, heavy work boots.

"No! No! Go away!" he yelled, anticipating with horror the feel of those boots on his frozen hands. A light beam illuminated his face. Then a hand closed around his wrist.

Crandall shrieked.

"Hold on, hold on. I've got you."

Another hand closed on his wrist. The hands were blissfully warm, and then he felt himself being pulled up. He scrambled with his feet as he was raised until he was balanced on the beam, then he stood. He swayed and fell forward against the person who had helped him. A flashlight, sitting on the beam, sent a long, thin light out into the darkness.

"You're all right now," said the man. "Come on, walk in front of me. I'll help you."

They walked slowly back along the beam to the ladder, using the flashlight to see their way. Crandall paused, rubbing his hands together. They were still so cold they felt frozen.

"Go ahead," the man said. "You can climb a ladder, right?"

"My hands," Crandall mumbled. "They're stiff."

"Oh! Probably from hanging on that beam. Here, let me see."

The light beam shown on Crandall's hands, and he saw with horror they were blue with cold.

"What the hell?" said the man. "What happened to your hands?"

"They're cold."

"Here." The man grasped them flat between his and rubbed them vigorously. It hurt, like needles stabbing him.

"Stop! No, don't do that. I can go down."

Crandall numbly made it down the ladder, followed by the worker. Once on the ground, the man guided Crandall back to the parking lot.

Now safely at the car, the man said, "What were you doing out there? This is dangerous. You can't just be walking around out there."

"I know that," Crandall snapped.

"You're lucky I came along," the man said reproachfully.

Some additional flashlight beams showed that others were heading that way.

"Yes, yes, I was. You're right," Crandall said, anxious to get out of there. "Sorry about that. Thank you. Thank you for your help. What's your name?"

"Darryl White."

The other men came up.

"What's going on?" one of them said. It was O'Mara, the construction superintendent. "Mr. Crandall! What are you doing out here? Who was that yelling?"

"It was me," Crandall said. "I almost fell off that building and White here yanked me back up."

"Good save, Darry. This is Mr. Crandall."

"Really?" Darry said, still not seeming to know who Crandall was.

"Why were you out there? Are you OK now?" O'Mara asked.

"Yes, yes. I'm fine. I thought I saw someone wandering around out there, and I went too far out."

"Crandall?" Darry said, surprised, recognition crossing his face. "Mr. Crandall? Wow."

"Yes, well, thanks again, uh, Darry. You men, don't let me hold you up. I'll be going now."

"OK, well, glad you're all right."

They all called good night as he got into his car. Although it was a warm night, he put the heat on full blast. He looked back at the skeletal structure. It all seemed like he had been in the grip of some kind of mad hallucination, behaving like a fool.

But as he watched, he thought he saw the pale figures of two people standing up in the shadows, and a huge, dark bird flying around the beams. He put the car in reverse and pulled out of the parking lot, fast.

Chapter 35

It had been five weeks and Derrick was bored with his job. In his mind, picking up dirty dishes was woman's work, and he couldn't tolerate Raffie's barking orders in the kitchen. Derrick pretty much ignored him, but he couldn't help but notice that others jumped at his commands, and it irritated Derrick to see his younger cousin rising to this esteemed position. Derrick felt he, himself, was much smarter, much more talented, much better looking. Yet, his attempts at making new connections here were, so far, failing.

He did have one promising meeting later that night, though. He had dropped his uncle's name and it allowed him the opportunity to buy a drink for Emilio Esponzio, an Italian investment manager who had a reputation for making some interesting deals. He had come a few weeks in advance of the grand opening, to scope out the place. Derrick hoped he could make a good impression, get in on some of the activity, and get out of the kitchen and this trained monkey suit.

He spotted the Haldermans coming into the restaurant. He had approached Mr. Halderman, a chemical exporter, earlier that week, offering his assistance, and was treated like some kind of a cockroach.

Once the Haldermans were seated, Derrick offered the harried waitress to get their drinks for them.

"A Johnny Manhattan and a Sapphire tonic," she said, acknowledging his offer on the way past.

Mr. Halderman's would be the Manhattan, Derrick guessed, but just to be sure, when he was in the small, dark area between the bar and the restaurant, he blew nasal mucus into both drinks.

"Johnny Manhattan?" he said, at the table. Halderman nodded. Derrick set the drink near his plate, then, saying, "Sapphire tonic," set down the other drink in front of Mrs. Halderman.

"Enjoy," he said, smiling at both of them. Halderman glanced at him and nodded.

Didn't even recognize me, the bastard, Derrick thought as he backed away and watched with satisfaction as they sipped their drinks.

A little later, he noticed the pretty waitress, Barbara, go into the dry goods room for some supplies at the end of her shift, and he followed her in. They had been flirting with each other for about a week, so no time like the present, he thought. He shut the door behind him, startling her. She was opening a huge can of fudge sauce with an industrial-sized can opener that was screwed down to the work surface.

"Let me help."

He walked up behind her and put both hands on hers, his body close enough behind her so she could feel his groin. This was one of those make-it-or-break-it shots that he was accustomed to taking. He was not one to waste a lot of time with niceties. Either she wanted him or she didn't. Easy.

This time, much to his satisfaction, she sunk back into him and made some lame joke about his boner. Good enough. He had guessed right. Easy.

In less than two minutes, it was over and she was scurrying around, looking for a rag to clean up with. He dipped his finger into the fudge, rubbed it on her lips, sucked it off roughly, said, "See you later," and slipped back out of the storage room, checking his fly.

He could hear Raffie having a screaming fit about some stupid recipe. Derrick decided that was enough for one night, stepped into the changing room, tossed his white uniform on the floor, got into his jeans and polo shirt and left through the back kitchen door.

One of the dishwashers was having a smoke near the large garbage container, just at the edge of the floodlights.

"Hey, Derrick," he said. "You taking off, man?"

It was Jorge, a tired-looking guy of around fifty who had probably reached the summit of his career here at the Crandall Resort restaurant dishwashing machines. His dark eyes were kind, but the bags under them, as well as the scar that ran from the corner of one to his chin, suggested a difficult past.

"Yeah, man."

"Must be nice, just leaving when you want."

"No doubt."

"Boss's nephew."

"Yep."

"Hey, you want a hit for the road?" Jorge raised the cigarette and Derrick noticed that it was hand-rolled. Marijuana.

"Yeah, sure."

He stepped into the shadows with Jorge and took a long hit and held his breath. Jorge took one, too.

"So, where are you off to?" Jorge said, in the odd, creaky voice of a person talking while holding his breath.

"Got a meeting," Derrick said, also holding his breath. Finally, he let out the smoke.

"Business?"

"Yeah," he took one more big hit and said, "Thanks, man. See ya," holding his breath again. He nodded at Jorge and stepped away into the shadows.

"Sure thing," Jorge said.

Derrick waved without turning around. He checked his watch and saw he still had a half-hour before meeting Esponzio at the Red Rock Lounge. He decided to slip off toward the stable to see what he could see.

Derrick had discovered the location of the stable girl's flat, above the barn, and a couple of times a week, he stood among the aspens on a knoll nearby and watched her move around before bed. She had placed lace curtains in front of the windows, unfortunately, so her form was just a silhouette. He could sometimes see her shape as she stripped off her clothes. He was interested in the fact that he never saw her put anything else on for the purpose of sleeping. He wasn't sure if he couldn't see that part, or if she slept nude. He preferred to think she slept nude. In fact, he preferred to think she did everything nude. When he watched her ride out on the trails, or in the arena by the barn, he saw her hips moving back and forth with the horse's strides and imagined her as naked as Lady Godiva. He liked to imagine he was sitting on the horse behind her.

He noticed that her car was parked by the stable, and he went quietly over to it. Unlocked. He slipped inside and opened the glove compartment, pulling out the contents and thumbing through them. Owner's manual, insurance and registration, blah, blah. Then he found an envelope addressed to Maddie Cunningham. Maddie? That name sounded familiar. He was quite sure that this woman was called Kathy, however. He pulled out the contents of the envelope. It was a note, scribbled on a sheet of paper, and a photo.

"Hey, Maddie, I found this old photo of us at your aunt's and I thought you'd like it. I was so sorry to hear about your aunt. This picture really brought back memories! Hope all is well. Love, Trish."

Derrick squinted at the picture in the dim light. It showed two girls, about 11, all arms and legs, a black and white horse between them and, next to them, a smiling lady of about 65. He turned it over and read the writing on the back.

"Maddie Cunningham, Aunt Clara Stanton, me and Bugle the greatest horse on the planet!" it said, in a young girl's exaggeratedly swirly handwriting, complete with hearts instead of "I" dots.

Things clicked into place for Derrick. He put the automobile documents back in the glove compartment. Stepping out of the car, he shut the door quietly, and slipped the photo and note into his coat pocket.

He smiled with satisfaction as he looked back up at her shadow moving around the flat.

Just you wait, Kathy Maddie Stanton Cunningham, he thought. I'm going to get you yet.

But now, it was time to go meet Esponzio, so he headed up the dark trail, which he had memorized, and back toward the bright lights of the resort.

He ordered a bourbon at the bar. Bottom shelf, but not much longer though, he thought. His lucky break was coming. He could sense it. Maybe tonight.

Esponzio kept him waiting for half an hour. Then he came in with a young blonde on his arm and a couple of bodyguards. He sat them at a table near the dance floor and came over to the bar.

"Mr. Esponzio!" Derrick shook his hand warmly. "What can I get you to drink?"

"Frangelico, iced and up," Esponzio said to the bartender, who nodded.

"That sounds interesting," said Derrick, who had finished his bourbon. "Make it two."

The bartender found the bottle of liqueur on an upper shelf, filled a shaker with ice, added the shots, shook it once and poured out two perfectly measured cordials. He delivered them with a blank expression and nodded when Derrick told him to add them to his tab.

Esponzio wasted no time on small talk.

"Crandall, isn't it?" He paused for Derrick's nod, then went on. "Your uncle owns this place?"

"Yeah."

"I thought so."

He could thank his bastard uncle for this meeting later.

Esponzio was looking him up and down and didn't seem to like what he saw.

"What do you want to talk about, if I may be direct? I'm busy."

"Yeah, sure. I know you are, Mr. Esponzio," said Derrick, smiling broadly and sincerely, knowing this was his best look and that it was pretty damn good. "Well, I'll get right to the point. I am interested in working for you."

"Oh? Why would I want to hire you?"

"Well, I'm smart. I know when to talk and when to keep my mouth shut, if you know what I mean." He searched Esponzio's face for a smidgen of understanding, saw none, and went on without pause. "People like me, and I know people. I've been around. I'm not afraid of a fight and I usually win. I can pick up anything you want me to do really fast. I'll go anywhere and do anything."

"Are you a felon?" Esponzio cut in. The question threw Derrick, but only for a moment.

"Yes," he said, knowing, if he lied, it would be too easy to detect with a quick background search.

Esponzio looked at him steadily. "I appreciate your honesty," he said. "But if you are a felon, it means you got caught."

"Well, yes, but I can explain how that happened, Mr. Esponzio."

"No need. I only work with those who don't get caught." He sipped the cordial and set it lightly back on the bar. "Thank you for the drink."

He nodded to Derrick, stepped away from the bar and walked across the room to his companions, who watched him keenly as he approached.

Derrick gazed after him, frowning. With his hand near his lap, he formed his forefinger and thumb into the shape of a gun and, keeping his hand low, pretended to fire at Esponzio. It was a small movement, but it was noticed by one of Esponzio's bodyguards. Without taking his eyes off Derrick, he shifted his jacket slightly so Derrick got a glimpse of the shiny handgun holstered there. Derrick smiled, tossed back his revoltingly sweet drink, then Esponzio's, dropped twenty dollars on the bar and crossed the lounge toward the door, the guard's eyes drilling holes in his back as he went. Just before reaching the door and without turning around, Derrick casually stuck up his middle finger near his shoulder, so the bodyguard would get a good look at it before Derrick was gone.

"Derrick!" Raffie yelled. The restaurant was closed. Derrick was supposed to be there to help during a late lesson. Raffie had designed his signature meals for the week with the intention of each building on the next. This way, nothing would go to waste, yet each meal would be distinctly different from the one served the night before. He wanted to show Derrick what he had in mind, more to impress him with his brilliance than with any expectation that Derrick would retain the information for the purpose of becoming a chef.

It was a total joke to think Derrick would ever learn this business, but that was the game they were playing, Raffie thought. Crandall and his mother expected it so he would give it something of an effort, albeit a mild one.

"Derrick!"

Jorge, who was mopping up out front, stuck his head in the door and said, "I think he's gone, sir."

"Gone? Where the hell has he gone?"

"Don't know, sir." Jorge ducked back out.

"A-hole."

He filled a four-gallon pot with hot water, shifted it to the soup burner and turned on the gas to get it boiling. This burner had been custom made for him, built lower than the others, so it was easy to move big pots on and off. It was one of the many luxurious pieces of equipment his uncle had supplied. He chopped some leeks and began to add them. He was making a demi-glace for Saturday night.

"Jackass." He started chopping celery. Normally, he would have his prep cook do this, but he had wanted to work with Derrick himself. "Jerk-off."

"Goodnight, Mr. Raffie." The waitresses left in a flock, half of them sticking cigarettes in their mouths to light the second they made it through the back door.

"Whores," he snorted, after they left.

He heard a strange noise behind him that made him stop in mid-chop. He looked around and tried to locate the source. It had sounded like a whine, from an animal, or a creaking door perhaps? He didn't see anything. He turned back to the vegetables and started chopping again.

This time, he heard a distinct growl. He turned around again and thought he saw a small, tan and white dog trotting behind the counters toward the door.

"Jorge!" he shouted.

After a moment, Jorge stuck his head in the door. "Yes?"

"Get that goddamned dog out of my kitchen!"

"What dog?"

"It went that way!" Raffie thrust his head around, chopping again.

Jorge started walking through the kitchen. Raffie could hear him whistling and making kissing sounds, trying to call the dog, opening doors. After a couple of minutes, Jorge came back around the counter.

"I don't see a dog, sir. The door was cracked. Maybe he went back out."

"He better have. I don't need any filthy dogs in my kitchen. And shut that door!"

"I did, sir. No dogs."

Jorge went back out to the dining room. Raffie heard the vacuum cleaner start. He continued to work in the warm quiet of the kitchen.

Then he heard the growl again. He spun around, looking sharply at the floor. He held his chopping knife up by his chest. He would chop that little sucker if he had to. He didn't see anything, but he heard another growl. Maybe it had ducked under the counter. He put down the knife and picked up a long-handled ladle. Bending down, he shoved the ladle under the counter, rattling it back and forth. No dog.

He stood back up. As he did, his eyes fell upon a huge paw on the countertop, right in front of his nose. He straightened slowly. An enormous white and tan dog was standing on the counter. It was just like the one he had seen, but much larger. Its teeth were bared and it was growling a low, deep, rumbling growl. Raffie dropped the ladle with a clang and started to back away slowly, his heart tightening.

The dog seemed almost to be glowing, and Raffie thought he could see right through it, noticing the neatly stacked pans in the cupboard directly behind it. Raffie's eyes grew wide.

"Jorge," he whispered, his voice failing him, his heart jumping. "Jorge."

The dog hunched down, about to pounce.

"Jorge!" He found his voice and screamed the name. He turned and tried to run, but his foot hit the ladle and slipped out from under him just as the dog pounced. Raffie felt an icy chill go through his body and a squeezing pain grip his chest just seconds before he fell, head-first, into the kettle of boiling liquid. After one futile little squirm, his heart gave a last clench, and he was dead, his head cooking slowly in the merrily bubbling broth.

When Jorge headed home, about thirty minutes later, he called a "good night" to Raffie, and, as usual, received no response. He went out the back door, pushed it tight, and lit a cigarette as he walked to his car.

Chapter 36

Maddie couldn't sleep. She kept thinking about what had happened out on the trail, the ghostly horse that looked like Bugle, the dead pony, the little girl who almost died, her aunt, and how she could possibly prove that Crandall had killed her. If she could only find some drive or disk that held Toby's file back-up.

"Damn it, Toby. Where is it?"

Finally, she got up and turned on her computer. Eduardo had e-mailed her some pictures that she decided to save on a small, detachable drive. As the pictures transferred, she watched the blinking blue light on the tiny, external drive, blankly.

It was amazing that such a little thing could hold so much information, she thought, ejecting it and pulling it out of the port. She held it between her finger and thumb. Such a little thing, holding so many important things, like a little treasure box.

A treasure box! Suddenly, she knew where Toby kept his backed-up files.

She got dressed and went down to her car, heading out the back way into town. She anxiously covered the twenty miles, going too quickly along some of the sharp curves. It was a cloudy night and no moon or stars emerged to provide extra light. It seemed like another storm might be brewing.

Once in town, she parked behind Toby's old office building. The third story was alight, and she guessed there might be an apartment up there. But Toby's old office, still unoccupied, was dark.

She checked the back door first. It was solid, and locked. Then she slipped around the front of the building and checked the front door, just in case the tenants had left it open. She ducked out of the lights of a passing car once before getting to the door. Also locked. She went back around the building and looked for a way in. An old, iron ladder descended the building, its bottom about ten feet up. It was a fire escape, and for security reasons, it didn't go all the way to the ground unless someone was climbing down it, at which point, it would slide down, allowing escape from a blaze. She pulled her car under it, and that made the jump doable. Maddie sprung up, grabbing a rung in both hands. The ladder shifted with a painful-sounding screech.

"What was that?" she heard from the apartment above. Maddie, who had climbed enough so her feet were now on a rung, was breathing hard with nerves and exertion. She heard footsteps above her and the third-floor window slid open.

"What is it?" came a female voice from inside.

"I don't know," said a male voice directly overhead.

Maddie continued to try to flatten herself against the building, not daring to breathe.

"Do you see anything?"

Maddie imagined him looking up and down the alley. If he looked directly down, he could probably see her.

"No," he said.

She heard the window slide shut. She climbed slowly, trying not to jostle the ladder, until she reached Toby's window. She slipped onto the ledge and used the strength of her legs to push up the heavy, old-fashioned window, praying it was not locked. It didn't feel like it was going to budge, but then suddenly, it creaked open, so easily it was as though someone had opened it for her. She held her breath and waited. The couple upstairs apparently hadn't heard the creak.

With a sigh of relief, she was through.

In the flashlight beam, the office looked pretty much as she remembered it, with Toby's furniture still in place. As soon as she saw Toby's old-fashioned desk, she knew right where to look. Toby always hid little trinkets for her in the secret drawer underneath. She didn't fit under there as well as she used to, but her hand quickly found the hidden drawer.

She slid it open and flashed her penlight beam into it. The light found the only object in the drawer. It was a three-inch external drive. Toby had backed up his files, and he had placed the backup in a safe place that he could easily access, but that others were unlikely to find.

Maddie picked up the drive, tucked it in her jeans pocket, and started to close the drawer. But as she did, she noticed the small flashlight beam reflect brightly off something there. That was odd. She shown the beam directly in the drawer and was astonished to see a crystal. It was clear and chunky, about the size of the top joint of her thumb. She held it up in her light and saw it had a beautiful, distinctively pink color.

That was odd. She was sure the drawer had been empty. Glass, probably, she thought, or rose quartz. It wasn't hers, but still, no one else would ever find it here, and it was so extraordinarily beautiful. Maybe Toby had left it there for her many years ago, and they had both forgotten the game before she found it. She felt so certain that it was meant for her that she smiled and tucked it into her jeans pocket. She closed the drawer and slid out from under the desk.

When she stood up, she noticed a fresh, spicy smell in the air, and it immediately reminded her of Toby. How odd. Where was that coming from? Maybe he had kept aftershave in his desk drawer, and she had disturbed the bottle with her activity.

She quietly crossed to the door, unlocked it and stepped out, allowing it to lock behind her, and hurried down the stairs. She slipped out the back door, jogged on tiptoes across the alleyway to her car, and started back toward the resort. She couldn't wait to see what was on that drive.

Chapter 37

Irma had just finished assisting a young woman who worked as part of the overnight cleaning staff. She had been trying to find a properly fitting uniform, and Irma deliberately had her try one that was too tight before handing her the correct size. The woman had left in a hurry, leaving Irma grinning in the locker room.

Irma caught a peek at her own face in the mirror, black hair and bright red lips in sharp contrast against her pale, dry skin. She blew herself a kiss before leaving, going back to her room. She noticed that the normally warm and mellow hallway had an unusual chill tonight, and she had the distinct feeling that she was being watched. She kept turning around and looking behind her, thinking she heard steps there. But, whenever she looked, there was no one to be seen.

She was glad to get in her suite. She locked the door and started to take off her blouse. When she turned around she yelled in surprise. There was a man standing in front of the bed, a tall man in the shadows, wearing a cowboy hat. Despite her initial start, a slow smile now spread over Irma's face.

"So here you are at last," she said.

He approached her, unbuttoning his shirt. He kept his head tilted down, so his face stayed in the shadow of his hat. His loose shirt revealed a lean but muscular chest and firm stomach.

"Mmm, you look yummy," Irma said. "You must be a real cowboy."

She reached for his chest but he stepped back.

"Oh, shy, are you?"

He nodded his chin up.

"Want me to strip?"

He nodded again.

"Strong and silent. I like that. Let me see your face, cowboy."

241

He slowly tilted his head up. She wondered what she would see, now that she finally had him close. She grinned as his square chin appeared, his full lips, straight nose and then, those eyes. He had unusual eyes, almost a golden green color.

"Well, aren't you pretty to look at," she said with enthusiasm. She couldn't believe her luck. This boy, in his cowboy outfit, looked like he could be up for some serious sexual gymnastics and it had been a long time since someone this young and handsome had shown interest in her.

He smiled at her, then nodded at her to continue taking off her blouse. She unbuttoned it and slid it off, revealing her large breasts, cupped rigidly in a somewhat pointy bra.

She looked at him expectantly. He nodded at her and she chuckled.

"You are a devil, aren't you?" She unhooked the bra and let her breasts loose. They flopped down and spread outward.

"You like?" she said. The cowboy nodded, most of his face again in shadow.

This was too much fun. A man of mystery. She noticed he had an old-fashioned, holstered gun on one hip and a long-bladed knife in a leather case on the other.

"Woohee," she said, "You sure know how to do it right, don't you?"

In her excitement, she could feel a little sweat break out on her brow and under her breasts. "I have a feeling it's going to get hot in here," she said. "Mind if I open the window?"

She walked to the window and slid it opened. She liked standing half-naked in the window, overlooking the garden where guests might be walking, and anyone who happened to look up would see her standing up there, chest bare, like Queen Cleopatra. Feeling regal, horny and unusually beautiful, she turned back to the room to see the cowboy walking slowly toward her. He was totally naked, she saw with delight, except for his boots.

"You forgot the spurs," she said.

He continued to walk, and as he did, he started to change. She couldn't really see what was happening at first, in the dim light, but it seemed like his skin was changing color, becoming gray, starting to peel off in places.

Her first thought was that he had some kind of disgusting disease. But then she realized that something was terribly wrong. His skin was literally falling off him and now she could see his organs, and they started dropping out of his body, onto the floor, first his lungs, then his heart and stomach. Then his intestines fell out in a big tangle.

Irma felt a scream building in her throat. She pushed herself against the ledge, backing as far away as she could, but he kept coming. His penis was black with decay, and it dropped off his body like an overripe banana. The smell of rotting flesh and bowels filled the air and she finished the scream. It started low, then switched to a high-pitched shriek. As the skeletal cowboy lifted his shadowed face again, she saw his eyes hanging by thin, rotting cords and his tongue a bluish, slug-like blob behind his lipless, grinning teeth.

Irma fell backward out of the window.

She fell fifty feet, her breasts floating up like nippled balloons. When she landed, she took out a glass table and a nearby croquet set. She bounced once and ended up bent, face-first, over an iron garden bench, her top half on one side, her backside in the air on the other, as though she were still waiting for her cowboy to come for a ride.

Chapter 38

Crandall was having a hard time getting to sleep. The events at the construction site had unnerved him, and his hands were freezing. They were still bluish and icy. He would have to get to a doctor to see if he had damaged them while he was hanging onto the beam. Strained the tendons or something. Or maybe he was starting to suffer from poor circulation, and this event had aggravated it? He wasn't sure, but even though he soaked them in hot water and was now wearing warm gloves, they still felt frozen.

He had the television on in his suite, but he wasn't watching. He paced around the room in his pajamas and robe. He went to the window and looked out. It was a moonless night, and it seemed like a storm was coming.

As he was turning away from the window, something caught his eye. Crandall peered through the glass. It couldn't be. It looked like the figure of a small, elderly woman, shuffling toward him across the lawn, emitting a slight, whitish glow. As he watched, she seemed to fade away. Crandall went pale. After all he had experienced tonight, he knew he couldn't pretend any longer that this wasn't happening.

She was coming for him.

"Do you think we should start planning our wedding?"

Rachel was lying naked on the bed, her round, silicone-filled breasts perched on her chest with a somewhat unnatural poofiness.

Emerson, who had been stretched out in the groggy haze of sexual satisfaction, was suddenly fully alert.

"A wedding?" He couldn't keep the shock and irritation out of his voice. It was late. They had listened to a band that played until after 2, then came up to her room and fooled around. Now he just wanted sleep.

"Well, yes, Emmer."

She called him "Emmer." He didn't like that. But, in fairness, Emerson was hard to make into a nickname. That was why he went by Emerson.

"Why wait? I don't see any reason for dragging things out, when it's obvious we are so well suited for each other."

They were well suited for sex with each other, that was definite. They had been having it once or twice a day for the past few weeks, and it had been great, no doubt. But marriage? He racked his brain to identify a single conversation they had had that ever strayed from topics Rachel preferred, which appeared to remain rigidly on what type of car was best this year, where to go shopping and what to buy there, and who was getting a private jet and flying to what resort.

They had not talked about a single book, a single idea, not politics, not philosophy, and most especially, not bugs. In fact, her only mention of bugs came amidst screams if she happened on one unexpectedly, together with demands that he kill it. Which he didn't do. Instead, he would drop the offending bug out the window or put it in a potted plant, or just generally reposition it out of her sight, behavior she definitely found abnormal.

And now she mentioned marriage? It would have been funny if it weren't so aggravating. The idea of spending his life with this beautiful bore was a bleak one. Even she must know that they did not have the faintest idea whether they were well-suited as partners. How could they? All they had done was have sex.

It was at this moment that Emerson suspected for the first time that he had been the victim of a well-planned attack. A full-frontal-nudity attack, and the pillage she was planning to claim was him. He had been so overwhelmed by the idea that this beautiful woman found him attractive, and so appreciative of being able to have sex with someone who could almost be a supermodel, that he hadn't seen it coming.

Emerson had always been tongue-tied and shy around women, especially beautiful women, and this had been true with Rachel as well. But at this moment, he had no trouble being direct.

"There is no way we're getting married."

When he left the room ten minutes later, it was with his body fairly bruised, his shirt in his hands and without his shoes, but his spirit greatly relieved. He heard something hit the door as it closed behind him. His shoe, no doubt. He slipped his T-shirt over his head, but didn't bother putting on his button-down over it.

It all made sense. His confidence, which had soared because of her constant flattery, had just hit the ground like a crashing jet. He now realized that she was just hunting for what she perceived as a wealthy, jet-setting husband. Man, had she picked the wrong playboy.

Really, all along, he knew something was wrong with the situation, and he was actually glad to have finally figured it out. Of course, it took her being blatantly obvious, but the sex had obscured his reasoning. He saw now that he had been part of her formula: Go to the new, elite resort being run by single son of wealthy developer. Find son. Have sex with son. Marry son. Be rich wife of said son and live a life of luxury, or get huge alimony in a divorce. It was probably all the same to her. Never mind having the slightest clue about who your spouse was. That would be an incidental nicety, but not at all necessary.

He heard another enraged wail and something else hit the door behind him. After waiting a moment, he used his master key card to swiftly open the door, reached his arm inside and grabbed his shoes.

"Thank you."

He let the door shut as he heard another, more furious wail. Admitting to himself that grabbing his shoes that way had been obnoxious, he was nonetheless happy to have them on. He hustled down the hall, heading to the night office to collect Courtney, the one female he could count on at the moment.

Courtney was playing quietly on the floor in the back room of the office. She had slept for a while, but then awoke, and now she didn't feel tired. So, as she waited for her dad, she played with a plastic horse she had brought with her to Mrs. Gamino's. She trotted the horse around the pattern on the carpet, letting it jump over an obstacle she had made out of hotel pens and note pads.

Mrs. Gamino popped her head in the office. "Not sleepy?"

"No. Is my daddy coming soon?"

"I think you'll be asleep by the time he gets here," she said. "Give me a couple minutes and I'll come read a bedtime story to you. It's very late."

"OK."

She ran the horse over the carpet and made a little whinnying sound.

To her surprise, the whinny was answered by a real whinny. She froze, listening. She heard it again. It was definitely a horse's whinny. She got up and ran to the window and looked out into the darkness. This window, in the front of the building, looked over the valet parking lot, but she could also see a garden and the swell of the grounds beyond a wall. She heard the whinny again.

There it was! A loose horse trotted out on the grounds. It looked up at her and reared, like it was upset and trying to get her attention. Could it be Cocoa? Maybe Karla was wrong about him being dead! Maybe he was just knocked unconscious and now he was lost and he needed her help.

"Cocoa! I'm coming!"

Courtney ran out the back door of the office, wearing her nightgown and slippers, and hurried out through the nearest side exit into the garden. She ran across to the wall. It was tall, but she used the pot of a hibiscus tree to climb to the top.

She paused up there and called, "Cocoa!"

At first, she didn't see him, but as she strained her eyes through the dark, she spotted the horse again, pacing back and forth, tossing its head. It had run farther out across the grounds, nearer to the wild mesa. The horse had a strange, whitish glow around it.

"No, Cocoa! You're going the wrong way!" she yelled. "Come on! The stable is the other way!"

Courtney leaped down off the wall, and started running.

Maddie pulled into the stable lot with the headlights out. She didn't want to bother Karla, who lived in a small home at the other side of the parking lot, across from the barn. It wasn't until after she parked that she remembered Karla was away for the night. Hurrying up to her apartment, she pulled the small external drive out of her pocket and inserted it in the port on her laptop.

As she waited for the drive to open, she examined the pale pink crystal. It was exceptionally beautiful and clear. It was curious, as large as it was, it didn't seem to have facets the way quartz normally did. And the color was distinctive.

Finally, the drive finished loading. As hoped, it appeared to contain backups of Toby's client documents. She scrolled quickly to "Stanton, Millicent Clara" and opened the folder. She sorted the files by date, so that the most current would be on top. The second file down was the last will and testament. She noted that the date and time it was last saved was March 14 at 2:47 p.m. She thought about it for a minute. That was the day before Toby had left to go on his vacation, just before the big storm that had buried the region in snow. And it was the day Clara had died.

She saved a copy to her hard drive, so as not to change the date on the file, and opened the copy. It was short and simple, just like the one she had seen in Hector's office. However, this will was distinctly different.

Instead of the sentence that said Clara had sold her land to Crandall and all the proceeds from the sale after her death would go to Maddie, it said:

> I want to be clear in this last will and testament that my land is to stay in the Stanton-Cunningham family. This land has been in my family for many years, and it is the belief of my family that it contains the potential for great wealth, both spiritual and physical, and it should not cross out of our family's hands for any reason. Therefore, I entrust this land to my niece, Katherine Madeline Cunningham, under the condition that it will never be sold, not wholly or in part, and that it should pass only to her blood relatives. If no relative is born and the line should end, then the land is to be entrusted to a wildlife and land conservancy, in full.

Maddie sat back, horrified, yet also satisfied. She was right! The Crandall will was a fake. The police report had stated that, after her appointment with Toby, Clara was seen leaving town for home on the 4 p.m. bus. There was no way physically possible that a new will could have been generated by Toby and Clara before he left for New Mexico and before Clara died. Would this be enough to take to the probate court? Would it be enough for criminal charges?

She looked back at the folder and saw a file called "Stanton Notes." She saved a copy of this to her hard drive and opened it up. As she scanned the document, she felt great joy. Toby had kept notes dating back for years, documenting his meetings with Clara and his recommendations made to her. Included in the most recent notes was one saved on that same day. It said:

> I have again urged Clara to sell her land to Crandall, as the price he is offering is much higher than the going market rate, and having the money will lift her out of what is obviously a state bordering poverty. Despite my urgings, Clara has repeatedly refused to consider this proposal. She has also alluded to being in possession of documents she

refuses to share with me that are pertinent to the property. I'm sure that the original abstract or deed is among them, but there may be other documents that she feels she needs to protect. I have recommended that she place them in the security of a safe-deposit box, but she refuses.

"Yes!" said Maddie. Another nail in Crandall's coffin.

She settled in to read the other documents.

Still aggravated from his exchange with Rachel, Emerson decided to walk across the gardens to get some air, instead of tracking through the hotel hallways, on his way to pick up Courtney.

The clouds had blown off and it had become a beautiful clear night. The moon was almost full, and a light breeze blew from the south. He sat down at a table near the pool. It was closed, but a few green lights illuminated the bottom. He could hear the cheerful sound of partiers, across the way in the bar. He sighed, taking a deep breath, and felt some of the tension leave his upper back. He noticed he had not tied his shoes, so he bent to do so, just as a ratty piece of blue paper, tossed by the wind, tumbled by his foot.

Something on it caught his attention. It was the word, "Maddie," in large, fragile letters.

The paper blew into the pool, and Emerson lay on his belly to scoop it up. He held it carefully, smoothing it out on the tabletop. The paper was dirty and torn, the writing faded, but he could still make out the message.

Maddie,

Crandall has killed me. He has taken the land illegally. This is your land. Take it back. Protect it! Look at the base of the tree.

Emerson read this note several more times. A clammy sweat beaded at his brow, and his heart, which had just started to slow down, now pounded again. The question that had dogged him since speaking to the sales clerk at the sporting goods store now spread through his body, chilling him.

"Crandall has killed me."

He looked up in the direction of his father's window. The lights were still on and he saw a silhouette pass the sheer curtains. He looked at the note again.

"Look at the base of the tree."

There was no question which tree it meant. Emerson jumped up and strode to the ponderosa, where it still towered above the hotel in the center of the courtyard. Its base was now adorned with flowering annuals. He dropped to his knees and started scrabbling at the dirt. He worked his way around the base, feeling through the loose topsoil, scraping it away. Finally, his hand felt a rope. He grasped it and yanked hard, leaning back with his body to pull open a small door. It was a hinged lid, covering a square container, stuck firmly in the ground at the base of the tree. He reached inside and his hand found a metal box. He grasped it and lifted, but it would not move far. He continued feeling around and discovered it was chained in place. He yanked and jerked at the chain, but it was thick and heavy, and he could not get it to yield.

He sat back on his thighs, thinking, then stood. He hurried to the gardener's shed at the back corner of the pool garden. It was locked, but this was easily fixed with a sharp kick. He went in and emerged with bolt cutters and a flashlight. Holding the light in his teeth, he snapped through the chain with the powerful tool. He yanked the box out of the hole and carried it back to the light of the pool patio. Using the bolt cutters, he beat on the metal hinges until they gave way. He peeled back the lid and peered inside.

He saw a thick envelope, a jar of crystals and a pink silk bag. He opened the bag and pulled out two pendants, their strings braided carefully together. They each held a large, pink stone, one in a gold, heart-shaped setting and the other artfully woven to its setting with fine silver wire. He tucked them back in the bag and picked up the small jar, holding it up against the light. The stones shimmered, some tiny, but some as big as marbles, some pink, some clear. He put the jar and the bag in his jeans pockets. Then he opened the envelope and unfolded the contents. A map, a deed and a letter. His hand now shaking, he began to read.

Dear Maddie,
I want to tell you a story that is wonderful and exciting and maybe hard to believe.

He went on to read Clara's story of Asa and Mayla. When he finished, Emerson tucked the documents back in the envelope. Then he looked again at the scrawled note he had pulled from the pool, now dry and fragile on the poolside table.

He put his face in his hands. He wished he didn't know. He didn't want to know. Suddenly his stomach lurched, and he hurried to the edge of the poolside garden, where he got on his hands and knees and vomited.

When he was done, he slid into a sitting position, gasping for breath. He felt like he had been punched in the stomach. Then he stood up. He had to get Courtney. That was the only thing he could think about right now.

Chapter 39

Maddie had just finished looking through all of her aunt's legal files when she heard a noise in the stable. It sounded like a frantic horse, blowing and stomping. She closed the small drive and ejected it, putting it in her pocket. The noise continued. She hurried down the outside stairs that brought her to the stable door.

Some of the stabled horses nickered nervously, agitated and looking down the aisle. She turned on the overhead lights, but they were the type that were very slow to come on. Hurrying down the aisle, she looked around to find out what was wrong. In the dim light, she saw a terrible sight. The horse, Bop, was tied in his stall, and a man was whipping him across the face and neck with a riding crop. The horse was pulling back against the rope, trying to escape.

"Stop that!" Maddie shouted.

The man turned around and smiled. She recognized him as the person who had watched her that day a few weeks back, the one who had made her so uncomfortable.

"Oh, it's you," he said, smiling as though he had happened on her at a cocktail party.

The lights were coming on fully now, casting a creepy blue glow about the stable and buzzing loudly. He quickly approached the stall door, smiling and holding the crop. She could see that his eyes were very red, his pupils unusually large. It didn't take an expert to see that he was high on something. Without looking away from him, she quickly moved out of his reach and pulled out her cell phone. She dialed 911 and hit "send" just before he flew at her.

"Put that fucking phone down," he said, knocking it out of her hand furiously. It hit the wall and then fell on the cement aisleway, smashing apart.

She turned to run, but he shoved her hard from behind and she fell forward. She hit the floor, slamming her chin, and rolled onto her back. He was trying to hold her by the legs and she kicked him hard in the nose. She scrambled up and ran.

"Everything go OK?" Emerson asked Mrs. Gamino.

"Oh yes. She was as good as gold, just like always, but she woke up and couldn't get back to sleep," said Mrs. Gamino. "When I checked on her last, she was playing with her horse on the carpet. She said she wasn't ready to go back to bed yet, and I didn't push it."

"That's fine. Thanks for watching her." He gave her fifty dollars, which she accepted.

"You're too generous," she said. "I used to only make a dollar an hour when I babysat."

"You're worth it."

She looked at him with concern.

"Are you OK, Mr. Crandall? You don't look so good."

"Tough night." He tried to smile, but just couldn't muster it. "I'll go get her. Hopefully, she's asleep."

He went into the back office and opened the door. The room was empty.

Unnerved, Crandall decided to take a walk through the hotel. He wanted to be around other people. There would be someone in the office, and maybe some other insomniac out in the gardens.

He started down the hallway, but he felt that he was not alone. He cast a fearful glance back and thought he saw the shape of an elderly woman down the hall. He quickly turned and hurried away from it. Up ahead, he was certain he saw a figure ducking into a doorway of a room. When he approached it, he stayed on the opposite side of the hall, and cast a wary look toward the doorway. There was no one there. But as he turned back, he saw the translucent figure of an American Indian woman standing in the doorway of the room right next to him. In the brief glance he had, he saw her face stretched in a terrible gape and she held a hatchet high

254

over his head. Crandall ran down the hall to the stairway door. To his horror, the hatchet hit the door jamb right by his head, burying itself an inch into the frame.

He wrenched the door open and cast a look behind him, expecting to see the woman closing in on him. But there was nothing. The hallway was empty. Looking up at the door jamb, he saw the hatchet was gone. The metal frame was solid and undamaged. With a moan, he opened the door and hurried down the steps.

Emerson called Security, then ran up to his suite to see if, by some chance, Courtney had gone back up there by herself. It was well past 3 a.m. Where could she be? His mind raced with terrible images of her getting out into a hallway and being collected by some pedophile who might be staying in the hotel. He started yelling her name as he ran, disturbing the guests, but he didn't care. If she was in someone's room, he wanted to know.

The two security guards were in the office when he got back down.

"Help me find her!" Emerson said. "Search the place. She could be anywhere."

He ran outside into the garden, yelling her name. Maybe she had gone down to the stable.

He started running across the garden. Just ahead, he saw the shape of a man, a man in a cowboy hat, hovering just out of sight in the trees.

"Hey!" he yelled.

But then the figure seemed to vanish before him. A terrible, creepy feeling filled Emerson, but he kept going. Courtney was all he could think about.

Then he felt a rumbling under foot. In a split second, the ground was shaking and rolling under him and a branch fell, hitting him hard on the shoulder. He dropped to his knees, rubbing the injury. His shirt had torn. The rumbling stopped and he realized that he had experienced an earthquake.

When he stood up, the cowboy was standing in front of him. But instead of flesh and blood, he saw a terrible, rotting skeletal figure, its teeth grinning in front of an oozy, black tongue. The figure fell at him and Emerson ran, panicking, through the garden. He burst into a small clearing and noticed a pale figure leaning over a cast iron bench. Small, pink lights lit the garden prettily, and in this dim light, he was terrified as he approached the figure. He didn't want to look, but felt compelled. He reached out and touched the woman's ice-cold shoulder. The slight touch sent the body tumbling off the bench onto its back and he saw his Aunt Irma's face, frozen in an expression of terror.

Emerson yelled and continued running. He groped for his cell phone as he went. He ran past a decorative rock outcrop that slanted up at a sharp angle away from the garden. As he was fumbling with his phone, he heard another rumbling sound. Looking up to his left, he saw a basketball-size rock tumbling down the outcrop. He dove to the left, his phone sailing out of his hand, and hit the ground at the same time as the rock hit his foot with a nauseating crack.

"Holy crap!"

He sat up and felt his foot. Maybe broken. He fumbled around for his phone and saw it under the rock, crushed.

He rolled onto his hands and knees, then tried to stand. He eased himself up and gingerly tried to put some weight on the foot. He was in excruciating pain. He heard another rumble from the outcrop. Looking up, he saw the figure of the cowboy near the top, and as he watched, it seemed like the whole side of the outcrop was starting to slide. Pain or not, he got up and ran. He got clear just as the mountain of rock crashed across the garden path.

Racing out of the garden as fast as his pain allowed, he entered the road that would take him to the stable. When he looked back, he saw the shadow of a figure watching him from the edge of the garden.

"What the hell is happening?" he said aloud, his voice sounding high and strange.

He turned and started toward the stable.

Derrick barely felt the blood running from his nose. He touched it and examined the thick, glistening drop on his finger. If anything, it revved him up even more for the hunt. After he left Esponzio, he had downed a half a quart of bourbon, popped four amphetamines, and snorted two lines of coke. Once he felt fully charged up, a raging bundle of energy, he had headed for the stable.

He had found the horse Maddie rode the most, tied it on two sides and started to hit it, knowing it would eventually make enough noise to bring Maddie down. Beating the horse had given him a brutal satisfaction and revved his anticipation for Maddie.

He had not anticipated the broken nose, but it only increased his appetite. He lit a cigarette, took a couple long drags, then dropped it. He stepped on it as he walked quietly in the direction she had run. He had not fully extinguished it, though, and it burned slowly, next to some loose hay that had been missed during the daily sweep of the barn aisle.

"Kathy," he called in a high, sing-song voice. "Kathy. Or should I call you Maddie? Yeah, I know who you are. Come out now and play." He walked casually down the aisle, completely certain that he would get what he wanted in the end, and, in his high state of mind, looking forward to the fight.

Maddie crouched by the tack room door. She had run this way, thinking it was the fastest way to get to Karla's house, and a phone, but she remembered too late that the door was locked from outside every night. She was trapped.

She was holding a shovel. It was light enough for her to swing, but heavy enough to knock a man out cold, given a good enough hit. She was counting on a good enough hit. She heard the man calling her name. Jesus, he was jacked up. She knew the drugs made him twice as dangerous.

As he approached, he grew quieter. She listened, trying to gauge the right moment, every nerve on end.

Courtney had followed the horse onto the mesa. But when she was so far out she could no longer see the lights of the resort, it vanished. Scared, alone, and lost, she was wandering around, crying and calling for her father.

She could feel the earth shaking occasionally, and she wondered if this was an earthquake.

Then she heard a terrible screaming cry from above. Looking up, she saw a giant bird, talons bared, diving at her with what looked to be fire trailing behind it. She screamed and ducked, and at the moment it should have struck her, she felt a fiery burning against her skin.

She started to run. The fiery bird was flying behind her, swooping at her, filling her with burning pain. As she ran, she heard the sound of hoof beats behind her. Turning hopefully, she saw a pale, spotted horse giving chase as well, charging at her. She ran faster, her little legs churning. Every time she turned to look behind her, it seemed that the horse was right on top of her, rearing up over her, about to dash her head open with its hooves. She screamed and ran on.

Then, she realized where she was running. She was heading right toward the same cliff that Cocoa had gone over. The burning bird and the bad horse were trying to chase her off the cliff! She stopped at the edge and turned back. The horse bore down on her, rearing up over her again, and the bird flew straight at her head. She stood at the edge of the cliff, trying to balance, her arms circling. Then the edge crumbled and she started to fall.

Emerson got to the stable. Looking behind him, he could see the shape of the cowboy coming along the path at a steady pace. He ran through into the lighted aisle.

"Courtney!" he yelled.

Derrick heard a man's voice yelling in the stable, but it was as though from another dimension, not in the same one as Derrick. He slid along the wall. She would have found a weapon, he thought. She was smart. She knew how to fight.

As he got to the corner of the wall, he crouched. She leapt out. She yelled and swung the spade where his head would have been if he hadn't crouched at the last minute. It hit the wall above his head and he leapt on her. He flattened her under him on the hard cement floor and started groping madly at her jeans, trying to yank them down. She kicked at him and yelled again, fighting and wiggling. He slammed her head against the concrete and she lay still for a moment, then moaned.

"Courtney!" came the frantic male voice.

"Help! Help! Emerson! Help!" She started to struggle again.

The figure of a limping man appeared in silhouette.

"Hello?" he called.

"Jesus!" said Derrick. He punched Maddie hard, then got up, picking up the shovel at the same time. He ran at Emerson, swinging wildly at his head.

"Hey!" Emerson said, ducking.

The shovel hit his shoulder, and he fell. Derrick raised the shovel and drove it at Emerson's neck. Emerson rolled aside and the spade hit the concrete with a sharp sound. Emerson stood and Derrick hit him again with the spade, knocking him face forward, and he lay still. Then Derrick felt a slam on the back of his head and he saw a flash. Maddie had hit him from behind, and now she was running.

He got up and ran after her. He caught her near the stall where the beaten horse was tied. A small flame was burning on the floor. He dove at Maddie and took her down from behind. Her wrist made a sickening snap. She screamed in pain. He tore her shirt open and grabbed at her breasts roughly from behind.

Crandall ran down two flights of stairs. He paused at the landing and looked up. Looking over the bannister at him, smiling mildly, was the ghostly face of Clara Stanton. Crandall yelled and ran down another two flights. He caught his foot and fell flat at the bottom. Cursing, he looked at the door and noticed that he was at the kitchen level. He stepped through the doors.

"Hello?" he called. Of course, the kitchen was silent. No one was there at that hour. It was too early for the morning staff and too late for the evening staff. He made his way toward the back door of the kitchen. He was surprised to see lights on.

"Hello? Is anyone here?" He walked through the kitchen, hurrying, almost on tip toes, listening for any unusual sound.

As he approached the cooking area, he smelled something strange. He looked cautiously around the corner of the cabinets and saw Raffie's body, head still in the pot. Crandall approached him, and pulled back on the cold body. Raffie fell onto the floor. His body was stiff and cold, his face boiled beyond recognition.

Crandall shrieked. He heard a noise behind him. He leapt over Raffie's body and darted toward the back of the kitchen.

Looking madly for someplace to hide, he wrenched open a door and bolted through. He immediately realized he had made a mistake. He had run into the freezer. It was large and stacked high with five-gallon containers of ice-cream and large boxes of food, all frosted over slightly in a temperature kept at a steady, zero degrees Fahrenheit. Like all walk-in freezers, it had a handle on the inside to prevent anyone from getting trapped. However, this freezer also had a lock on the outside, which had been special-ordered by Crandall himself, to prevent theft. As Crandall was turning around to leave the freezer, the lock turned on the outside, as though moved by an invisible hand. He was trapped.

Emerson sat up, heard the sounds of a struggle and picked up the shovel. In the bright light of the stable, he saw Derrick on top of a woman, and a fire burning near them. Emerson continued toward Derrick and swung the shovel handle hard in a sweeping movement, smacking Derrick's chin, knocking him backward. The woman rolled over groggily and Emerson was astonished to see it was Maddie.

"Watch out!" she yelled, just as Derrick launched himself at Emerson. The two men hit the ground and rolled.

"Fire!" Maddie yelled.

Emerson realized that he and Derrick were rolling right toward the growing flame. He shoved himself away from Derrick. He noticed Derrick's eyes were wild and red, and his actions were unnaturally animated. Derrick swung the shovel at Emerson.

"Derrick, stop! It's me! It's Emerson!"

Derrick paused and said, "Why, it's Emerson. The most eligible bachelor. My egghead cousin who gets to work up on the second floor."

He pulled the shovel back like a baseball bat. He put a lot of hatred into the swing.

"With Daddy!"

Emerson partially blocked it, so it didn't hit him full on the head, but he went down.

"You always got everything you wanted, you little shit," Derrick said, stepping over Emerson and kicking him in the face on the way.

Maddie tried to scramble away from him but he stopped her with a boot to the back. The flames were spreading. The horses were trapped in their stalls, stomping and spinning in terror.

Emerson stood shakily, then leapt onto Derrick, who fell forward, into the stall where the terrified horse was still tied. The flames climbed up the far wall. Emerson hurried to Maddie.

"We have to get out of here," he said.

"Hurry," she said. "The horses!"

She seemed woozy, so he picked her up, carrying her as fast as he could, out the door and far from the stable. He set her down gently, where she leaned against the fence of the paddock.

"Are you all right?"

"The horses! Let the horses out!"

He turned and ran back into the barn, still limping. One by one, he opened the stall doors, and the horses ran through the big open door and out. The one horse was still tied up, and the flames were starting to burn around the entrance of its stall. Emerson grabbed a bucket of water from the next stall and dumped it over his head so it soaked his hair and shirt. He darted through the flames to the horse and started to untie it, working on the knots while the horse yanked back and forth.

He finally untied the last knot and felt a hand on his leg. Derrick had come to, still fighting.

"No!" Emerson said. "The building is on fire!"

Just then the white horse struck out with its front hoof in a lightning fast motion that hit Derrick squarely on the forehead.

It was the last blow that Derrick would take. He was killed instantly.

"Jesus," said Emerson, looking down at his cousin's vacant expression.

The timbers creaked overhead. Emerson grabbed a hold of the horse's mane near the top of its neck, and the horse jumped over

Derrick's body and galloped out the barn door, partly dragging Emerson as he tried to run along with it.

Once clear of the barn, Emerson let go and fell rolling on the dusty ground. With a frightening crack, the roof of the stable fell in. Flames poured through the open door, fed by the light morning breeze, raging thirty feet in the air.

He crawled over to Maddie and flopped down next to her. Her face was dirty. Her cheek was bruised and her eye was swollen from Derrick's punch.

"That man?"

"Dead."

"You knew him?"

"Yeah."

"You saved the horses."

"Yeah."

They watched the fire. After a moment, Emerson tensed. He was sure that he saw the image of the cowboy, standing in the flames, right in the stable door, watching him steadily.

"Holy Christ," Emerson said, tense, wondering what was next.

The cowboy turned toward him.

"You saved me, too." Maddie said.

"Yeah," he said, still focused on the figure. He pushed himself upright, getting ready. For what, he did not know.

"Do you see that?" he whispered.

She looked at him, then followed his frightened stare.

"See what?" she asked, tensing, too.

The cowboy stepped out of the flames and Emerson could see him more clearly. He couldn't believe his eyes. Instead of the horrifying, rotting, skeletal figure he had seen before, now he saw a lean and rugged man. The man pushed his hat back and Emerson saw his golden green eyes. Like Maddie's eyes, he thought, startled.

Then the cowboy smiled, tipped his hat at Emerson, and turned, walking casually off into the dawn, gradually disappearing as he went.

Emerson noticed the sense of anxiety he felt for months suddenly lifted. Without knowing why, he could tell he didn't need to be afraid anymore.

"See what?" Maddie whispered again, urgently.

"Nothing," Emerson said. "Never mind."

He groaned to his feet, feeling every bump and bruise. His ankle still throbbed, but he guessed it was not broken, after all.

"My daughter is missing. I have to find her. You didn't see a little girl down here, did you?"

He looked at the burning stable and his stomach tied up in a ball. What if she was in there? No, impossible. He would have found her by now. She would have come out when she heard the voices.

"No, Courtney wasn't down here tonight."

Emerson looked at her sharply, suddenly remembering that Courtney had identified Maddie as the person who saved her just before her pony went over the cliff.

"Have you been working down here?" he said in wonder.

"Yes. But not any longer. I quit, so you don't have to fire me. I found the proof I need. Your father stole this land from my aunt, and he may have even killed her and her lawyer."

The words hit Emerson like cold water, the sick feeling knotting his stomach again. "I found something too," he said.

He pulled the envelope out of his pocket and handed it to her.

She looked at him in wonder and started to read quickly by the light of the burning stable.

"My daughter," he said. "Do you have a car?"

He saw headlights coming from the resort. Someone must have seen the flames.

He realized that Maddie's shirt was ripped open, and he could clearly see her white lace bra over her breasts and her pale, flat stomach. He stood and quickly took his T-shirt off and held it out to her. She was still reading, and didn't notice.

"Here," he said, touching her with it. "Where's your car?"

She lifted her face toward him a little, but her eyes still focused on the letter.

"Well?" he snapped.

She looked up at him with a furious satisfaction. "I knew it."

"My daughter is missing," he said angrily, still holding the shirt out to her. "I need to find her. I need a car. And put this on."

She seemed to hear him for the first time. She took the shirt and slipped it over her head, pulling her torn one off from underneath. She wrapped the torn one tightly around her wrist, gasping with pain. She started to stand and he quickly held out his hand to help her.

"We'll take the ATV," she said. "It can cover more ground."

Chapter 40

Crandall tugged at the handle of the freezer. He pounded. He yelled.

"Help! Get me out of here! I'm trapped! Help!"

"It's cold, isn't it?" said a gentle voice behind him.

He stopped in mid-pound, all his senses on the alert.

"Oh yes, it's very cold," said the voice.

He turned around slowly. There was the body of Clara Stanton, sprawled out on the freezer floor next to him. Her eyes were frozen open, the eyeballs looking hard and icy. Her lips, too, were frozen solid, slightly parted. Crandall's feet slid out from under him and he sank to a sitting position, but he scrambled to get up, trying to get away from the terrible sight. He put his hands over his eyes and yelled, "No!"

When he opened his eyes, her body was gone.

He was shaking uncontrollably. He wrapped his robe around him and sat down, tucking his legs up to his chin. He was going to die here, he knew. They had caught him at last and there was nothing he could do. Clara Stanton was going to get her revenge after all.

"Damn you," he moaned, tightening the robe around him. "I didn't even kill you. The power went off anyway."

Crandall saw his hopes for the resort, the money, the power, all sailing away from him.

"Damn you!" he said.

"Don't worry," whispered a voice next to his ear. "It's not so bad, freezing to death."

He turned his head slowly and saw her icy body sitting right next to him, a frozen smile on her glazed face. Then, the freezer went dark.

Crandall screamed.

Emerson drove the ATV as fast as it could go to the resort. A thunder storm was rolling in from the west. Lightning flashed soundlessly through the dawn, and thunder rumbled.

As they approached the hotel, Emerson noticed some of the kitchen staff arriving, telling him it was nearly 5 a.m. Just then, a police car pulled up, lights flashing. Two officers emerged, and one of them spotted Emerson.

"Mr. Crandall!" he said, hurrying over, his hand on his heavy belt to keep the tools there from hitting him as he ran. "What the hell is going on up here?"

Emerson got out of the ATV.

"My daughter is missing."

"I'm going to keep looking for Courtney," said Maddie, driving away.

Emerson noted that she headed around the perimeter of the hotel grounds, then turned north toward the rocky cliffs.

"We have gotten three separate calls from here," the officer was saying. "The first was a 911 call that got disconnected before we could speak to the caller, the next reported a body in the kitchen and another reported a body in the garden."

"Yes, my aunt, she's dead," Emerson said vaguely, still looking after Maddie. "In the garden." The officers' words suddenly hit him. "A body in the kitchen?"

"Your aunt? Did you make the call?"

"Whose body is in the kitchen?" Emerson said frantically, starting to run toward the hotel.

"Mr. Crandall, wait,"

A bright flash of lightning lit the sky, accompanied immediately by a deafening crack of thunder. On the south side of the cliffs, there came the distinctive, distant sound of a blast of dynamite. And then, the earth began to shake.

This time it wasn't just a tremor. The ground moved so much that Emerson was thrown backward. A deep crack in the earth started 300 yards away, in the rocky cliffs north of the resort, and it ran along the earth, right toward the hotel. The ground began caving in directly under the center of the hotel, and the huge structure started to quiver.

With a splitting sound, the entire center section of the hotel dropped straight down into the earth.

Emerson paused in horror, watching it go. Then, the screams of people inside caused him to start running again. The guests. The employees. He ran, knowing he had to try to get as many out as he could.

Crandall, hunched in the freezer, barely breathing, felt the earthquake as though from a different world. He was unable to react. He had stopped shaking a while ago, and his body had stiffened around him. Then he felt the hotel start to move, and he heard the cracking and snapping of boards and metal as the walls quaked and the hotel sank. The freezer abruptly tumbled onto its side. Shelves of frozen food crashed across the room. The freezer seam split open and a gap appeared in the corner.

Crandall was tossed around, and this caused him to revive. He saw the opening and crawled toward it. As he went, the blood started circulating in his body again, and he shook uncontrollably. The hotel heaved again like a giant, sinking ship. He eased through the split in the corner of the freezer and started climbing, still on his hands and knees, toward the light of the dawn. All around him, walls were making popping sounds and things were crashing, but all he could think of was getting out of the building, away from the freezer. Away from Clara Stanton.

He climbed over debris blocking the back of the hotel, and up the rocky edge of the fissure. When he reached the surface, he slowly stood, still shaking, and gazed around in wonder and horror at the hotel. People were screaming and running away from it. Nearby, someone was trapped under the giant, granite front desk, yelling for help.

Crandall was standing in the garden. He suddenly realized that he not only had escaped the freezer, but he had escaped death during the earthquake.

Still shivering, he started to laugh.

"I beat you, you old wench!" he yelled. "I beat you anyway!"

Just then, he heard an ominous creaking. It was close, but not coming from the hotel. He turned his head, and so, he saw it coming. The giant ponderosa, its roots loosened by the earthquake, crashed upon him, crushing him to death.

Chapter 41

Emerson scrambled frantically through the debris of the hotel, yelling for Courtney. Guests were hurrying out of their rooms, trying to find a way out of the building. This wing of the hotel had shifted to a steep angle, with the center of the hotel underground in the wide crack that had opened in the earth.

"That way!" Emerson yelled, pointing up the hallway. "Go up. Get out the fire door by the stairs!"

Any doors that were closed, he opened with his master key. When he found guests, most confused and scared, he helped them out, directing them toward the exit. Soon, he noticed some of the guests were staying to help him, and so now he could hurry through the hallways, opening doors while others came in behind, guiding those inside toward the nearest exit. Firefighters appeared, also helping with the rescues.

As he reached the rooms at the end of the wing, he realized that the fastest way out for those in this part of the hotel was to smash their room windows and crawl out onto the ground.

He heard screaming inside the last room and opened the door. To his shock, he found Rachel in there, dressed only in a man's T-shirt. She was screaming hysterically. On the floor nearby, investment expert Emilio Esponzio sat naked, looking bewildered, blood trickling down his forehead, his round belly perched on his stumpy genitalia.

Rachel stopped screaming abruptly and stared at Emerson, eyes wide with a new fear. It took Emerson a few seconds to grasp what he was seeing.

"You have an interesting way of getting over a broken heart," he said, hurrying past her and kneeling by Esponzio. She started to run out the door.

"Not that way. Too dangerous."

He got up and grabbed a marble-based lamp from the bedside.

"Cover your face."

He threw the lamp through the window, wrapped his arm in a blanket and broke away the glass shards. He laid the blanket across the sill and held out his hand, glaring at her.

She took it, cast him a frightened look and, with his help, jumped up to the ground. He went back to Esponzio, who was still dazed.

"Come on. Time to go."

Emerson gently helped him stand, wrapped him in a sheet and guided him up through the window.

"Rachel!" he yelled. "Get him to the paramedics. Rachel!"

She was gone.

"Nice," Emerson said. "Mr. Esponzio, go to that ambulance."

The man looked back at him, not comprehending, a tear dripping off his chin. A concussion, Emerson thought, or maybe Rachel had screwed his brains out. She was good at doing that. He pointed toward the main entrance, across the lawn.

"Walk that way, toward the flashing lights."

Esponzio nodded and started off obediently, the sheet draped over his shoulders, trailing behind him like a baby blanket, his pudgy backside jiggling as he walked.

Emerson noticed that, somewhere along the way, he had gained bloody scratches on his chest and stomach, so he grabbed one of Mr. Esponzio's clean T-shirts and put it on. Blood immediately dotted the white shirt. He left the room and hurried to the next floor.

Maddie's wrist throbbed with every bump the ATV went over. She drove around the perimeter of the grounds, then veered off to the north, looking for Courtney. She was driving near the pale yellow and red cliffs by the waterfall.

"Oh please," she said to herself. "Please don't let her be hurt."

She was heading in the general direction of the place where Cocoa had landed when the earthquake started. The ATV rocked and shook, and the steering wheel was momentarily yanked out of her hand. Just then, the fissure that would, within seconds, destroy the hotel, opened up, right under her wheels. She pressed the gas pedal to the floor, but before it could gain traction, both back wheels dropped over the edge of the crack. She gunned the motor, but though they spun, the front wheels couldn't hold the weight of the vehicle, and down it went, with Maddie, into the crack. About five feet down the vehicle got wedged against the dirt sides of the crack, and Maddie was dumped downward until she hit bottom.

Her wrist hurt, and she was bruised and scraped, but she had worse trouble. She knew it was probable that this fissure would close up again and crush her to death.

She heard a deep, ominous rumbling. The rocky hill above her was breaking up. There was a crunching, rushing, freight-train-like sound and then a huge boulder the size of an elephant fell down into the fissure, smashing the ATV to splinters and wedging itself firmly in the crack.

Maddie screamed and covered her head with her arms, ducking from the falling pieces of metal and chunks of the rock wall.

Hoping this gigantic boulder would hold the fissure open long enough for her to get out, Maddie started to crawl along the debris-strewn ground. Her knees and shins scraped painfully along the sharp rocks. She looked up to the top of the crevice. It was about twenty feet, almost straight up. An experienced rock climber, she could have done it on a normal day. But it was not a normal day. Her wrist was broken. She would not be able to do it.

The ground creaked. Dirt, pebbles and rocks crumbled from the walls of the crevice.

The sun was just starting to come up over the mesa when Emerson climbed out of a window of the hotel that had once been three stories high, but now was almost at ground level.

Emergency services, ambulances, police and fire trucks, had come from all the towns and cities within 100 miles of the resort. The hotel seemed to be empty of people now. Those who were rescued were mostly just bruised and scraped and receiving first aid. There were very few major injuries, and they hadn't found any bodies inside, except for the one presumed to be Raffie's.

Emerson's body was scratched all over. His head, face and body were bruised from his fight with Derrick, and he was exhausted. He scanned the ground for signs of Courtney, Maddie or the ATV. Nothing. Then he noticed that the fissure that had engulfed the hotel ran to the north rocks, the same place he had seen Maddie driving just before the hotel had sunk.

With a fresh panic, he set off at a run toward the hill.

"Maddie!" he yelled as he ran. "Maddie!"

He paused a ways up to catch his breath, bending over with his hands on his knees, panting, feeling desperate. Then he heard it.

"Help! Emerson! Help!"

It was faint. He lifted his head with a burst of hope.

"Help! Emerson! Down here!"

He ran. The ground was strewn with loose pebbles and sand, making it difficult. He got to the edge and looked down. It felt like his heart stopped beating for a moment when he saw her, he was so relieved to see she was OK. But then the ground made a threatening creaking sound.

"I'll be right back."

He thundered to the edge of the hotel grounds and grabbed a coil of snow fencing. He hurried back to the crack and unrolled it, feeding it down toward her. She grabbed it and prepared herself for what would be a slow and painful climb. He wanted to climb down and help, but there was nothing to which to secure the fencing, and it would have fallen in without his weight at the top.

The sun was climbing slightly higher, and as he watched, he noticed a strange sparkling behind Maddie's head. The light was starting to hit down inside the crevice. He gazed around Maddie. The ground and stony walls were ablaze with sparkling light.

"Maddie, look!"

She followed his gaze and looked around her. A brilliant blazing vein of sparkling stones lined the crevice. She bent down and picked up some rocks from the bottom. Amid the stony debris, she found clear crystals, some pink, some colorless, and many were large, clear and gorgeous.

She looked up at him and grinned.

Just then the walls of the crevice creaked and shifted. Maddie stuffed the stones in her pocket and grasped the fencing, trying to climb, but her wrist could not hold her weight. The walls started moving.

"I can't do it!"

"Just hang on."

Emerson leaned his weight back and, hand over hand, he hauled the fence out of the quivering crevice. Finally, she got close enough to the top for him to grab her arms. The ground made one last powerful rumble and, as quickly as it appeared, the crack started to close. With a final burst, Emerson yanked her clear and they scrambled away from the crevice. It closed with a squeal and a pop. The large bolder that had held the crack open just long enough for him to get her free still remained, sticking out of the ground like a giant bookmark.

The noise suddenly coming from the hotel was thunderous, and they sat up and watched, in time to see the center section that had dropped into the crack being crushed as the ground closed in around it. The two wings flanking the fallen section now collapsed inward, imploding and blasting out a cloud of dust that hid the hotel from view for a moment.

"Oh no. All the people!"

"I think we got everybody out."

For the first time, Emerson wondered where his father was.

"Courtney?" she said.

"I haven't found her."

His mind went temporarily numb, needing a break from the anxiety, fear and pain he had been experiencing for the last few hours. His gaze rose blankly out over the expanse of mesa, where the sun was now rising. Then he noticed something, a speck on the horizon. It took him a moment for his brain to make sense of it, but then he focused on it sharply.

Maddie noticed his expression and swung her head around. She, too, saw it, a shape approaching at a steady jog. It looked to be a person on a horse. Specifically, it looked to be a girl on a mostly white horse with black spots. The haze of heat made it difficult to focus, and as the figure got closer, the image changed weirdly to that of a little girl running toward them.

"Courtney!"

Emerson ran to her, scooping her up and hugging her hard. Maddie pulled herself upright, tears welling in her eyes.

Courtney hugged her father, but then started squirming when Emerson held on too long.

"Daddy! It's OK! Put me down."

He didn't, but instead propped her away from his body so he could look at her face.

"Are you OK? You're not hurt?"

"No! I'm OK."

He hugged her again and kissed her hair, pressing his cheek against her head.

"Daddy! Put me down!"

He finally did and she went to Maddie, giving her a big hug.

"Bugle brought me home!" she whispered. "He didn't try to hurt me anymore."

The tears that were welling in Maddie's eyes now spilled over. She didn't know what to say, or what to make of this comment.

Emerson had followed Courtney over, and now he pulled her into another hug and kissed her cheek again. Maddie noticed tears in his eyes, too.

"You wait here with Maddie," he said to Courtney.

To Maddie, he said, "Don't move. I'll be right back."

He limped off toward the crowd at the hotel, emerging within a couple of minutes, driving an ATV from the storage garage.

"Climb on, kiddo," he said.

Courtney jumped up onto the seat. Emerson went to Maddie and helped her climb in next to Courtney. He got behind the wheel, so they were all three crushed together on the narrow bench seat.

He turned and hugged Courtney again, and kissed the top of her head.

"Daddy!" Courtney protested, giggling. "Stop it!"

He laughed and looked over at Maddie. Despite the signs of her tough night, a scratch on her bruised cheek, the T-shirt torn and filthy, her golden-green eyes tinged with exhaustion, he thought she might be the most beautiful thing he had ever seen. On impulse, he reached over and briefly closed his hand over hers as she rested it on the seat. She looked sharply at him, surprised, then smiled a funny, halfway smile.

OK, he'd take that. He grinned at Courtney, then Maddie. He turned the ATV around, heading back toward the hotel.

But then Maddie saw something that made her yell, "Stop!"

He did, sitting up, alert, ready, once again, for action. "What?"

At about the same spot where Courtney had started running to them, Maddie thought she saw the hazy outline of an old-fashioned, buckboard wagon. Yes, there it was, hitched to a black-

and-white spotted horse. As the image became clearer, she saw a cowboy was helping an elderly woman up onto the seat, next to a pretty American Indian woman already seated there, a small white and tan dog standing up on her lap, wagging its stubby tail rapidly and smelling the air. Once the elderly lady was settled, the cowboy looked over his shoulder at Maddie and touched his hat. Then he walked around and climbed up on the other side. The elderly woman turned and smiled at Maddie as the horse started trotting.

"Aunt Clara!" Maddie murmured. She could actually hear the creaking of the seat springs, the clomping of the hooves and the crunching of the hard metal wheels. The wagon made a half-turn and started away from them, gradually disappearing into the hazy glare of the October sun.

"Goodbye," Courtney said.

"Goodbye," Maddie whispered.

Emerson sighed. He was exhausted, confused and in pain. The day had just started, and one glance over his shoulder at the hotel told him it was going to be a long one.

Yet, his heart was happy. He lingered a few moments more, just enjoying having them both next to him for this one, sunny moment, with no one, absolutely no one else, around.

Finally, he started the ATV again, toward the hotel.

"Here we go."

Whatever else awaited him, he was fairly certain that the spirits were finally at peace.

The End

Note from the author:

I hope you enjoyed *The Crandall Haunting*. If you did, please remember to leave a positive review at the site from which you purchased it. Positive reviews help others to find and enjoy this book.

Read on for a preview of its terrifying sequel, *For Sissy*!

For information about me and my work, please visit my webpage, www.ahgilbert.com, and sign up for updates!

Thanks for choosing *The Crandall Haunting*!

– A.H. Gilbert

For Sissy

~|~

Martin paused in his work.

Why did that little girl look familiar?

His hands were wet and sticky as he fumbled for his cigarettes in the dim room, which was lit only by the television and a single-bulb lamp in the corner. He lit one and sat back, squinting through the smoke at the TV. The local news was sharing a clip from its national affiliate about a trial, soon to start, in a county just outside of Denver. Martin didn't care about the trial—something about a hotel that collapsed—but that girl caught his attention.

He knew her face.

Martin shuffled his feet, making room on the cluttered floor, the black plastic rustling under his sneakers. The shoes, once white, were now stained. He would throw them out shortly and get a new pair. He leaned against the stiff wooden chair, found the TV remote, stopped the news, and hit "Reverse." There she was. He hit "Play."

A tall, dark-haired man—presumably the girl's father—stared at the camera as he walked with the girl, holding her hand as they attempted to hurry down the sidewalk, looking startled by the aggressive approach of the reporters with cameras. The shot lingered briefly on the girl before going back to the man, who, the screen caption said, was the hotel's owner. Martin reversed the feed again and paused it on the best shot of the little girl.

A slow smile spread over his scarred face, which was pocked from the cystic acne that tormented him until a few years ago.

Yes, it was the same girl.

Martin's dark brown eyes narrowed with focus as the realization settled in. He reversed the news story again and watched it with interest now, taking in all the details, such as when the trial was expected to start, and more important, the street and surroundings where the little girl was walking with her father.

The caption under the man's name said, "Emerson Crandall." The little girl wasn't named, but he knew who she was. She was the one person who could identify him.

He finished the cigarette as he thought about what he needed to do next, then stubbed it out in an already-full ashtray. The cigarette filter was smeared red.

Reaching again for the saw, Martin continued his work, methodically separating the dead woman's leg from her torso, cutting through the strong tendons at her hip, and then stuffing the leg, along with its partner, in an extra-strong, black, lawn-and-leaf bag.

Well, well. It looked like he would be applying for work in Denver.

A cell phone's ring jarred Emerson's frayed nerves, causing him to jump as though a gun had gone off next to his head. Detective Lotu looked at him curiously as he answered the call.

"Lotu," he said, his eyes on Emerson.

Emerson hadn't slept well for the last two nights. He stared dully at Lotu, watching his round, tawny face and wide mouth as the detective grunted a couple affirmative answers into the phone. Lotu hung up. Emerson's vision blurred, and he felt like he could just lean his head against the dingy yellow wall of the interrogation room and drift off. Then his body jerked involuntarily.

"You okay, man?" Lotu asked.

"Yeah."

"You seem a little jumpy."

The cheap, molded plastic chair in the interview room didn't fit Emerson's tall, lanky frame, and he shifted, uncomfortable. He realized that Lotu was waiting for more of a response.

"Yeah. I just didn't sleep well the last couple nights. It's catching up with me."

"Oh, sure. I see."

Emerson returned the detective's gaze, his vision blurring again slightly, his brain screaming for sleep. The other detective, Sheen, watched him warily, his expression confirming that Emerson was acting a little goofy. The detectives might be seeing his exhaustion as something else. Drugs? Mental illness? He had to focus. He sensed some change behind the large mirror, in the observation room it guarded, but when he looked that way, there was nothing. His gaze fell on his own reflection. He saw the wariness in his deep blue eyes, his dark, unkempt curls pushed back from his forehead impatiently, his long, straight eyebrows pressed low in a scowl, the muscle in his angled jaw pulsing as he clenched his teeth, his shoulders slouching defensively. The short beard he allowed to grow, mainly because he hated shaving, looked scruffy.

The unexpected glimpse forced him to see himself as the two sheriff's detectives did, and he didn't like it. He looked like a slapped dog. He sat up straight, drawing a breath that opened his broad shoulders and stretched his hard torso. At six-foot-two, Emerson was much taller than Lotu, but only a little taller than Sheen. Sheen, a graying redhead, was built like a mountain gorilla with a broad chest, powerful arms and thick, muscular legs.

Sheen noticed the change in Emerson's posture and became alert, radiating aggressive energy. Emerson's exhaustion made him want to return that hostility. But he needed to suppress that and focus.

Lotu had opened the conversation by asking Emerson questions about his trips to New Mexico. Confused, Emerson let them know – several times – that he was never there. With that line of questioning going nowhere, Lotu circled to worn-out questions about Mrs. Stanton's death.

"Just to be sure we're square on all this, remind us. When did you learn that your father planned to kill Mrs. Stanton?"

"I never learned that," Emerson said, annoyed, but striving for civility. He thought of calling Jeff, the lawyer representing Emerson and all of Crandall Enterprises, but didn't want to bother him on a Sunday. Besides, the police could get nothing new from Emerson on this. They already knew it all.

Emerson found himself drumming his fingertips on his thigh, humming a tune that rattled around in his brain.

Lotu raised his eyebrows in little, pointed arches, his round head, receding hair and soft features making him look more like a friendly friar than a homicide investigator. Emerson refocused on the question, wishing he could catch a nap.

"I only learned much later that it was even possible that he had planned to kill her. I'm not even sure what did happen the night Mrs. Stanton died. I thought she froze to death, right?"

Why did he feel so guilty? He had nothing to do with Clara Stanton's death. But his tendency to accept blame made him feel responsible, especially when it came to his family's bad behavior.

"Really? All you needed to do was get rid of her, and then you and your father could go on and build the biggest casino resort in Colorado. You were on the brink of becoming a millionaire. Except you needed her land. She was in your way. And now look at you. You've got no job, you're probably broke, and if you're not, you will be after the lawyers get done with you. You're going to trial, and you'll most likely spend the rest of your life locked away at Canon City with the most dangerous felons in Colorado. What will happen to your daughter?"

The idea scared and angered Emerson as he thought about his seven-year-old daughter, Courtney. He knew he had to regain control, but his exhaustion was causing him to overreact. Sheen watched him steadily, looking like a mutt that was expecting him to drop a morsel of food. Emerson didn't like that look or Sheen. He pegged Sheen as a bully when they first met a couple months ago. He usually combatted bullies with his wit, rather than his fists. But he was too tired to have his usual filters. This was a bad day to come here, he realized, way too late.

He had heard about police constructing false cases against innocent people.

He stretched his head back, looking at the ceiling, and took a deep breath before finally responding. "The last I knew, nobody is being charged with homicide. Not me, not my father, not his company."

"Not yet, but I think there was a homicide. I'm betting the jury will, too. Even if you're not formally charged with it, they could try to nail you on the other charges. And there could always be a civil suit. You could get off a whole lot lighter if you cooperate."

Lotu let it sink in, then softened his tone. "Look Emerson, you're a good guy. We know that. We know you're not a murderer. All you want to do is make sure your daughter's safe. Is that how your father got you to help him kill them?"

His anger bubbled.

"Don't try to manipulate me," he said. "I'm exhausted, but I'm not stupid."

"Just answer the question," Sheen said.

Emerson appraised him moodily. He had trained himself to be mild and flexible in most circumstances. But to stay that way, he constantly cooled a deep, smoldering fury that he could never quite extinguish. It churned, deep inside.

Sheen took a small step closer. Emerson wondered what it would be like to pound that jowly pink face and the bulbous nose. Sheen smiled, his face reddening, with a look that said, "Bring it." Emerson shook the thought away and yawned abruptly.

"Mr. Crandall?" Lotu said. "You with me, man?

"Yeah. Sorry." Emerson looked back at Lotu, still conscious of Sheen's heavy presence, too close. "Like I told you, I didn't know anything about what my father was doing at the time Mrs. Stanton died. I was in Syracuse, doing research. Invasive insects."

Sheen snorted derisively.

"For the government," Emerson added, wondering if that made it sound more credible or less. Impatiently, he reached for his phone, remembered it was off, per the detectives' instructions, and flipped it around in his hand a few times, staring at it blankly. His thoughts wandered back to that day in October when the Crandall resort was destroyed, and he learned about his father's treachery, the day that he and Maddie discovered the location of the diamonds that Clara Stanton had protected. These were some of the same thoughts that forced him awake the past couple nights.

"Everything OK?" Lotu asked.

"What kind of name is Lotu, anyway?"

"It's short for Lotulelei." He pronounced it "Lo-too-lay-lay."
"It's Tongan. But people have trouble saying it."

Despite his patient answer, Lotu and Sheen grew more
intense in their attention to him, as though he was acting just
strange enough for them to prepare themselves for something
unexpected.

"Huh," Emerson said. "Anyway, I hadn't talked to my father
in probably six months. But my research grant was canceled, and all
of a sudden Courtney came to stay with me, after her mother was
hospitalized."

Emerson flipped his phone, glanced at the mirror, wondering
who was in the room behind it.

"My father always told me he had a good job for me
whenever I needed it, but I never wanted to work for him. But then,
I needed a decent job for Courtney. So, I called him, planning to
work for him for a while, just until I could find a good job in my
field."

"Sounds like he had you just where he wanted you," Lotu
said. "What would you have done for that income? What would you
have done for that little daughter of yours? Would you have hurried
along an old lady's death? Would you have made her lawyer
disappear?"

Enough. Emerson stood up abruptly, accidentally knocking
over the flimsy chair. Lotu jumped up, too, in surprise, and Sheen
stepped closer, getting ready to pounce if needed.

Emerson quickly raised both palms. "Sorry!" he said. "It was
an accident." He picked up the chair and set it back in its proper
position.

"Please sit down, Emerson," Lotu said, trying to sound calm.

Emerson didn't sit. He was sick of this room, the detectives,
the questions hounding him for the past three months. He stretched,

letting his fingers skim the low ceiling, then walked over to the mirror. Cupping his hands against it to cut the glare, he peered inside, spotting dark shapes that might have been humans.

"Hello in there," Emerson said.

"Sit down, Crandall," Sheen said. "We're not messing around."

Emerson turned and saw them both standing on guard. He remembered they were trained to take down suspects far bigger and angrier than him. He sighed, sitting again and leaning back, hands behind his head, staring at Lotu.

"You have me for five more minutes," he said. "I have to pick up my daughter at three-fifteen."

"Are you taking medication?" Lotu asked, now sitting down again, too. Sheen remained standing and inched closer to Emerson.

"No. Nothing. I'm good."

"Because I have to say, you don't seem good. You seem distracted, edgy even. You're not normally like this."

"I'm just ready to get out of here. I haven't slept for two nights. I feel like I've answered these questions a hundred times. But, go ahead, Detective 'Lo-too-lay-lay.' Let's get this over with."

He could tell his attempt at a cooperative smile came off as a sneer. But Lotu smiled, the dimple reappearing in the loose flesh of his cheek.

"Yeah, sure." The detective sipped his coffee, then slid the paper cup aside.

"So, what was the deal with your father? He just thought it was okay to kill people to get his way, or what?" Lotu suddenly sounded rude. "You just went along with whatever he said, no matter who got hurt?"

This question provided the breeze that flamed Emerson's fury. "That's it." He started for the door.

Sheen stepped closer to him, not quite blocking him. Emerson could have stopped, but didn't, and his shoulder hit

Sheen's. Knocked off course, Emerson's leg Lotu's small table, tipping the paper cup, spraying coffee onto Lotu's face and white shirt.

Now Emerson felt his arm twisted painfully behind his back, and he fell forward as the cold steel of handcuffs snapped around his wrists. He was shoved to the floor on his stomach.

"Don't move!" Sheen's voice was near Emerson's ear, his elbow in his back.

Lotu, annoyed to find himself wet with cold coffee, stood at the ready. Two uniformed deputies rushed in.

"What do you think you're trying to pull?" Sheen said, pressing Emerson's face into the filthy, gray, concrete floor. "That's assaulting an officer."

"What are you talking about? You jumped in front of me," Emerson said, trying to swallow the rage, his voice muffled with his cheek against the gritty floor. His shoulders felt yanked out of the sockets. His hips were painful against the cold concrete.

"Let me up. I have to get my daughter."

Lotu wiped his face with his handkerchief and frowned at the big, wet stain on his shirt.

"Nice going," he said mildly. "You just earned yourself a night at our place. What is wrong with you, Crandall?"

"I didn't do anything!" Emerson said, panicked. "Don't put me in jail! My daughter needs me!"

"You should have thought of your daughter before you attacked a sheriff's detective," Sheen said, sitting back and removing his sharp elbow from Emerson's spine. "Get him out of here."

The deputies grabbed Emerson roughly on either side and yanked him up, pulling him out the door.

"Stop it!"

"What has gotten into you, Emerson?" Lotu said calmly. "You never acted so strange before. You know better than to hit a sheriff's detective like that."

"I have to call her babysitter, please!" He looked to Lotu.

Lotu appraised him, frowning.

"Yeah, okay. Let him make the call."

"I want a copy of that recording," Emerson said.

Then the door closed, and Emerson was on his way to jail.

End, Preview

Want more? Buy **For Sissy** at Amazon, Barnes and Noble, or your favorite online bookstore!

About the Author: A.H. Gilbert
www.ahgilbert.com

Listening: Podcasts

Brain Science; Hidden Brain; Horses in the Morning; Listen Money Matters; Locked Up Abroad; Love + Radio; My Dad Wrote a Porno; Mysterious Universe; No Such Thing as a Fish; On Being with Krista Tippet; Savage Love cast; Sword and Scale; Ted Radio Hour; The Dough Roller Money; The Guardian's Science Weekly; The Moth; The New Yorker: Fiction; The Vanished Podcast; True Crime All the Time (and TCAT Unsolved); Unfictional; Writing Excuses

Listening: Music

Leonard Cohen; Grace Vanderwaal, Annie Clark (aka St. Vincent); Tom Waits

Doing

Photographing insects & nature; Horseback riding; Hiking; Golf

Binge Watching

Better Call Saul; Chopped; Stranger Things; The Fall; The Forest (The French series, with subtitle); *The Killing; The Walking Dead*

Recent Reads:

The Good House, by Ann Leary; *The Road,* by Cormac McCarty; *The Girl with All the Gifts,* by M.R. Carey; *John Dies at the End,* by David Wong; *The Dry,* by Jane Harper; *All the Birds Singing,* by Evie Wyld; *Confession of a Serial Killer: The Untold Story of Dennis Rader,* by Katherine Ramsland